10·6·2017

mity & the
ishing Well

NANCY ATHERTON

Aunt Dimity & the Wishing Well

headline

First published in 2014 by
HEADLINE PUBLISHING GROUP

1

Cataloguing in Publication Data is available from the British Library

ISBN: 978 1 4722 1631 1

Printed and bound in Great Britain by
Clays Ltd, St Ives plc

Headline's policy is to use papers that are natural, renewable and recyclable
products and made from wood grown in sustainable forests. The logging and
manufacturing processes are expected to conform to the environmental
regulations of the country of origin.

HEADLINE PUBLISHING GROUP
An Hachette UK Company
338 Euston Road
London NW1 3BH

www.headline.co.uk
www.hachette.co.uk

For Meg Ruley and Annelise Robey,
who've been by my side every step of the way

One

*I*t was a fine day for a funeral. Rain plummeted from a leaden sky and a blustery wind blew the chill of mortality through the mourners clustered in St. George's churchyard. It was early May, but it felt like the raw end of March.

The funeral was well attended, despite the dismal weather. CLOSED signs dangled in shop windows throughout the small village of Finch, and cottage curtains, so often twitched aside to allow one inquisitive neighbor to observe another, hung motionless. Everyone who was anyone stood shivering in the churchyard, and in Finch, everyone was someone.

Short, plump Sally Pyne, tearoom owner and baker extraordinaire, shared an umbrella with her equally plump fiancé, Henry Cook. Christine and Dick Peacock, the pub's well-fed proprietors, served as a human windbreak for the more slightly built retired railroad employee, George Wetherhead. Ruddy-cheeked Mr. Malvern, a local dairy farmer, stood beside Grant Tavistock and Charles Bellingham, whose business was the purchase, sale, and restoration of fine art.

Near the three men, draped in a black woolen cape that hung to her ankles, stood Finch's resident witch, Miranda Morrow, who'd left her holistic health hotline unattended in order to pay her respects to the deceased. The presence of a pagan at a Christian burial might have raised eyebrows in a less tightly knit community, but Miranda's neighbors were accustomed to her funny little ways.

Four women—two widows and two spinsters, all retired—huddled together for warmth in the lee of a marble angel. Elspeth Binney, Opal Taylor, Selena Buxton, and Millicent Scroggins never missed a funeral if they could help it, but their patented piety was, on this occasion, undercut by the volley of resentful glances they cast at a fifth woman, Amelia Thistle. Amelia had wounded them grievously by winning the heart of the village's most eligible widower, who happened to be my father-in-law. The quarrelsome quartet had almost forgiven Amelia for succeeding so spectacularly where they had failed, but the cold rain had made them cranky.

Peggy and Jasper Taxman occupied their usual positions at the forefront of the assembly. Mild-mannered Jasper Taxman was a mere blip on the village's radar, but his wife was a supernova. Peggy Taxman ran the post office, the general store, the greengrocer's shop, and every village-wide event in Finch, and she did so imperiously, with an iron hand and a voice that could crack granite. None but the brave would dare to question Peggy's right to plant her Wellington-booted feet wherever she chose to plant them.

By contrast, Mr. Barlow, who was the church sexton and village handyman, stood at a respectful distance from the grave, while Bree Pym, the twenty-year-old New Zealander who'd helped Mr. Barlow to lower the coffin into its final resting place, rested her muddy hands on the headstone shared by her great-grandaunts, Ruth and Louise Pym, whose house and modest fortune she had inherited. Brave Bree rarely missed an opportunity to goad Peggy Taxman, but she'd sheathed her sharp wit for the day and watched the proceedings in solemn silence.

I, too, stood in the churchyard, along with my husband, Bill, and our eight-year-old twins, Will and Rob. My father-in-law, William Willis, Sr., had hoped to join us, but as he'd only recently recovered from a nasty inflammation of the lungs, he'd been ordered by his physician, his housekeeper, his gardener, his son, his daughter-in-law, and his sweetheart to stay at home.

My best friend, Emma Harris, had also been unable to attend the funeral because of illness, though in her case it was a horse's illness rather than her own. Pegasus, Emma's beloved chestnut mare, had been diagnosed with a mild case of colic, which had been all the excuse Emma had needed to spend the day in a nice, dry barn. She'd acknowledged the gravity of the occasion by canceling the day's classes at her riding academy, but since horses could not be relied upon to clean their own stalls, her staff and stable hands had been too busy to come to St. George's.

Theodore Bunting, Finch's vicar, stood in his customary place at the foot of the grave. While he struggled to control his prayer book's flapping pages, his wife, Lilian Bunting, attempted to shield him from the worst of the wind with a large black umbrella.

As the vicar spoke of dust and ashes, the eyes of the congregation darted furtively from the rain-dappled coffin to Lilian's umbrella, which tilted alarmingly with each passing gust. The men and women in the churchyard were too mature to speak their thoughts aloud, but my sons were not.

"Mrs. Bunting is going to fly straight over the church if she doesn't let go of that umbrella," Rob observed dispassionately.

"Like Mary Poppins," added Will. "Only older."

Bill emitted a brief but regrettably audible snort of laughter. I elbowed him in the ribs and quelled Will and Rob with a look, but the damage was done. Mr. Barlow snickered, Bree Pym giggled, and soon the only shoulders that weren't quivering with suppressed mirth belonged to Peggy Taxman, whose gimlet gaze eventually silenced the unseemly tittering.

The good people of Finch weren't given to giggling at funerals. Finch was a tiny hamlet set amid the rolling hills and the patchwork fields of England's Cotswolds region. Although Bill and I were Americans, we'd lived in a honey-colored cottage near Finch for a decade. Our sons had never known another home.

Bill's widowed father completed our family circle. Will and Rob had the run of their grandfather's splendidly restored Georgian mansion, but the wrought-iron gates guarding his estate kept less welcome visitors—Elspeth Binney, Opal Taylor, Selena Buxton, and Millicent Scroggins, to be precise—at bay.

While Willis, Sr., tended his orchids and courted Amelia

Thistle, Bill ran the international branch of his family's venerable law firm from an office overlooking the village green, the
twins attended Morningside School in the nearby market town
of Upper Deeping, and I juggled the ever-changing roles of
wife, mother, daughter-in-law, friend, neighbor, gossip moni-
tor, and community volunteer. Over the years, Bill, Will,
Rob, Willis, Sr., and I had become vital threads in the fabric of
our village and we did our best to keep the cloth intact.

We could do little, however, to repair the gaping hole left
by a villager's death. In a tiny place like Finch, the loss of a
neighbor usually sent shock waves of grief through every
household. As a rule, a death in Finch was regarded as a death
in the family, and no one with the faintest sense of decency
would laugh during a family funeral.

Mr. Hector Huggins, however, was the exception that proved
the rule. His death hadn't sent so much as a ripple of grief through
Finch, not because he'd been disliked, but because he'd lived
among us as a stranger. In a village where everyone knew virtu-
ally everything about everyone else, Mr. Huggins had managed
the miraculous feat of remaining anonymous.

A few useless things were, of course, known about him.
He'd been a senior partner in an accounting firm in Upper
Deeping. He'd patronized local businesses, attended local
events, and never missed a Sunday service at St. George's,
but he'd made neither friends nor enemies in the village. He'd
simply made no impression at all. Bill had once described him
as a wallpaper man, someone who hovered quietly in the

background, unable or unwilling to involve himself in other people's lives.

Upon his retirement, Mr. Huggins had taken to spending his afternoons sitting silently on the bench near the war memorial and his evenings fishing silently from atop the humpbacked bridge at the south end of the village green. No one knew how he'd spent his mornings, but it seemed likely that he'd spent them in silence.

Mr. Huggins had lived in Ivy Cottage, a modest stone dwelling across the lane from my father-in-law's estate, but since Ivy Cottage was completely hidden from view by a tall hedgerow, it was possible to drive past it many times without knowing it was there. Neighborly concern had prompted me to call on Mr. Huggins from time to time, but I'd never set foot inside his front gate. He'd always turned me away at the gate with a gentle smile and the soft-spoken assurance that he required no assistance.

Neither I nor my neighbors had known that Mr. Huggins was ailing until an ambulance had arrived at Ivy Cottage to take him on what had proved to be his final journey. He'd died ten days later in the hospital in Upper Deeping. Shortly thereafter, the vicar had received a letter from a London solicitor containing the payment as well as the arrangements for Mr. Huggins's funeral, but whether the same solicitor would handle the disposal of his late client's worldly goods, no one could tell.

A faint communal memory suggested that Mr. Huggins

had relatives living abroad, but none had shown up to bury him. Mr. Malvern, Dick Peacock, Henry Cook, and Grant Tavistock had volunteered to serve as Mr. Huggins's pallbearers, but it had been left to the vicar to eulogize him because no one else could think of anything to say.

The vicar had done what he could with an awkward situation, basing his sermon on a pair of verses in which St. Paul exhorted his brethren "to aspire to live quietly, to mind your own affairs, and to work with your hands . . . so that you may command the respect of outsiders, and be dependent on nobody."

Mr. Huggins hadn't worked with his hands, exactly, and the villagers had bristled slightly at the suggestion that they might have been regarded as "outsiders" by a man who'd never made the least effort to become a part of the community, but they couldn't deny that their late neighbor had lived quietly, minded his own affairs, and depended on nobody but himself. The general feeling seemed to be that, if self-reliance were a virtue, then Mr. Huggins had earned his place in Heaven.

What he had not earned was a place in our hearts. I doubted that anyone in the churchyard felt a deep and abiding sense of loss at his passing. They might have felt pity for a man whose family had, apparently, abandoned him. They might have regretted their failure to get to know him better. They might even have felt sorry for not feeling sorrier about his death. But no one was heartbroken.

I suspected that the vast majority of my neighbors had, like myself, come to Mr. Huggins's funeral out of a sense of duty, and a sense of duty could hardly be counted on to inoculate them against a contagious bout of giggling. Even so, we all looked a bit shamefaced after our indecorous descent into comedy, and redoubled our efforts to appear somber. A neighbor had died, he had no one to mourn him, and we owed it to the honor of our village to see him off properly.

The vicar was about to drop a morsel of mud on the coffin when he was distracted by a commotion in the lane. Heads that had been bowed rose alertly as a white Ford Focus splashed to a halt on the grassy verge beyond the lych-gate, and the vicar's hand fell to his side as a tall figure leapt from the car, vaulted the churchyard's low stone wall, and sprinted across the sodden grass, dodging nimbly between headstones and skidding to a halt mere inches from Mr. Huggins's open grave.

The newcomer was a young man—in his midtwenties, perhaps. He was dressed in a dark-brown rain jacket, khaki cargo shorts, and a pair of rugged hiking sandals, and though his clothes were slightly shabby, he was much more than slightly good-looking. His blond hair was like tousled corn silk, his eyes were as blue as a summer sky, and his deeply tanned face made his teeth seem almost too white. Even his toes, which were rapidly turning pink in the cold air, were handsome. As he paused to catch his breath I could sense hearts fluttering among the faithful, but though many mouths had fallen open, words seemed to be in short supply.

Once again, a child led us.

"Hello," Will said brightly. "Who are you?"

"I'm Jack MacBride," the young man replied in a broad Australian accent. "And I've come to say good-bye to Uncle Hector."

Two

The young man gave Will a friendly wink, then turned to face the vicar.

"I'm in the right place, aren't I, Padre?" he inquired anxiously. "St. George's church? In Finch? Only, Finch wasn't on my map, so I had to stop in Upper Deeping for directions and the bloke who gave them to me was a bit of a wally."

"Calm yourself, Mr. MacBride," the vicar said gently. "You are in the correct place. You may, if you wish, be the first to cast earth into your uncle's grave."

"Beauty," said Jack.

He scooped a heaping handful of mud from the mound near the grave and let it fall with a mighty splat on the coffin lid. The gruesome noise broke the spell he'd cast over the churchyard. Gaping mouths snapped shut, astonished gazes were averted, and the ancient ritual continued as if a golden-haired Adonis hadn't burst upon the scene like a ray of sunshine.

The women stepped forward to drop damp posies into the grave and the men contributed modest lumps of dirt, but Will and Rob, delighted by Jack MacBride's exuberance, had to be restrained from hurling great gobs of mud in the grave's general direction. Bill and I clamped our hands onto their shoulders until the vicar had pronounced the final blessing.

Amelia Thistle nodded sympathetically to Jack, then strode

off to visit her recuperating beau in his graceful Georgian home, but the rest of the villagers formed a line and shuffled past the newcomer, studying him covertly while murmuring impromptu words of condolence. Bill and I allowed the boys to throw one small mud-ball apiece into the grave, then joined the vicar and Lilian at the end of the line, while our neighbors lingered near the lych-gate to await developments.

"I'm very sorry for your loss, Mr. MacBride," the vicar began.

"Jack'll do," the young man interjected. "Mr. MacBride's my dad."

"I'm very sorry for your loss, Jack," the vicar began anew. "I'm Theodore Bunting, vicar of the parish."

"And I'm Lilian Bunting, Teddy's wife," said Lilian, furling her troublesome umbrella. "Please allow me to introduce our friends: Bill Willis, his wife, Lori, and their sons, Will and Rob."

"G'day," said Jack, with a nod to each of us.

"Your feet look cold," said Rob.

"They are, a bit," Jack admitted.

"Why don't you have socks on?" inquired Will.

"And why are you wearing shorts?" Rob added.

"Because it's hot where I come from," said Jack. "My warm clothes are at the bottom of my pack and I didn't have time to fish them out." He looked apologetically at the vicar. "Sorry for buggering up the ceremony, Mr. Bunting. I'd've been here sooner, but my plane was late getting into Heathrow and it took for-bloody-ever to rent a halfway decent car and traffic was a bloody nightmare because half the bloody roads were flooded and—"

"Apology accepted," the vicar broke in, with a sidelong glance at the children. Will and Rob were gazing up at Jack with stars in their eyes. *Bloody* wasn't a word they heard often, especially in a churchyard. To hear a grown-up use it three times in one sentence *at a funeral* was an undreamt-of treat. I exchanged looks with Bill and silently added a refresher course in appropriate language to the day's schedule.

"Mrs. Bunting and I are hosting an informal gathering in the schoolhouse in remembrance of your late uncle," the vicar continued. "We would be honored if you would join us, Jack."

"There's cake," Will piped up.

"And hot chocolate," Rob said, staring at Jack's pink toes.

"*Gallons* of hot chocolate," Will confirmed.

"Sounds like a proper feast," said Jack, grinning at the boys. "Lead the way, mates!"

Will and Rob grabbed Jack's outstretched hands and bounced along on either side of him, talking a mile a minute. As if on cue, the villagers flowed through the lych-gate and up the cobbled lane toward the old schoolhouse, which served as Finch's village hall. The Buntings, Bill, and I followed at a more sedate pace while Mr. Barlow and Bree stayed behind to fill in the grave.

"Did you know he was coming?" I asked Lilian.

"I didn't know he existed," Lilian replied.

"Mr. Huggins's family wasn't mentioned in the letter I received from the solicitor," said the vicar.

"Maybe Mr. Huggins didn't mention his family to his solicitor," I said.

"It seems an odd sort of thing to keep from one's legal adviser," said the vicar.

"Mr. Huggins was an odd man," said Lilian. "May he rest in peace."

"Amen," said the vicar.

"There have been rumors floating around," I said thoughtfully, "about relatives living overseas. If Jack MacBride is Hector Huggins's nephew and if he's as Australian as he sounds, he'd count as an overseas relative."

"I suspect our questions will be answered before too long," said Bill. "Young Jack doesn't know it yet, but he's about to be interrogated by the entire village."

Whether consciously or unconsciously, our foursome picked up its pace. I wasn't sure about the others, but I wanted to be on hand to hear my neighbors give young Jack the third degree.

The schoolhouse was blessedly warm and dry after the churchyard. We stashed our rain gear in the cloakroom and hurried into the schoolroom to help ourselves to steaming cups of tea. A coterie of influential women usually supervised the tea urn, so I was surprised to find a group of men lounging near it. Henry Cook, Dick Peacock, Jasper Taxman, and Grant Tavistock watched patiently while their significant others piled food on Jack MacBride's already crowded plate.

"Can't blame them, really," Henry said philosophically. "He's a good-looking lad."

"The accent helps, of course," said Grant. "Charles has always had a soft spot for Aussies."

"Peggy can't abide Australians," said Jasper. "She thinks they're loud and vulgar."

"It looks as though Jack's changed her mind," Dick observed.

"He hasn't," said Jasper, shaking his head. "She just doesn't want Sally's cake to outshine hers."

"She's fighting a losing battle there," Henry asserted. "My Sally is the best baker in the county."

"You'll get no argument from me," Jasper said morosely. "But you'll definitely get one from my wife."

"Perhaps there'll be a food fight," Dick said hopefully, and his companions perked up.

Potluck meals were competitive events in Finch, and since my neighbors had expected the schoolhouse gathering to be the highlight of Mr. Huggins's funeral, they'd gone all out to show off their culinary skills. The trestle tables along the walls trembled beneath the weight of savory casseroles, sausage rolls, quiches, and sandwiches, while the tables on the dais held a cornucopia of cookies as well as a truly magnificent parade of cakes. My own contribution, a modest seed cake, paled by comparison with the Dundee, Eccles, Madeira, and coconut cakes surrounding it. Devil's food cake, I'd learned through hard experience, was regarded as unsuitable fare at a funeral luncheon.

"Has Jack said anything interesting?" Bill asked the tea urn's guardians.

"He told us a pretty good joke before he was swept away," said Dick, "but he hasn't been able to get a word in edgewise since then."

"Your nippers are having a high old time of it," Henry observed. "They're like baby birds catching the crumbs falling from Jack's plate."

"Except that, in this case, the crumbs are macaroons, meringues, and brandy snaps," said Grant.

Visions of sugar shock danced in my head. I promptly abandoned Bill and scurried across the room to pull Will and Rob from the scrum surrounding their idol. After wiping powdered sugar from the boys' chins and whipped cream from their sticky fingers, I sent them straight home with their father. Bill didn't object to the prospect of being stuck in the cottage on a rainy day with a pair of hyperglycemic eight-year-olds because he knew it would be pointless. Nothing short of a burst appendix would pry me away from what promised to be the main topic of conversation in Finch for months, if not years, to come.

"Enough is enough," Lilian murmured. "The poor boy will be crushed to death if we don't rescue him." Raising her voice to be heard above the din, she called, "Ladies and gentleman!"

The babble of voices ceased.

"Shall we give our honored guest a chance to breathe?"

Before anyone could reply, Lilian marched across the

room, and gently but firmly extracted Jack from his legion of admirers. She then tucked his free hand into the crook of her elbow and guided him to a chair in a corner of the room. The vicar and I promptly slid into the chairs flanking Jack's and Lilian pulled one over to face his.

The legion, realizing that it had wasted a golden opportunity to question the newcomer, surveyed our defensive perimeter crossly and began to sidle slowly in our direction.

Jack brushed cake, cookie, and bread crumbs from his rumpled blue pullover and smiled gratefully at Henry Cook, who'd brought him a cup of tea.

"Eat up," said Lilian. "You must be famished."

"I could eat a horse and chase the jockey," Jack acknowledged. "Haven't had a decent bite since Bangkok."

He tried to balance his overladen plate on his knee, but finally gave up and placed it on the floor. We allowed him to wolf down a ham sandwich, three sausage rolls, a bacon butty, and a gargantuan hunk of Sally Pyne's Madeira cake before we got down to business.

"You must be tired after your long journey," the vicar began. "To come all the way from Bangkok—"

"I came all the way from Sydney," Jack corrected him. "Bangkok was a layover."

"Do you live in Sydney?" Lilian asked.

"Sometimes," Jack replied, "but I was born in Malua Bay—about 300 k's south of Sydney."

"Do your parents still live there?" I inquired. Behind the

question lay several others: Were Jack's parents alive? If so, why hadn't they come to the funeral? Had there been a rift in the family? Was that why Mr. Huggins had lived in England while his closest blood relations lived in Australia? And so on.

Sadly, Jack answered only the question I'd actually asked.

"You couldn't pry my parents away from Malua Bay with a crowbar. It's their little slice of paradise." Jack drank his tea, wiped his mouth with the back of his hand, and regarded me quizzically. "I can give you their phone number, if you want to check up on me."

I blushed, but Lilian chuckled.

"You must forgive our curiosity, Jack," she said. "Your late uncle never spoke of his family, and his solicitor failed to inform us of your plans to attend the funeral. If we'd known you were coming, we would have postponed it for another day, to allow you time to arrive at your leisure."

"No worries," said Jack. "I didn't know I was coming until a few days ago. It was all a bit of a rush. Aldous Winterbottom—"

"Your uncle's solicitor," the vicar interjected.

"Right," said Jack. "Old Aldous tottered out to meet me at Heathrow with the keys to Uncle Hector's digs and a pile of papers. He can vouch for me." He plunged a hand into a pocket in his cargo shorts. "I've got his number here somewhere."

"I have Mr. Winterbottom's telephone number," the vicar assured him, "but I feel no compulsion to ring him. You wouldn't have gone to so much trouble to be here if you weren't who you say you are."

"Have you a place to stay this evening?" Lilian inquired. "If not, you're more than welcome to spend the night with Teddy and me at the vicarage. We have bedrooms to spare."

"Kind of you, Mrs. Bunting," said Jack, "but I'll be kipping at Uncle Hector's for the next little while. Aldous Winterbottom tells me the electric's still on and the phone's still working, so I should be snug as a tick on a sheep's backside." His forehead wrinkled as he looked from the vicar to Lilian. "Trouble is, I'm not sure where Uncle Hector lived."

"He lived in Ivy Cottage," I informed him. "It's not far from here. If you'll drive me home, I'll point it out to you."

"Deal," said Jack. His brilliant grin widened suddenly into a gaping yawn. "Sorry," he muttered, raising a hand to cover a second yawn. "I reckon jet lag's caught up with me. I'm knackered."

"If you'll come to the vicarage, I'll give you tea, eggs, bacon—whatever you need for breakfast," said Lilian. "You can stock your pantry properly when you've recovered from your travels."

"You're one out of the box, Mrs. Bunting," said Jack, clapping her on the shoulder.

Sally Pyne stepped forward and said timidly, "I could pack up a bite or two for you, too, Jack."

"So could I," Opal Taylor said, sliding neatly in front of Sally. "You'll be too tired to shop tomorrow—"

"And we can't let you starve!" gushed Selena Buxton, jostling Opal to one side.

"Cheers, ladies, that'd be great," said Jack, winking at them.

Sally, Opal, Selena, and the rest of Jack's fans dispersed to prepare their special offerings for transport. Jack smiled good-naturedly, then focused his attention on a single, unassuming cookie on the edge of his plate. He picked it up and studied it for a moment, then popped the whole thing into his mouth. A faraway look came to his eyes as he chewed.

"Magic," he said, smacking his lips appreciatively. "I don't suppose you can tell me who made the Anzac biscuits."

"That would be Bree Pym," Lilian informed him. "You may have noticed her in the churchyard—the dark-haired girl with the nose ring."

"Bree's from New Zealand," I said.

"That would explain it," said Jack. "No one but a true blue Aussie or a can-do Kiwi can make a proper Anzac biscuit. I'll have to thank Bree for giving me a taste of home." He craned his neck to scan the room. "Is she here?"

"I'm afraid not," said Lilian. "Bree remained in the church-yard with our sexton, to fill in your uncle's grave."

"Bree helped Mr. Barlow to dig it, too," said the vicar. "She and Mr. Barlow shared the task of lowering the coffin into its final resting place."

"That little girl dug a grave?" Jack exclaimed. "She must be stronger than she looks."

"Word to the wise," I said. "Don't call Bree a little girl. She won't appreciate it and you might live to regret it because, yes, she's a whole lot stronger than she looks."

"Point taken," said Jack.

"Bree's very fit," the vicar observed, "but Mr. Barlow is of the opinion that coffin-lowering is a matter of technique rather than strength."

"Either way, I have a hell of a lot to thank Bree Pym for," said Jack. "And Mr. Barlow, too. Good thing I'll be staying on for a bit." He yawned again and a tide of tiredness dimmed his bright blue eyes.

"Come along," said Lilian, getting to her feet. "It won't take me a moment to fill a basket for you at the vicarage. Then you and Lori can be on your way."

"If Ivy Cottage is in any way deficient," said the vicar, "please feel free to accept my wife's invitation to stay with us."

"Thanks, Mr. Bunting," said Jack, "but to do my job, I need to be on the spot."

"Your job?" inquired the vicar.

"Didn't I say?" said Jack. "I'm here to settle Uncle Hector's affairs."

Try as I might, I couldn't imagine what kind of affairs a quiet, retiring man like Hector Huggins would leave unsettled, but I didn't press Jack for details. The drive home would give me ample time to conduct a proper interrogation.

Three

The good people of Finch bestowed a whole week's worth of food upon Jack MacBride as he exited the schoolhouse. The vicar and I helped him to tote the bulging bags and the brimming baskets to his rental car and I watched with interest as he pushed aside a beat-up khaki backpack and a rectangular black box to make room for his bounty.

The black box instantly caught and held my attention. It reminded me of the boxes Bill used to store legal papers for his English clients. I wondered if it contained the papers Aldous Winterbottom had delivered to Jack at Heathrow and whether those papers concerned Hector Huggins's unsettled affairs. Given half a chance, I would have taken a quick peek inside, but I wasn't given any chance at all.

Before I could so much as bend down for a closer look at the box, Lilian was beside me, placing the promised supply of staples in the trunk. With a sigh, I closed the trunk, climbed into the car, and waited for Jack to say his good-byes to the Buntings. I waved to Lilian and the vicar as Jack took his place behind the steering wheel, then directed him to drive toward the humpbacked bridge.

"I appreciate the lift," I said. "Bill took the boys home in our car. If it weren't for you, I'd have a damp two-mile walk ahead of me."

"My pleasure, Mrs. Willis," said Jack.

"I'm Lori Shepherd," I informed him. "I didn't change my last name when I married Bill, but it hardly matters because everyone calls me Lori. I hope you will, too, Jack."

"Right you are, Lori," he said with an amiable nod.

"Sorry about the lousy weather," I said.

"We have our fair share of rain in Oz," he said. "It buckets down during the monsoon. Rivers break their banks, flood towns. Rain's a bloody nuisance in the wet."

"The wet?" I repeated.

"The monsoon season," Jack explained. "We call it 'the wet' and it is. It's not so cold, though." He smiled ruefully. "Wish I'd taken the time to find my socks. My feet are bloody frozen."

"I prescribe a hot bath and a roaring fire," I said. "And a nice cup of tea. A cat in your lap would warm you up, too, but I don't think your uncle owned a cat."

"No," said Jack. "Uncle Hector wasn't one for pets."

We bumped over the humpbacked bridge and I advised Jack to slow to a crawl. "See the big, shaggy hedgerow?" I said, pointing ahead and to my right. "Ivy Cottage is behind it. The narrow gap is for the front gate and the wider one is for the driveway."

"Ta," said Jack.

I gestured to my left. "My father-in-law lives across the lane. He wanted to attend your uncle's funeral, but he's recovering from a bad chest cold and we didn't want him to risk a relapse. To tell you the truth, we had to lock him in his bed-room and hide the key."

"Really?" said Jack, looking surprised.

"No, not really," I admitted. "But he does regret missing the funeral. He has strong feelings about participating in communal rituals."

"Poor old cobber," said Jack. "Hope he's fighting fit again soon."

"Thanks," I said, smiling at the mental image of my genteel father-in-law brandishing boxing gloves at a brutish opponent. "William's housekeeper would have been there, too, but she had to stay at home to keep an eye on him."

"In case he found the key, eh?" said Jack.

"More or less," I said. "Her name is Deirdre Donovan. If you need anything—a cup of sugar, directions to the gas station—she'll be happy to help."

"Helpful sort of place, Finch," Jack commented.

"We try." *And we try a lot harder for someone with your good looks and sunny disposition,* I added silently. Aloud, I said, "Two miles to go to my cottage. Then you can drive straight back to Ivy Cottage and hit the sack."

"That's the plan," he said.

"I hope your uncle didn't leave too much for you to do," I said.

"Not too much." Jack shrugged nonchalantly. "No worries."

"Excellent," I said, hiding my disappointment behind another smile. A generalized "not too much" wasn't the sort of in-depth personal information I'd hoped to glean from Jack during our time together, but I gave it another shot. "Did you know him well?"

"Well enough," Jack replied.

I began to suspect that Jack was too tired to give my questions the answers they deserved, but before I could try again, he turned the tables on me.

"You're a Yank, aren't you?" he asked. "A Pom would've said 'petrol' station."

"I am a Yank," I confirmed. "Bill is, too, but we've spent the past ten years in England."

"Why?" he asked.

"I inherited property here, and since my husband's clients live in Europe, we decided to make England our home base," I replied. "But, mainly, we moved here because we fell in love with Finch. It's a great place to raise a family."

"I'll bet it is," said Jack. "Quiet, safe, lots of room for the kiddies to run about, no yobbos to set them a bad example."

"No," I agreed. "No yobbos."

"Except for me," said Jack, giving me a sheepish glance. "I'll have to clean up my act while I'm here. Wouldn't want the ankle biters picking up my bad habits."

"Well," I allowed, "if you could use words like *bloody* sparingly, or not at all, Bill and I would be grateful. We know our children hear worse language in the school yard, but we do our best to cultivate civility at home."

"Consider it done," said Jack.

"No offense," I added anxiously.

"None taken," he said. "When in Rome——"

He interrupted himself with a gigantic yawn and I brought the question-and-answer session to a close. There was nothing to be gained from hammering away at a man who was too sleepy to finish his sentences, so I spent the rest of the short trip pointing out notable landmarks. Jack studied Bree's red-brick house carefully as we passed it, but he barely glanced at Emma's curving drive, and he seemed unmoved by the lush, green, sheep-dotted pastures that popped into view between the dripping hedgerows.

"I'd rather be counting them than looking at them," he admitted. "Jet lag's a bugger."

I winced inwardly, but Jack seemed to hear himself because he immediately rephrased his comment.

"That is to say," he said, in a plummy English accent, "jet lag's a *dreadful* bore."

I grinned and gave him an approving thumbs-up, then suggested that he slow down again as we approached my cottage. A moment later, he pulled into the graveled drive, switched off the ignition, and turned to face me. Upon closer inspection, his sky-blue eyes were bloodshot and there was a hint of pallor beneath his deep tan. The sooner he went to bed, I thought, the better.

"May I beg a favor, Lori?" he asked.

"Beg away," I told him.

"The thing is," he said, "I'll never finish all the tucker the ladies piled onto me. Would they mind if I asked you to take some of it off my hands?"

"Yes," I said without a moment's hesitation. "Gifts, once given, may not be re-gifted and they must never, under any circumstances, be returned. Not in Finch, at any rate."

"It could be our little secret," he said imploringly. "No one would have to know."

"Everyone would know within the hour," I said flatly. "Don't ask me how it happens. It just happens. There are no secrets in Finch, Jack, and the sooner you accept this fact of life, the better off you'll be. If you want to get rid of the excess, uh, tucker, I suggest you bury it in the woods in the dead of night, but even then there's a fifty-fifty chance that someone will see you."

He frowned for a moment, then brightened.

"I could invite people to lunch," he suggested. "Are you and Bill and the twins free tomorrow?"

"Sorry," I said, shaking my head. "Sundays are family days. We spend them with Bill's father."

"Just as well, really," Jack said resignedly. "I'll be bumping into walls until I adjust to the time change. How about Monday?"

"The boys will be in school and Bill will be at the office," I said, "but I'd be happy to join you for lunch on Monday."

"You think Bree Pym might come, too?" Jack asked. "It'd give me a chance to thank her for looking after Uncle Hector's grave."

"I'll extend an invitation to her in your name. In the meantime . . ." I took a pen from my purse, scribbled my phone number on a scrap of paper scrounged from the bottom of my trench coat pocket, and handed it to Jack. "If you need anything, give me a call. We may be temporary neighbors, but we're still neighbors."

"And in Finch, neighbors help neighbors." Jack nodded. "I'm beginning to see why Uncle Hector loved it here. See you on Monday, then, around noon or thereabouts?"

"I'll be there." I opened the car door. "Are you sure you're alert enough to get back to Ivy Cottage in one piece? The curve by Bree's house can be a little tricky, especially when the roads are slick."

"No worries," he assured me. "Thanks for the tour, Lori."

"Thanks for the lift," I said, getting out of the car. "And welcome to Finch."

I waited to make sure he was driving toward the village rather than away from it, then splashed up the flagstone path and let myself into the cottage.

An ominous silence greeted me.

I hung my trench coat on the coat rack, stepped out of my rain boots, placed my shoulder bag on the hall table, and tiptoed into the living room, where I found my menfolk—including our sleek black cat, Stanley—asleep in a heap on the couch.

Stanley raised his head briefly at my entrance, but Bill, Will, and Rob didn't stir. The sugar high had apparently become a sugar low and Bill, worn out from the former, had clearly taken advantage of the latter. I left the four of them to their naps and crept quietly into the kitchen to prepare a simple, nourishing dinner.

With no dessert.

Bill and I spent after-dinner time looking through books about Australia with the boys. As we marveled at pictures of kangaroos, wallabies, and cassowaries, we also made it clear that people from other countries were allowed to use words little boys living in England were not. I couldn't tell if the message sank in, but it was a start. Jack's willingness to change his ways for the sake of the ankle biters would, I hoped, render remedial lessons unnecessary.

Once Will and Rob were in bed, Bill and I snuggled up on the couch in the living room, with a fire crackling in the hearth and Stanley curled into a black ball on Bill's favorite armchair. While the wind swirled around the chimney and raindrops splashed against the bay window, I told Bill what I'd learned about Hector Huggins's nephew.

He was unimpressed.

"Are you joking?" he scoffed. "You had Jack MacBride at your mercy for a solid fifteen minutes and all you managed to find out was that Uncle Hector didn't have a pet?" He wagged a finger at me in mock outrage. "If you go on like this, you'll be drummed out of the gossips' guild."

"What about Malua Bay?" I demanded. "And his parents still living there? And the mysterious black box?"

"Lilian Bunting dug the Malua Bay nugget out of him," Bill pointed out. "I'll give you a couple of points for the bit about his parents, but none for the black box. If Jack has to resolve his uncle's affairs, it stands to reason that he'd have a box full of legal papers." He shook his head. "It's not much to show, by Finch's standards, and it hardly makes my sacrifice worthwhile. While you were out there with Jack, learning very little, I was peeling Will and Rob off the ceiling."

"Sorry," I said, snuggling closer to him.

"No worries, mate," he said, in a truly dreadful Australian accent.

"I'll have another crack at him on Monday," I reminded him.

"Ah, yes, lunch at Ivy Cottage," said Bill. "You'll be the envy of every woman in the village." He nuzzled my ear. "I suppose you'll want to bring a certain person up to date on today's exciting turn of events?"

"Do you mind?" I asked.

"No," he said. "As long as you don't stay up too late. Stanley is a very nice cat, but I'd rather share my bed with my wife."

"I'll keep it short," I promised.

"Good." Bill kissed me until I ran out of breath, then headed upstairs, with his faithful feline padding after him.

I loosed a quivering sigh, then went to the study, to give a certain person the day's news.

Four

The study was as silent as it could be with raindrops dashing themselves against the diamond-paned windows above the old oak desk. The strands of ivy crisscrossing the windows shivered beneath the onslaught and I felt a chill creep through me on their behalf. Though I hadn't intended to light a fire, I struck a match, held it to the tinder in the hearth, and waited until the flames were dancing before I paused to say hello to my oldest friend in the world.

"Hi, Reginald," I said. "If it doesn't stop raining soon, the river will overflow, Finch will be flooded, and the villagers will be forced to abandon their homes and flee to higher ground. And I'll have to wait until the summer drought to ride my new bike."

Since Reginald was a small, powder-pink flannel rabbit, I didn't expect him to reply, but the gleam in his black-button eyes seemed to suggest that he understood how much my new bike meant to me. The bicycles of my childhood had been purchased from thrift stores or garage sales, and I'd bought the bicycle I'd ridden as a young adult from a guy at a flea market. My new bike was the first brand-new bike I'd ever owned. The thought of turning pedals no one else had turned thrilled me to the core.

Reginald looked very snug in his special niche in the

floor-to-ceiling bookshelves beside the fireplace and snug was how I liked to keep him. Reg and I went way back. He'd been made for me before I was born by a woman I'd met only after her death.

The woman's name was Dimity Westwood and she'd been my late mother's closest friend. The two women had met in London while serving their respective countries during the Second World War. The shared experience of living in a city under siege created a bond of affection between them that was never broken.

When the war in Europe ended and my mother sailed back to the States, she and Dimity strengthened their friendship by sending a constant stream of letters back and forth across the Atlantic. After my father's sudden death, the letters became my mother's refuge, a quiet retreat from the daily pressures of teaching full time while raising a rambunctious daughter on her own.

My mother was extremely protective of her refuge. She told no one about it, not even me. As a child, I knew Dimity Westwood only as Aunt Dimity, the redoubtable heroine of a series of bedtime stories invented by my mother. I was un-aware of the real Dimity's existence until after both she and my mother had passed away.

It was then that Dimity Westwood bequeathed to me a comfortable fortune, the honey-colored cottage in which she'd spent her childhood, the precious postwar correspon-dence, and a curious blue leather–bound book filled with blank pages. It was through the blue journal that I finally met my benefactress.

Whenever I opened the journal, Aunt Dimity's handwriting would appear, an old-fashioned copperplate taught in the village school at a time when pupils practiced their penmanship on slate tablets. I stopped breathing for a full minute the first time it happened, but it didn't take me much longer than a minute to realize that Aunt Dimity's intentions were wholly benevolent.

I couldn't explain how Aunt Dimity managed to bridge the gap between this world and the next—and she wasn't too clear about it, either—but I didn't much care. The important thing, the only thing that mattered, was that Aunt Dimity was as good a friend to me as she'd been to my mother. The rest was mere mechanics.

I twiddled Reginald's pink ears, took Aunt Dimity's journal from its shelf, and curled up with it in one of the tall leather armchairs facing the hearth. The fire crackled cozily as I opened the blue journal and gazed down at it.

"Dimity?" I said. "It's still raining."

I smiled as the familiar lines of royal-blue ink began to curl and loop across the blank page.

Really? And here I was, thinking I heard fairy fingers tapping on the windowpane.

"Very funny," I said. "Honestly, Dimity, I've never been to a wetter funeral."

I believe I have. Fanny Preston's grave was so waterlogged we had to wait a week to bury her, and even then we were afraid she might float out of it.

"You win, Dimity," I said, grimacing. "At least we got Hector Huggins in the ground today."

God rest his soul. Was the poor man's funeral well attended?

"Naturally," I said. "Everyone was there, including a surprise guest."

Splendid! There's nothing more intriguing than a surprise guest at a funeral. Come along, now. Fill in the picture. Man or woman? Young or old?

"A young man," I said. "Midtwenties, blond, blue-eyed, adorable, and Australian."

An adorable Australian? Oh, dear. I do hope he won't turn your head.

I blushed. I couldn't help blushing. Aunt Dimity knew all too well that I had, in the past, allowed my head to be turned by a certain kind of male charm. Nor could I deny that on one or two—possibly three—occasions, she'd felt distressed enough by my behavior to remind me of my marriage vows. I could, however, recall with some pride that she hadn't had to trot them out in quite some time.

"My head is screwed on as tightly as a lid on a Mason jar," I assured her, "but nearly every other head in Finch is spinning because our visitor is as nice as he is adorable. His name is Jack MacBride and he claims to be Hector Huggins's nephew."

Claims to be?

"The vicar's willing to take his word for it, but I'd like him to prove it," I said. "I would have asked him for proof this afternoon, but he was so wiggy from jet lag that it seemed unfair to badger him. Never fear, though. I'll have another chance to wangle the truth out of him on Monday."

Will he still be within wangling distance on Monday?

"Yes," I said. "Jack's staying in Ivy Cottage while he sorts out his uncle's affairs."

Affairs? What kind of affairs would a man like Mr. Huggins leave unsorted?

"I asked myself the same question," I said, nodding.

Canceling a magazine subscription? Retrieving a suit from the dry cleaner? Emptying the refrigerator? Mr. Huggins's solicitor could have sent a minion to attend to such trivialities. They scarcely merit the onsite oversight of an Australian relation.

"I agree," I said, "which is why I'm having lunch with Jack on Monday. I want to know who he is and what he's up to."

You're also dying to take a peek inside Ivy Cottage.

"True," I acknowledged equably. "It would be a feather in my cap to go where no villager, apart from the late Mr. Huggins, has gone before. But my main goal will be to find out why Jack's here. I'd also like to take a look inside the very interesting black box I saw in the trunk of his car. Bill thinks it's filled with legal papers, but I'd prefer to see for myself before I decide."

A wise policy. For all we know, it might contain a treasure map. Mr. Huggins may have buried a cache of gold doubloons beneath his bed.

"If he did, I'll find out," I said confidently.

I'd rather you stay out of the bedroom.

"Ho ho ho," I said, rolling my eyes.

I'm not joking, Lori. Though I was joking about the treasure map and the doubloons. I can't think of a man less piratical than Hector Huggins.

"Neither can I," I said, "but you know what they say about the quiet ones—they always have a dark secret to hide."

It's hardly ever true, more's the pity.

"Nevertheless," I said, "Jack MacBride must have had a good reason to travel halfway around the world and I intend to find out what it is."

I have no doubt that you will.

"Thank you, Dimity," I said. "And there's no reason to worry about . . . anything. Jack is a pretty boy, but Bill's the man for me."

I'm glad to hear it. Bill is worth more than all the pretty boys in the world put together. It's getting late, Lori, and you'll want to arrive at church early tomorrow, in case any news about Jack has surfaced overnight. I suggest that you lay your unturned head upon your pillow and get some sleep. Who knows? The skies may be clear by morning. You may be able to ride your shiny new bicycle to church.

"Ever the optimist," I said pessimistically. "Good night, Dimity."

Good night, my dear. Sleep well. And keep me informed!

"I always do," I said.

I waited until the graceful lines of royal-blue ink had faded from the page, then returned the blue journal to its shelf, tamped down the fire, touched a finger to Reginald's snout, and ran upstairs to finish the kiss Bill had started.

The skies did not clear in the morning and I did not ride my bicycle to church. Thanks to a lost shoe, an unfortunate incident with a glass of orange juice, a broken umbrella, and two last-minute trips to the toilet, I was also unable to get myself and my family to St. George's any earlier than usual, which was, as usual, halfway through the processional.

I wasn't as attentive as I should have been during the service, but at least I stayed awake, which was more than could be said for Dick Peacock, Grant Tavistock, Henry Cook, and Bill. They dozed off as the vicar commenced his learned sermon and awoke, looking refreshed, the moment he finished it.

I couldn't claim the moral high ground, however, because I didn't listen to the vicar's sermon, either. While the men slept, I studied my neighbors, searching for the telltale signs of a gossipmonger bursting with news. I found nothing, not a flushed cheek, a knowing smile, or an arched eyebrow, to indicate that anyone had dug up anything worth repeating about Jack MacBride.

I hadn't reckoned with Lilian Bunting's poker face. When she took me aside after the service, I expected her to ask me if I'd learned anything about Jack on the drive home after the funeral luncheon. Instead, she had a million-dollar tidbit to share with me.

"In case you were wondering," she said, as we huddled beneath her oversized umbrella, "Jack MacBride is exactly who he says he is."

"I was wondering," I acknowledged, "but I didn't expect you to come up with the goods. How did you find out? Did the vicar ring Mr. Winterbottom after all?"

"No," Lilian replied. "I did. Teddy's a trusting soul, but I'm a scholar. In my world, facts aren't facts until they're confirmed by a reliable source."

"Well done," I said admiringly. "Did Mr. Winterbottom tell you anything about Mr. Huggins's unresolved affairs?"

"He did," said Lilian.

Her gray eyes twinkled as she pulled me farther into the churchyard, where we were less likely to be overheard by prying ears. It was clearly a gesture born out of habit rather than necessity because the only people left to overhear us were too far away and too preoccupied to do so. Our husbands, my sons, my father-in-law, and Bree Pym were engaged in a lively discussion of the upcoming cricket season in the relative comfort of the church's south porch. Everyone else had scurried home as fast as their wellies could carry them.

"Did you happen to notice the black box in the boot of Jack MacBride's motor?" Lilian asked.

"I might have caught a glimpse of it," I allowed. "Bill thinks it's filled with legal papers."

"There may be legal papers in it," Lilian conceded, "but it contains something else as well. Apparently, Mr. Huggins wrote a memoir. In his will he asked his nephew Jack to prepare the manuscript for publication."

My jaw dropped.

"*Hector Huggins?*" I said, flabbergasted. "A *memoir?* I don't mean to speak ill of the dead, Lilian, but who on earth would want to read a memoir written by the world's most innocuous man?"

"I know," she said, smiling delightedly. "I couldn't believe it, either."

"And what does a kid like Jack know about preparing manuscripts for publication?" I went on. "I can imagine him hiking in the Outback or surfing in Samoa, but . . . editing a manuscript?" I shook my head. "Nope. Can't picture it."

"He must have hidden talents," said Lilian.

"One thing's for sure," I said. "Jack won't stay in Finch for more than a day or two."

"What makes you say that?" Lilian asked.

"Because Mr. Huggins's memoir must be the shortest one on record," I said. "'I worked. I fished. The end.'"

Lilian's snort of laughter would have won a disapproving sniff from Peggy Taxman, but, luckily, Peggy wasn't there to hear it.

"We really shouldn't make fun of the poor soul," Lilian said, with a contrite glance at the mound of freshly dug earth on Mr. Huggins's grave.

"I'd feel guilty if I weren't so stunned." I stared incredulously at the grave, then looked at Lilian as a bright idea occurred to me. "Maybe Mr. Huggins made the whole thing up. Maybe he wrote a fake memoir filled with wine, women, and song to compensate for a life filled with water, fish, and silence."

"I hope he did," Lilian said. "He always struck me as a rather lonely man, but a man with a vivid imagination is never lonely."

"I'll find out what I can from Jack," I said. "I'm having lunch with him tomorrow. Which reminds me . . ." I caught Bree's attention with a wave of my hand. She strode over to join us, rain streaming from her camouflage rain poncho and splashing onto her bumblebee-striped Wellington boots, her nose ring glinting dully in the diluted daylight.

"What's up?" she asked. "You two look like you're conspiring. Are vicars' wives allowed to conspire, Mrs. Bunting?"

"It's the first thing they teach us at vicars' wives' school," Lilian replied.

"I suspected as much," said Bree, nodding wisely.

"What's up," I said, "is an invitation to lunch at Ivy Cottage on Monday. Jack MacBride would like to thank you for a number of things, including his uncle's grave and your Anzac biscuits."

"Did he eat the biscuits?" Bree asked, her dark-brown eyes narrowing in suspicion. "Or did he sneer at them?"

"Why would he sneer at your biscuits?" asked Lilian.

"Because he's on the wrong side of the great Anzac biscuit debate," Bree replied. "They were invented in New Zealand, of course, but Aussies claim them for Oz. The Aussies are delusional, but they'll never admit it, not to a Kiwi, at any rate."

"Jack made no such claim," I assured her. "He loved the biscuits and he'd love to meet you. Will you come?"

"Sure," said Bree. "It'll be a novel experience, hearing an Aussie thank a Kiwi. What time?"

"If it's raining, I'll pick you up at noon in the Range Rover," I said. "If not, I'll still be at your place at noon, but I'll be on my bicycle. I'd offer you a seat on my handlebars, but you'd probably be safer jogging alongside."

"No fear," said Bree. "I'll be ready and waiting for you on my bike. We can race to Ivy Cottage." She thrust a fist into the air. "The first stage in the Tour de Finch!"

Since Bree was a good deal younger, ten times more energetic, and in much better shape than I, I excused myself and went back into the church. It suddenly seemed like a good idea to pray for a little more rain.

Five

My prayers were answered. The first stage of the Tour de Finch was canceled, due to inclement weather.

Though the rain slackened during the night, it returned in full force at the dawn's early light. I smiled as I sent Bill off to work, sang as I drove the boys to school, and skipped merrily from room to room while I completed my morning chores. The pangs of guilt I felt when I thought of the rising river were assuaged by the knowledge that my journey to Ivy Cottage wouldn't leave me with strained hamstrings and a badly bruised ego.

Bree was waiting for me when I pulled up to her house in my canary-yellow Range Rover. She splashed down her front walk, clambered into the passenger's seat, gathered her billowing poncho into a manageable bundle, and gave me a commiserating look.

"Too bad about the weather," she said.

"A real shame," I agreed, shaking my head regretfully.

I waited until she'd fastened her seat belt, then drove slowly and carefully through the small streams flowing across the lane. I'd once slid into a ditch while negotiating the tricky curve near Bree's house and I did not intend to give Bill a reason to remind me of my mishap.

"I was looking forward to seeing your new toy," Bree continued.

"She's a beauty," I said.

"She?" said Bree, raising an eyebrow.

"Definitely," I said. "She's what used to be called a girl's bike, but the man at the cycling shop informed me that they're now referred to as 'low-entry' bikes."

Bree snorted, but I ignored her.

"Her name is Betsy," I went on, "and she's the most gorgeous shade of blue. Twenty-one speeds, a rattan basket, a two-tone brass bell, a generously padded seat, and tires that will handle everything from dirt to gravel."

"Do you and Betsy plan to do much mountain biking?" Bree asked skeptically.

"We plan to stay on paved roads," I replied, "but you never know. An emergency might crop up. I might be forced to ride cross-country to save a life. Best to be prepared."

"I hope it's not my life you're saving," Bree muttered. Before I could muster a stinging retort, she continued brightly, "It was great to see William at church yesterday. He looks as fit as a fiddle."

"We can thank his housekeeper and his sweetheart for his recovery," I said. "Deirdre and Amelia have taken excellent care of him."

"Which is a polite way of saying they've locked him in his bedroom for the past month," said Bree.

"Needs must," I said. "They'll let him resume his normal routine as soon as the weather settles down. I know he misses his country walks."

"He'd catch pneumonia if he stepped outside today," said Bree, squinting at the cloud-covered sky. "Our Aussie's teeth must be chattering," she went on. "I'm sure his lips were turning blue on Saturday. Serves him right for wearing shorts and sandals."

"Be nice," I scolded. "The poor guy's plane was late and he was in such a tearing hurry to get to the funeral that he didn't have time to change into sensible clothing."

"Aussies aren't known for being sensible," said Bree. "What's he doing here, anyway? The funeral's over and done with. Why is he sticking around?"

"According to Lilian, who heard it from Mr. Huggins's solicitor, Jack MacBride came to Finch to complete a project mentioned in his uncle's will." I glanced at Bree to catch her reaction. "Jack's preparing his uncle's memoir for publication."

Predictably, Bree burst out laughing.

"Priceless," she said when she finished guffawing. "What's it called? Adventures in Accounting? Thrills and Gills? The Spoken Word: How to Get Along Without It?"

"Your guess is as good as mine," I said. "But please try not to laugh if Jack mentions the memoir to us. It must be a labor of love for him. He can't imagine it'll be a best seller."

"A labor of love?" Bree scoffed. "If you ask me, it has more to do with money than with love."

"What do you mean?" I asked.

"I'll bet Mr. Huggins left Jack an inheritance," said Bree. "But Jack gets it only if he agrees to tidy up the memoir."

I recalled Jack's beat-up backpack, his shabby clothing, and his last-minute decision to attend his uncle's funeral, and nodded thoughtfully.

"You may be right," I said. "He doesn't dress like someone who can afford to splash out money on impromptu flights to England."

"No, he doesn't," Bree agreed. "The bequest must have included travel expenses. I'll bet Jack wouldn't have come if his uncle hadn't paid his way *and* tucked in a little bonus cash to make the journey worth his while."

"I'd hate to think that Jack's motives are purely mercenary," I said, "but I guess I'd understand it if they were. You couldn't pay me enough to read Hector Huggins's memoir, but Jack's pockets may not be as plump as mine. Can't blame a boy for trying to make a buck."

"I suppose not," said Bree. "Still, it's a bit despicable. Jack may not have been rich enough to visit his uncle, but if he cared for him at all, he could have written to him."

"How do you know he didn't?" I asked.

Bree snorted. "When was the last time our beloved postmistress kept her mouth shut about a piece of foreign correspondence? Peggy Taxman would have crowed like a rooster if she'd seen letters from Australia addressed to Mr. Huggins."

"True." I sighed. "You're painting a grubby picture of our visitor. Which makes me a little sad, because I thought he was a nice guy."

"He may be a nice guy," said Bree, "but he may be a money-grubbing ocker. I'm keeping an open mind."

"Glad to hear it," I said. "What's an ocker?"

"A boor," said Bree. "A big-mouthed, pushy jerk. In other words, a typical Aussie."

I glanced at her in surprise. "What have you got against Australians? Is there a blood feud between your countries or is it a personal quarrel?"

Bree's lips compressed into a thin line.

"Here's a little joke Jack told at the funeral luncheon," she said. "Why are so few crimes solved in New Zealand?"

"I give up," I said. "Why are so few crimes solved in New Zealand?"

"Because everyone has the same DNA," she said grimly.

The punch line took a couple of seconds to sink in. When it did, I had to bite my lip to keep myself from smiling. If Bree was determined to be offended by a fairly harmless quip, there was nothing much I could do about it. But I tried.

"I'm sure he meant it in good fun," I said.

"Exactly," said Bree. "He was telling jokes meant in good fun *at his uncle's funeral.*" She tossed her head. "Typical Aussie."

"Believe it or not," I said, "you and Peggy Taxman have something in common. She doesn't like Aussies, either. She thinks they're loud and vulgar."

"Peggy hasn't spent enough time around Australians to form a valid opinion of them," said Bree. "I have."

"Well, I've spent some time around Jack," I said, "and I don't think he's vulgar. Boisterous, perhaps, but not vulgar. He very kindly offered to rein in his language for the boys' sake, and he's holding today's feast in your honor."

"I'll try to keep an open mind," Bree promised again, unconvincingly. "Who knows? Jack may surprise me."

I sincerely hoped he would. Bree had a sharp wit and an even sharper tongue. If Jack displeased her, our luncheon at Ivy Cottage could prove to be more challenging than the Tour de Finch.

The untrimmed hedgerow had overwhelmed the verge in front of Ivy Cottage, so I parked the Range Rover on the manicured grass on Willis Sr.'s side of the road. Bree and I piled out of the Rover and crossed the lane, scarcely bothering to look for oncoming cars. Traffic was not an issue in Finch.

While a few of my neighbors locked their doors against intruders, Hector Huggins had locked his tall, wooden gate. When I'd dropped by to check on him, I'd had to ring the intercom he'd installed on one of the gateposts to summon him, and even when he'd answered it, he'd never opened the gate far enough for me to see past it.

The gate was still locked when Bree and I reached it, but I addressed the intercom with a greater sense of anticipation than I ever had before. After years of frustration, I was confident that I would be admitted at last to the land beyond the hedgerow.

"Jack?" I said. "It's Lori Shepherd and Bree Pym. May we come in?"

"No worries." Jack's voice crackled through the speaker and a click signaled the lock's release.

Smiling broadly, I opened the gate, strode boldly into the front garden, and came to a stumbling halt. Bree moved forward cautiously to stand beside me.

"I think we've found Sleeping Beauty's cottage," she murmured. "And her garage."

I knew exactly what she meant. Ivy Cottage wasn't a ruin. It was a pretty place, two stories tall, with a pair of bay windows on the ground floor and a pair of dormer windows protruding from its wavy slate roof. Tall chimneys bracketed the roof, faded green-and-white checked curtains hung in the windows, and a shallow porch sheltered a front door made of weathered oak. Ivy Cottage would have been worthy of a picture postcard had it not been left to languish in the most unkempt front garden I'd ever seen.

Nature had run riot in Mr. Huggins's realm. The shed that served as a garage seemed to be drowning in a congested mass of shrubs, vines, weeds, and flowers. Slender brick paths leading from the gate and the garage to the front door were barely discernible beneath the overgrowth, and a thick mat of ivy had colonized the cottage's stone walls. The ivy had been pruned around the windows and the porch, presumably to allow for light and access, but it had otherwise been allowed to do exactly as it pleased.

Jack had chosen to park his rental car in the weed-infested gravel driveway instead of in the decrepit-looking garage. Smoke rising from both chimneys suggested that he'd heeded my advice to warm himself before a roaring fire. I suspected he'd needed the warmth rather desperately after he'd fought his way barelegged through the sodden jungle to enter his home away from home.

"We should have worn waders," Bree commented, as we walked in single file along a brick path obscured by dripping greenery. "And brought a machete."

"Not everyone's a gardener," I allowed.

"Anyone can use a machete," said Bree.

"G'day, ladies!" Jack called to us from the doorstep. "Come in, come in!"

I was happy to accept his invitation and happier still when he closed the door behind us. My jeans were soaked through from the tops of my rain boots to the bottom of my rain jacket and Bree's were similarly saturated, but the cottage was deliciously warm and dry. It was, in those as in many other respects, the exact opposite of the front garden.

I'm not the best housekeeper in the world, nor am I the worst. I'd like to think that, on an average day, the tidiness level in my home rests somewhere between Untouched by Human Hands and This Property is Condemned. Mr. Huggins had evidently favored the sterile end of the bell curve. The rectangular room in which we stood had been created by removing the wall between the front and back parlors. It was simply furnished, excruciatingly clean, and absolutely devoid of clutter.

Jack's brown rain jacket hung from a row of hooks mounted on the wall beside the door. Below the hooks lay a utilitarian rubber mat, presumably a resting place for damp or dirty footwear. A sagging armchair upholstered in a drab brown fabric sat before the hearth and its twin faced a large, multi-paned picture window overlooking the back garden, which was, if anything, even more of a wilderness than the front.

A pole lamp and a small table sat beside each armchair, a small bookcase with glass doors rested against one wall, and a sisal rug covered most of the parquet floor. There were no pictures on the plastered walls, however, no framed family snaps on the bookcase, no knickknacks on the windowsills, nothing that might reflect the personality of the man who'd lived there.

Except that the room was probably a perfect reflection of Hector Huggins's personality, I told myself sadly. A blank room for a blank man.

Jack was wearing his rumpled blue pullover and his sandals, but he'd covered his bare feet with a pair of thick woolen socks and swapped his cargo shorts for khaki trousers. He beamed at us as if we were old friends.

"Good to see you, Lori," he said. "Good to meet you, Bree. Nice nose ring."

"Nice tan," said Bree. "Did you come by it honestly or is it sprayed on?"

My heart sank, but Jack didn't bat an eye.

"It won't rub off," he replied good-naturedly. "I spent the summer doing conservation work at Uluru. Not much shade out there and the sun's hot enough to scorch rocks." He shrugged. "Sunblock can only do so much."

"Oh," said Bree, and I was pleased to see that she was disconcerted.

Our meal was waiting for us on a round oak table in the center of the room. A straight-backed wooden chair at the table was flanked by two folding chairs that seemed very familiar.

"I had to borrow the folding chairs from the schoolhouse," Jack said, following my gaze. "As I explained to Mr. Barlow when he opened the schoolhouse for me, Uncle Hector didn't do much entertaining, so my seating options were limited. Nice bloke, Mr. Barlow."

The oak table looked like a rainbow in the midst of a dull brown desert. Though its three place settings were composed of plain white china, the spaces in between were filled with the covered casserole dishes Jack had received from the villagers. I'd seen the dishes at so many village events that I could identify their owners as well as their contents by their colors alone.

The blue dish invariably contained Peggy Taxman's shepherd's pie; the yellow, Sally Pyne's chicken in sherry sauce; the green, Charles Bellingham's braised lamb shanks; the red, Christine Peacock's beef in beer; the orange, Opal Taylor's sausage and apples; and the purple, Miranda Morrow's solitary vegan offering of lentils with sweet potatoes. The savory fragrances rising from the dishes added a homey touch to a room that couldn't, by any stretch of the imagination, be considered homey.

"Right, then," said Jack, clapping his hands together. "Sling your jackets on the hooks, hop out of your boots, and help yourselves to the fire. Tea for two is on its way."

I waited until he'd left the room, then turned to glare at my companion.

"Is it sprayed on?" I parroted back at her in a hissing whisper. "Really, Bree?"

"Sorry," she said, pulling her poncho over her head.

"Open mind, remember?" I said. "You're keeping an open—" I interrupted myself with an exasperated huff when I saw what my young friend was wearing. The navy blue sweatshirt emblazoned with the New Zealand flag was about as subtle as a declaration of war.

"It seemed like a good idea at the time," she said, gazing down at her shirt. "I could take it off, but I'm not wearing anything underneath."

"Keep it on," I advised her wearily. "There's such a thing as being *too* welcoming."

Jack returned, carrying two plain white teacups on two plain white saucers.

"Great shirt, Bree," he said, handing each of us a brimming cup. "The Southern Cross is my favorite constellation. There's milk and sugar on the table, courtesy of Mrs. Bunting. Would you like to tuck in now or wait until you've dried out a bit?" He peered ruefully at our soaked trousers. "Sorry about the rain forest."

"No worries," Bree said as Jack strolled with her to the fireplace. "Not everyone's a gardener."

"Uncle Hector didn't like to impose his will on nature," Jack explained.

"He imposed his will on fish," Bree pointed out.

"He always threw them back," Jack countered.

I placed myself between them before Bree could decide to lecture our host on the pain suffered by a hooked trout.

"How's the jet lag?" I asked.

"Gone," said Jack.

"In one day?" I sighed wistfully. "Oh, to be young again . . ."

"You're not exactly in your dotage," said Jack.

"I'm a lot closer to it than you are," I returned, smiling. "Tell me about Uluru."

"It's a great big rock in the middle of Australia," said Bree.

"Too right, it's big," Jack said, then turned to me. "Uluru's what they call an island mountain—a hunk of sandstone a thousand feet high and a thousand feet long, with another thousand feet hidden belowground. It stands alone in a great, wide-open landscape and at sunrise and sunset it turns a thousand shades of red. The Anangu—the local Aboriginal tribe—regard it as a sacred place. Uluru is their name for it, but you might know it by another name. In 1873, a surveyor named William Gosse christened it Ayers Rock."

"I've heard of Ayers Rock," I said, nodding, "but I didn't know it was called Uluru. It sounds impressive."

"It is," said Jack. "Have you seen it, Bree?"

"No," said Bree. "Seems a long way to go to see a big rock."

"Some things are worth going a long way to see," Jack said lightly. His gaze rested briefly on her face, then he grinned and said, "Who's hungry?"

"I am," I declared. "There's something about damp, gloomy

days that makes me want to eat nonstop. I'll probably weigh three hundred pounds by the time summer arrives." I glanced morosely at the rain streaming down the front window. "If it ever does."

Jack scurried over to the table to pull out the wooden chair for Bree, then seated me in one of the folding chairs and took the place opposite mine for himself. He removed the lids from the casserole dishes, invited us to help ourselves, and made sure our plates were full before he filled his own. He was, I thought, behaving like a perfect gentleman. I hoped Bree was taking note.

My comment on the weather sparked a pleasant conversation about weather in various parts of the world, to which Bree contributed little. Jack seemed entirely at ease, though I couldn't help noticing that he toned down his Australian accent and used Aussie slang less often than he had when I'd first met him, as if he sensed Bree's aversion to his rowdy countrymen and wished to set himself apart from them.

Our talk soon turned from worldwide weather to English weather and from there it was a short leap to the English countryside and the charm of English villages. Jack reserved special praise for Finch and the many kindnesses the villagers had shown him since his arrival.

"I enjoyed spending time with Mr. Barlow this morning," he said. "He thinks the world of you, Bree."

"I'm fond of him, too," said Bree. "He's a good man and he's taught me a lot of useful things."

"Like grave digging," said Jack. "I hope you know how

grateful I am to you for looking after my uncle's grave. I wish I'd gotten here in time to dig it myself."

"I wish you'd gotten here before your uncle died."

Bree spoke in an undertone, but she might as well have slapped Jack in the face. I glanced at him apprehensively, but he met Bree's reproachful gaze without flinching.

"I didn't know I had two great-grandaunties until they were on their deathbeds," she continued. "They were the sweetest old ladies on earth and I would have given absolutely *anything* to have had one more day with them. Why didn't you come here sooner, Jack? Your uncle didn't have any friends. A nephew would have come in handy. Why did you wait until after he was dead to show your face in Finch?"

"Bree," I began in a low voice, but Jack waved me to silence.

"No worries, Lori," he said. "Bree's only saying aloud what everyone else in Finch must be thinking."

"We'd appreciate a few answers," said Bree.

"I'll give them to you," said Jack, "but it's a sad story."

"No fear." Bree set her knife and fork aside and folded her arms. "I'm tougher than I look."

Six

My better self was dismayed by Bree's bluntness, but the Finch-trained gossip in me was perfectly willing to cut to the chase. When Jack replaced the covers on the casserole dishes, I took it as a sign that a long and satisfying yarn was in the offing, and when he leaned back in his chair, I couldn't keep myself from leaning forward. Full disclosure seemed imminent and I was all ears.

"First off," he said, "I'm sorry about your great-grandaunts, Bree. It must have been rough to lose them so soon after finding them."

"It was," Bree said stiffly, "but we're not talking about me at the moment. We're talking about you."

"I'd better get talking, then," said Jack. He thought for a moment, then began, "The long and the short of it is, my dad didn't have much use for Uncle Hector."

"Why not?" asked Bree.

"Dad doesn't have much use for any man who isn't just like him," said Jack, "and Uncle Hector was as unlike him as anyone could be. Dad's a big, strapping bloke, all muscle and mouth. Uncle Hector was a soft-spoken, shy little guy. Dad's the CEO and founder of a prestigious property development firm. Uncle Hector was a bean counter at a small-town accounting firm. Dad catches marlin and has them mounted as

trophies. Uncle Hector caught trout and tossed them back."
He smiled mirthlessly. "Got the picture?"

"I think so," I said. "How does your mother fit into it?"

"Mum is Uncle Hector's sister," Jack replied. "His only sibling. Helen, her name is. Hector and Helen." He sighed. "Grand-
dad was a fan of Greek literature, but his children didn't live up
to their heroic names. Mum is just as shy and self-effacing as
Uncle Hector was. Which is fine with Dad because he likes to
have the spotlight all to himself."

"Opposites attract," I said, nodding. "How did they meet?"

"Dad was in London, making deals," Jack replied, "and
Mum was in London, working as a bank clerk. There she was,
going about her business, when a brash Aussie bloke came
along, promising to take her away from her gray, cramped
little island to a land where the sun always shines." He
grimaced apologetically. "Dad doesn't have much use for
England, either."

"So your mum married your dad and emigrated to Australia," said Bree. "Didn't she miss her brother—her only sibling?"

"Mum was too dazzled by her new life to spend much time
thinking about her old one," said Jack.

"It must have been like going from black and white to
Technicolor," I remarked.

"Dad's Technicolor, all right," said Jack. "He's bloody
blinding. I reckon he picked Mum because he could dazzle her.
Big houses, big cars, big boats, everything bigger and better
than she'd ever imagined it could be. She kept her part of the

bargain by producing not one, but two sons to carry on the family name."

"You have a brother," I said interestedly. "Are the two of you close?"

"No," Jack replied. "Conor, Jr., is a chip off the old block. I'm the disappointment."

I surveyed his rumpled pullover and raised an interrogative eyebrow. "Would I be correct in assuming that your father's high-flying lifestyle doesn't agree with you?"

"Let's just say that Dad and I didn't see eye to eye when it came to arranging my future," said Jack. "It was his way or the highway and I chose the highway. When I left school, I left home, and Dad cut me off without a cent. I've been making my own way in the world ever since."

"Good for you," I said.

"Good for my soul, maybe," Jack said wryly, "but not so good for my bank balance." He turned to Bree. "The jobs I've held are jobs worth doing, but they've never paid much. If they had, I would've visited Uncle Hector more often."

"More often?" Bree repeated skeptically. "Did you *ever* visit him?"

"I did," said Jack. "When I was six and Conor was nine, Mum and Dad brought us over to meet Uncle Hector."

"Impossible," Bree declared, shaking her head. "If you and your family had ever come to Finch, someone here would have remembered you."

"Dad? Come to Finch?" Jack threw his head back and

laughed. "Now *that's* impossible. Dad'd never waste time in the wop-wops, Bree, not unless he was planning a land grab. We didn't come down here to see Uncle Hector. Uncle Hector came up to London to see us. It was a bit of a disaster, really, because he spoiled Dad's plans."

"How?" I asked.

"By being himself," said Jack. "He came to our posh hotel and he didn't seem to notice it. It wasn't beneath his notice, it just wasn't important to him. He wanted to see his sister and to meet his nephews. Everything else was just window dressing." A wicked twinkle lit Jack's eyes. "It drove Dad mad. He took us to a flash restaurant for dinner and Uncle Hector ordered fish and chips. Dad flapped his jaws about his newest yacht and Uncle Hector sat there, playing with a piece of string." Jack looked toward the fire and smiled reminiscently. "Uncle Hector showed me how to tie seven different knots with that piece of string. I can still tie 'em."

"You admired your uncle because he refused to be overawed by your father," I said.

"It wasn't that he *refused* to be overawed," Jack elaborated. "He just . . . wasn't. He and Dad didn't value the same things. Dad wrote Uncle Hector off as a loser, but I didn't think he was a loser. I thought he was a nice bloke who looked me in the eye and listened to what I had to say. He paid attention to me. That sort of thing means a lot, when you're six and your big brother's a bullying git."

"Was that the only time you met your uncle?" said Bree.

"Yep," said Jack. "Dad never brought the family over again and he didn't invite Uncle Hector to visit us in Oz. He told Mum that her brother was a bad influence on Conor and me, and in my case, he was right. Dad wanted me to go into the family firm, but Uncle Hector encouraged me to do all sorts of things before deciding for myself what to do with my life." He smiled wryly. "No prize for guessing whose advice I took."

"You seem to know a lot about your uncle," said Bree. "He didn't eat the fish he caught, he didn't like to impose his will on nature, he didn't entertain, he didn't share your father's values, he encouraged you to make your own decisions . . . How could you know so much about him if you met him only once, when you were a little boy?"

"We may not have met face to face," said Jack, "but we wrote to each other. Letter writing is old-school, I know, but so was Uncle Hector. He and I——"

"Sorry," Bree broke in brusquely, "but if you'd written to your uncle, all of Finch would have known about it. As you'll find out if you spend any time at all here, our local postmistress isn't the soul of discretion. Letters to or from Australia would have been a big-ticket item for Peggy Taxman. She would have told *everyone* about them."

"Crikey," said Jack with an air of enlightenment. "That would explain it."

"What would explain what?" Bree demanded.

"Uncle Hector didn't like to draw attention to himself, Bree," said Jack. "He must have known he'd be the center of attention if Mrs. Taxman found out about his family in Australia."

"He would have become a local celebrity," I confirmed.

"Which is the last thing he would have wanted," said Jack. "So he bypassed Mrs. Taxman." He smiled quizzically at Bree. "I didn't send my letters through the post office in Finch. I sent them to a post office box in Upper Deeping."

"Your uncle had a post office box in Upper Deeping?" Bree said uncertainly.

"That's right," said Jack.

"Your uncle was a clever man, Jack," I said, chuckling. "Not many of us can say we've outfoxed Peggy Taxman, can we, Bree?"

"Not many of us, no," Bree murmured, looking discomfited.

"Uncle Hector and I lost track of each other after I left home," Jack went on. "I haven't had a permanent address since then. That's why it took Aldous Winterbottom so long to find me. He tried to reach me when Uncle Hector became ill, but I didn't get his letter until . . . too late. When I found out that Uncle Hector was gone, I was gutted." He tilted his head toward Bree. "If I'd become a VP in Dad's firm, I could've visited Uncle Hector as often as I pleased. But if I were the VP type, I wouldn't be the sort of bloke who'd *want* to visit a bloke like Uncle Hector. My uncle understood why I couldn't come here, Bree, and he didn't mind. He encouraged me to work for love, not money."

"Oh," Bree said quietly.

"Uncle Hector left me enough to cover my travel costs," Jack went on, "because he wanted me to take care of a few things for him. There was no one else he could rely on."

"Right," said Bree, more quietly still.

"What did he ask you to do?" I asked.

"He wrote a memoir," said Jack. "I'm to read it, give it a tune-up if it needs one, and publish one copy of it privately. Uncle Hector wanted just one copy made." Jack's voice trembled slightly as he added, "For me."

I stared down at my plate, abashed. Lilian Bunting, Bree, and I had treated Hector Huggins's memoir as a big joke. We'd never considered the possibility that it might have been written as a farewell gift from a loving uncle to a favorite nephew. I felt thoroughly ashamed of my frivolity and I knew that Lilian would feel equally mortified when I told her the whole story.

Bree must have been experiencing similar emotions because she unfolded her arms and said somberly, "I wish I'd known your uncle better, Jack. I think I would have liked him."

"He would have been terrified by you," said Jack, but his crooked smile took the sting out of his words. "People terrified him, Bree. He preferred the company of birds, badgers, butterflies, trout. You may find it hard to believe, but he was a happy man."

"I'm glad," said Bree. "It gives your sad story a nearly happy ending." She cleared her throat, then inquired with exquisite courtesy, "What kind of conservation work did you do at Uluru?"

"Removing invasive plants, mostly," he replied. "Good preparation, as it turns out, for the second project Uncle Hector left me." He swept a hand through the air to indicate Ivy Cottage. "I'm to tidy the place up and get it ready to put on the market. The house seems to be in good nick, but the land needs a lot of work. And that's left me in a bit of a bind. Uncle Hector didn't own any gardening tools, apart from a dodgy-looking lawn mower, and I'll need more than that to restore order around here. Is there a place I can hire——"

"Don't be stupid," Bree interrupted. "I've got all the tools you'll need. What if I bring them 'round tomorrow morning?" She turned to me. "I'll haul them in my own car, Lori, so the Rover won't get mucky."

"Thanks," I said. "I have a hard enough time keeping it clean as it is."

"I could stay on and pitch in," Bree continued, turning back to Jack. "I've no plans for the day."

"I'll help, too," I piped up. "I'm not much of a gardener, but I can pull weeds if someone points them out to me. I'll see if I can recruit Emma Harris as well. She lives up the lane and she knows a lot about gardens."

"I'll take all the help I can get," Jack said gratefully. "Nine o'clock tomorrow morning suit you?"

"Could we make it ten?" I asked. "My mornings tend to be a little hectic."

"Fine with me," said Bree.

"Ten it is," said Jack. He sat upright and surveyed our empty plates. "You choose: dessert or a breath of fresh air?"

"Fresh air," Bree said promptly. She gave him a shy, sidelong look as she added, "And a fresh start?"

"Sounds good," he said, and his smile was bright enough to blind the sun.

Jack led us through the spotless, old-fashioned kitchen and out the back door. We stood beneath the cottage's overhanging eaves, letting the rain-cooled air clear our heads, until Jack suggested a modest expedition.

"I was poking around out here this morning, taking the lay of the land," he said, "and I bumped into something you might find interesting. Want to see it?"

"Absolutely," said Bree.

"Then grab your rain gear," said Jack, "and come with me."

Seven

*T*he back garden was a shadow of its former self. A few reminders of its glory days were still visible—a tumbledown stone wall at its outermost boundaries, a broken pergola framing the gap that had once held a gate, a ruined trellis swallowed by a rampant rosebush—but in its present state it was nearly indistinguishable from the untamed meadows that surrounded it.

Bree and I followed Jack along a trail of flattened greenery he'd left behind during his early morning rambles, to a spot in the center of the garden, where a tall mound of ivy rose like a bristling hillock from the matted vegetation. When we reached the mound, he motioned for us to stand back, then seized a handful of vines and drew them aside like a swathe of drapery to reveal his discovery.

Bree's face lit up like a child's on Christmas morning.

"It's a well!" she exclaimed.

It was a well, but it wasn't a plain old workaday well. It was a well straight out of a fairy tale, round in shape and made of smooth river stones as large as cantaloupes, with a shingled roof resting on a pair of wooden posts. A wooden spindle spanned the posts, but there was no rope wound around it, and the crank, if it still existed, was concealed by vines.

"Is it a real well?" I asked. "I mean, is there water in it or is it just there for decoration?"

Instead of answering me directly, Jack plucked a pebble from the ground and let it fall into the well. I listened closely and felt a shivery thrill of delight when I heard a distant splash.

"Let's give it some air," Bree proposed, and stepping forward, she began to tear vigorously at the ivy with both hands.

"Hold up, Muscles," Jack cautioned. "The posts may come down around your ears if you go at it full-bore."

"Right, Boss," Bree agreed. "Easy does it."

Jack produced a fierce-looking folding knife and proceeded to slice through the tough vines as if they were strings of spaghetti. Bree and I removed the detached strands as gently as our eagerness would allow, and as the pile of discarded vines grew, my hopes rose. It looked as though at least one of the garden's features had survived Hector Huggins's reign of benign neglect.

"I don't see any holes in the roof," Bree announced, "and the posts seem to be sound."

"The crank's still attached," I said happily, uncovering the spindle's business end.

"I reckon the rope rotted a long time ago," said Jack, gazing into the well. "It's probably down there, with the bucket."

"They can be replaced," I said confidently.

It took us thirty minutes to free the well from its tangled shroud and though the shingled roof shook from time to time, nothing came down around our ears. We were as wet as dishrags by the time we finished, but no one complained. Jack looked exhilarated, Bree seemed utterly enchanted, and I felt as giddy as an archaeologist excavating a treasure-filled tomb.

While Jack and I stood back to survey the fruits of our

labor, Bree remained on her knees, clearing the last few vines from the side of the wellhead nearest the cottage.

"I wonder how long it's been since anyone set eyes on it?" I mused aloud.

"I wonder how long it's been since anyone used it?" said Jack. "You'll have to have the water tested," I advised. "It might not be safe to drink. And you might consider putting a lid on it."

"We don't want Will and Rob to make a splash," Jack said, with an understanding nod.

"We most certainly don't," I said fervently. "And they will, given the smallest opportunity."

Bree sat back on her heels suddenly and gave a short gasp of surprise.

"What's up?" I asked.

"Look," she said, beckoning to us. "There are words. Words carved into the stone."

I sank to my knees beside her and saw that a bulbous river stone beneath the well's rim had been chiseled flat to form a kind of plaque. Seven words had been engraved on the flattened stone, in a rough but readable Celtic script:

speak and your wish will be granted.

"It's a wishing well," Bree said wonderingly. "A real, live wishing well." She craned her neck to peer up at Jack, who'd bent over us to read the inscription. "You mustn't put a lid on it," she said urgently, "not a solid lid. If you do, the well won't be able to hear you."

For a moment it looked as though Jack would lose what-ever ground he'd gained with Bree by laughing at her, but he bit his lip, straightened, and gave a passable imitation of taking her seriously.

"I'll put a *removable* lid on it," he assured her. "That way, it'll be safe for the nippers, but accessible to, um, well wish-ers. Have a wish in mind, Bree?"

Bree's rosy cheeks became rosier as she looked away, mut-tering, "Don't be stupid. There's no such thing as a wishing well. It's just a . . . a silly game."

"I'm always up for a silly game," I said brightly. I sprang to my feet, leaned low over the well, and bellowed into its black depths, "I wish it would stop raining!"

Bree and Jack laughed—Bree, somewhat sheepishly.

"Problem solved," Jack declared. He gave Bree a hand up and tilted his head toward the cottage. "Tea, anyone? And brandy snaps? I'd offer you Anzac biscuits as well, but I've al-ready scoffed the lot."

Bree's face went from rose to beet-red as the compliment registered and she looked more confused than ever as Jack turned his back on her and strode jauntily into the cottage.

The fresh pot of tea arrived too late in the day for me to take full advantage of it. I had things to do at home before I picked Will and Rob up from school—not the least of which was to change into dry clothes—so I gulped the scalding brew, gobbled a brandy snap, thanked Jack for his hospitality, and promised to return the following morning to begin work on Hector Huggins's gardens.

Bree seemed relieved rather than disappointed when I cut our tea party short. She thanked Jack politely, though without quite meeting his gaze, and scampered out to the Rover like a rabbit pursued by a wolf.

Our return journey was conducted in a Hector Huggins-esque state of silence. Bree was absorbed in her own thoughts, and since anything I said would have sounded like "I told you so," I kept my mouth shut. Though we had a cornucopia of fresh subjects to discuss, we didn't exchange a single word until we reached Bree's house and she turned to me, looking perplexed.

"What's he up to?" she asked.

"Jack?" I hazarded. "Why should he be up to anything?"

"Because I was a complete cow," she stated flatly, "and he was a complete . . ." Her voice trailed off.

"Gentleman?" I suggested.

"Yes, he was a gentleman," she admitted, frowning. "It doesn't make sense, Lori. I was horrible to him. Why was he so nice to me?"

"Because he's a nice guy," I said mildly. With heroic self-restraint, I refrained from adding, *And because not all Aussies are ockers, you young idiot!*

"He does seem like a nice guy," Bree acknowledged reluctantly, "but I still think it's weird."

She undid her seat belt, hopped out of the Rover, said she'd see me at Ivy Cottage in the morning, and trudged through the pouring rain to her front door.

I opened my own front door ten minutes later and threw a hasty greeting to Stanley, who was in the living room, curled into a sleek black ball on Bill's favorite armchair. I ripped off my rain jacket, kicked off my boots, tore upstairs to change, and tore back downstairs to turn on the lights in the study, pat Reginald's pink flannel snout, snatch the blue journal from its shelf, and drop into one of the tall leather armchairs before the hearth, opening the journal as I fell.

"Dimity?" I said, panting slightly. "I'm back from Ivy Cottage and I have tons to tell you!"

Good afternoon, Lori. Your fact-finding luncheon was a success, was it?

"It was like bathing in a waterfall of gossip," I confirmed. "I'd intended to draw Jack out gradually, but Bree went straight for his jugular and as a result, I now know three thousand times more about him than I did this morning. I know about his mousy mother and his blowhard father and his bullying big brother, Conor, Jr., and when he met his uncle and how they kept in touch and why Jack never came to Finch and where he got his tan and—" I broke off to catch my breath and Aunt Dimity took advantage of the pause to ask a question.

What did you mean when you said that Bree went straight for Jack's jugular?

"I meant that she more or less accused him of being a rotten, no-good, absentee nephew," I said. "It was more than a little tactless of her, but it worked. In order to defend himself, Jack had to tell us all sorts of things about his family and himself." I sighed happily. "Oh, Dimity, it was wonderful!"

I'm sure it was, my dear, but I'd be grateful to you if you'd give me an intelligible account of what, exactly, Jack told you.

"One intelligible account, coming up," I said. I distilled Jack's long, sad story into a more compact version, but by the time I finished, Aunt Dimity knew as much about Jack Mac-Bride as I did.

What a touching tale. Hector Huggins looked into the eyes of a six-year-old boy and saw someone quite different from himself, but instead of denigrating the difference—as Jack's father did—he accepted, admired, and nurtured it. By doing so, he helped Jack to become the fine young man you've described.

"He certainly did," I said. "Jack seems to be aware of the debt he owes his uncle."

It's a debt of love and gratitude, which he has already begun to repay. You and I might be bored to tears by Mr. Huggins's memoir, but I doubt Jack will be. I believe Jack will treasure every word. Yes, indeed, a very touching tale, and at the same time, as you put it, a waterfall of gossip! Jack painted a remarkably detailed picture of his past and present circumstances for you and Bree. I wonder why he was willing to explain himself to you?

"He wasn't just explaining himself to us," I said. "He was explaining himself to the whole village and it's not hard to understand why. He doesn't want people to see him as a vulture swooping in to pick his uncle's bones."

I don't believe anyone who met him on Saturday regarded him as a vulture.

"Maybe not," I said, "but they've had time to reconsider. Who knows what nasty notions have occurred to them since then?"

Very true. He was wise to enlist you and Bree as his ambassadors. You'll both be fearless in his defense, should the need arise.

"I wouldn't count on Bree just yet," I said. "She thinks Jack's up to something."

What sort of something?

"Who knows?" I said. "She doesn't. If you ask me, she's miffed with Jack for confounding her expectations. She wanted him to be a foul-mouthed, beer-guzzling Aussie lout, but his charm offensive disarmed her."

It can be unsettling to have one's prejudices undermined.

"Prejudices *should* be undermined," I stated firmly. I hesitated, then added, "I have to agree with her about one thing, though. Jack was preternaturally nice to her. He shrugged off every poisoned dart she threw at him and kept on smiling."

Yes, well, she's the only young person he's laid eyes on since he arrived in Finch, and she happens to be an immensely attractive young person. Jack, too, is young, he's a long way from home, and he and Bree do come from the same hemisphere. It's entirely understandable that he should be drawn to her. Wouldn't it be splendid if they fell in love?

"Matchmaking from beyond the grave," I said, clucking my tongue. "You simply can't help yourself, can you, Dimity?"

Old habits die hard. So to speak.

I laughed out loud.

"I'll let you know if I detect any softening on Bree's part," I said. "I won't be able to observe her on the way to Ivy Cottage tomorrow, though, because she'll be driving her car and I'll be riding my new bike."

Through the rain?

"It won't rain tomorrow," I said.

You sound very sure of yourself.

"I am very sure of myself, because——" I stopped short and started over again, feeling foolish. "Sorry, Dimity. I forgot to tell you about the wishing well." I hunkered down in the tall armchair and repaired my omission. When I was done, Aunt Dimity's handwriting resumed.

I seem to recall a well at Ivy Cottage——the Sandersons lived there in my time, and Mrs. Sanderson used to take tea with my mother in the back garden——but I don't remember it as a wishing well. Mr. Sanderson had trained ivy to grow up the sides, though, so the inscription you mentioned must have been hidden from view.

"What a pity," I said airily. "You missed your chance to make a wish. I, on the other hand, spoke, so my wish will be granted. The soggy season ends tomorrow."

Naturally.

"Do I detect a note of sarcasm in your response, Dimity?" I inquired.

You detect an entire symphony of sarcasm in my response, my dear. Did Bree make a wish?

"Certainly not," I said. "She's much more grown up than I am."

In some ways, perhaps. Jack MacBride may help us to see just how grown up she is.

"Stay tuned for further developments," I said. I glanced at the mantel clock and scrambled to my feet.

"Gotta run, Dimity. Will and Rob will have to flag down a cab if I don't leave right this minute."

Drive carefully, my dear. I don't want you to end up in a ditch again.

"You and Bill will never let me forget the ditch incident, will you?" I grumbled.

I sincerely doubt it.

I smiled wryly while Aunt Dimity's handwriting faded from the page, then returned the journal to its shelf, gave Reginald's ears a quick twiddle, and took off in the Rover for Upper Deeping.

It may have been wishful thinking, but as I dodged puddles and braved rushing rivulets, I could have sworn the rain was slacking off.

Eight

"You're proud of yourself," Bill said during breakfast on Tuesday morning. "You're actually proud of yourself."

He shook his head in disbelief as he stared at me across the kitchen table.

"Why shouldn't I be proud of myself?" I retorted. "The sun's shining, isn't it? The wind has stopped howling and there isn't a cloud in the sky." I buttered a triangle of toast and pointed it at him as I continued, "You should be grateful to me for making such a wise and benevolent wish. If I hadn't, you'd have half the river running through your office right now."

I'd spent much of the previous evening telling Bill about the luncheon at Ivy Cottage. Like Dimity, he'd reacted skeptically when I'd mentioned the wish I'd bellowed into Jack's rediscovered well, and I'd spent the entire, sun-drenched morning reminding him of how wrong he'd been to doubt me.

"You did not stop the rain, Lori," Bill stated unequivocally.

"I didn't do it *alone*," I acknowledged through a mouthful of buttered toast. "The wishing well—"

"Lori," Bill interrupted, glancing meaningfully at Will and Rob, who'd been following our conversation with great interest.

"Oh, all right," I conceded. I paused to swallow my bite of toast before saying solemnly, "I can't control the weather. A wishing well can't control the weather. A wish can't keep the rain from falling or make the sun shine."

"Thank you," said Bill.

"But you have to admit," I added, eyeing him mischievously, "it's a corker of a coincidence."

"What's a coincidence?" Will asked.

"Did you use a corker to stop the rain, Mummy?" asked Rob.

Chastened by Bill's accusatory glare, I spent the next few minutes explaining to our sons that I'd been playing a game with Daddy when I'd said those silly things about the wishing well and that intelligent young men knew better than to believe in silly things. I then scooped their dishes from the table and headed for the sink, leaving the definitions of *corker* as well as *coincidence* to Bill.

Since Emma Harris's mornings were even more hectic than mine, I waited until after the school run to telephone her. She sounded harassed when I reached her, so I was slightly surprised when she jumped at the chance to put her vast expanse of gardening knowledge at Jack's disposal.

"It'll be a relief to get away from the stables for a while," she said.

"Are you still nursing Pegasus?" I inquired, recalling her chestnut mare's convenient case of colic.

"Rosie's fine," she assured me, "but not much else is. I had to cancel today's riding lessons as well as tomorrow's because the south pasture is flooded, the riding rings are knee-deep in mud, and half the hands are off sick. It's nothing we can't handle, but I won't mind putting it behind me for an hour or two."

"Come whenever you can," I said. "We'll have a nice cup of tea waiting for you."

"Sounds heavenly," she said. "I'll try to get away around noon."

"See you then," I said, and rang off.

I'd dressed for the day in an old T-shirt, an old cardigan, a very old Windbreaker, and a pair of nylon hiking trousers that were old but still water repellent. I'd donned a pair of sneakers as well, but I'd tucked my trusty wellies into the rattan basket on Betsy's handlebars, along with a pair of gardening gloves and a wide-brimmed straw hat. I was, I thought, ready to deal with whatever Hector Huggins's gardens could throw at me.

My beautiful bicycle was waiting for me where I'd left her, leaning against the garage door, with a matching helmet dangling from her handlebars. After donning the helmet, I settled myself on Betsy's well-cushioned seat, pushed off, and rang her brass bell to express the sheer joy I felt at finally taking her out for a spin.

There is nothing quite as exhilarating as riding a spanking new bicycle through the English countryside on a perfect day in May. The warm sun caressed my face, a self-generated breeze cooled my brow, and birdsong filled my ears as I pedaled swiftly along the twisting lane. I felt as if I were flying, and though the road surface was still quite damp, I handled the tricky curve near Bree's house without slowing.

I wasn't entirely sure what to do with Betsy's twenty-one gears, but the gear she was in seemed to be working well enough for my needs, so I didn't worry about changing into another. I arrived at Ivy Cottage feeling exultant, gave the hand brakes a firm squeeze, and tumbled over the handlebars and into the shaggy hedgerow.

A few unfortunate words escaped my lips.

"Lori?" Jack called over the hedge. "Is that you?"

He raced through the gateway, ran to my side, and hovered anxiously while I extricated myself from a web of springy branches. I noted vaguely that he'd donned his cargo shorts and sandals again, but I was too mortified to savor my close-up view of his shapely legs.

"Are you all right?" he asked.

"No worries," I said, spitting out a mouthful of hawthorn leaves as I hauled myself to my feet. "I had a soft landing."

"It's a good thing we put off the hedge trimming," he observed.

"Agreed," I said. I gestured to the modest sedan parked on the verge near Willis, Sr.'s, wrought-iron gates. "I see Bree has arrived."

"With far less drama than you," said Jack.

While he collected the items that had fallen from Betsy's basket, Bree emerged from the gateway. She, too, was wearing shorts, but hers were denim cutoffs, and her feet were protected by her bumblebee-striped wellies. I was pleased to note that her short-sleeved purple T-shirt bore no national symbols, and though her tattooed arms were on full display, I considered the tattoos' floral motifs to be politically neutral.

She surmised from the scene what had happened and had the good grace not to laugh.

"Are you sure you're okay?" she asked, pulling Betsy upright.

"I'm embarrassed, but unbroken," I told her.

"No need to be embarrassed," she said. "I reckon the only cyclists who haven't taken a spill are cyclists who leave their bikes at home." She squatted to examine Betsy, pronounced her fit to ride, and stood. "You're right, Lori. She's gorgeous."

"She?" said Jack.

"Don't ask," said Bree.

"Lori!" cried another voice, and I looked up to see short, plump Sally Pyne trotting toward us from the direction of the humpbacked bridge.

"Great," I muttered. If Sally had witnessed my fall, the whole village would know about it before lunchtime.

"Good grief, Lori," she exclaimed as she drew nearer. "Should I ring Dr. Finisterre? I saw you sail over your handle-bars and I was sure you'd killed yourself."

"Not dead," I said, spreading my arms wide to display my undead body. "Not even concussed. Nothing but a few scratches. It's the hand brakes. I'll have to get used to them."

"I should think so," said Sally. She turned immediately to Jack and pressed a hand to her ample bosom. "Sally Pyne, in case you've forgotten."

"How could I forget you, Mrs. Pyne?" said Jack. "You own the tearoom and you made the delicious chicken in wine sauce."

"I do, I did, and I'm Sally to you," said Sally, blushing with the pleasure of being remembered by someone as young and handsome as Jack. "I'm sure you have lots to do, Jack, so I won't beat about the bush. I don't want you to feel pressurized in any way, but it dawned on me last night that you might not know how to return the casserole dishes once you've finished with them. So I thought I'd pop in and tell you whose dish is whose."

"You beauty," said Jack. "That's a great idea. I'll show you to the kitchen." Jack dumped my possessions into Betsy's basket and presented his arm to Sally. "Allow me to assist you, Sally. The front garden's a bit wild and I wouldn't want you to turn an ankle."

"One crash landing per day is enough, eh?" Sally said, peering up at him roguishly. She placed her hand in the crook of his elbow and bounced through the gateway as gaily as a young girl on prom night.

I took Betsy from Bree, began rolling her through the gateway, and stopped short.

"What happened to the intercom?" I asked, gazing at the dark patch on the gatepost where the device had been mounted.

"Jack dismantled it," said Bree. "He plans to leave the gate unlocked as well. He wants the villagers to feel free to knock on his front door."

"They'll knock *down* his front door," I said, pushing Betsy into the jungle. "Everyone's dying to poke their noses into Ivy

Cottage. Take Sally, for example. If she gives two hoots about casserole dishes, I'll eat Betsy's tires. Sally came here to snoop."

"The first of many," Bree said, nodding sagely.

"When did you get here?" I asked.

"Twenty minutes ago," she replied. She pointed to an impressive array of tools piled on a blue tarpaulin stretched across the ground between the garage door and the front bumper of Jack's rental car. "We unloaded my car and made a start on clearing the path between the garage and the cottage, but we haven't gotten very far. Is Emma coming?"

"She hopes to be here by noon," I said.

"Good," said Bree. "I don't mind clearing the paths because the paths are already there, but I'm not sure about the rest of it. Emma will know what's worth saving and what isn't."

"Forget the paths," I told her. "Let's snoop on the snoop."

I propped Betsy against the cottage, hung my helmet on her handlebars, took my wellies from her basket, and shooed Bree indoors. We entered the kitchen in time to hear Sally assign Miranda Morrow's name to the purple casserole dish.

"Shall I go over it again?" she asked.

"I think I'll remember," Jack replied.

"Good. When you're ready to return them," she concluded, "you can ask anyone in the village where to go and they'll point you in the right direction."

"Thanks, Sally," said Jack.

"Not at all," said Sally. She strolled casually to the wide-open back door, peered into the garden, and exclaimed, "You have a well, Jack! I didn't know there was a well at Ivy Cottage." She glanced over her shoulder at him. "Do you mind if I pop out for a peek?"

"Be my guest," said Jack.

Bree and I exchanged speculative glances as Sally made a beeline for the well.

"Jack," I said, "have you spoken with anyone in the village since Bree and I were here yesterday?"

"I spoke with Mrs. Taxman," he replied. "I went to the post office yesterday afternoon to mail a water sample to a testing lab in Oxford, and since the post office is inside Mrs. Taxman's general store, I had a look around the shop while I was there. I didn't find the bucket or the rope I wanted, but Mrs. Taxman offered to order them for me. She was very helpful."

I nodded. "Did you tell Peggy about the well when you ordered the bucket and the rope?"

"Of course I did," said Jack. "I'm prepping the cottage for sale, remember? The well's a selling point."

"Did you tell Peggy about my wish?" I went on patiently.

"I may have made a joke about it," Jack admitted. "It's pretty hilarious, after all. Lori Shepherd wants the rain to stop and—*bam!*—it stops raining! I think I said we could use someone like you back home in the wet."

I groaned and Bree heaved a dolorous sigh.

"Why the long faces?" Jack asked.

"You don't know what you've done," I said.

"Enlighten me," said Jack.

"Where do I start?" I said, gazing at him pityingly. "What you have to understand, Jack, is that everyone in Finch is frothing at the mouth to sneak a peek at Ivy Cottage because no one's set foot in it since your uncle moved in."

"They would have come calling for that reason alone," said Bree, "but you've given them an even better reason."

"The well?" Jack guessed.

"The *wishing* well," I clarified. "The villagers will be trooping through here morning, noon, and night to make a wish in your well."

"You can't be serious," Jack scoffed. "No one over the age of six believes in wishing wells."

"I'm not saying they believe in it," I temporized. "Not all of them. Not deep down. But the ones who aren't superstitious will be intrigued."

"When they hear about Lori's wish coming true," said Bree, "they'll think to themselves, 'Why not give it a go?'"

"In short," I concluded, "you're about to be trampled by a herd of villagers."

"What's wrong with that?" said Jack. "Let 'em come. The more, the merrier."

"Famous last words," I intoned.

Bree put a finger to her lips and we fell silent as Sally Pyne came in from the back garden.

"It's a wonderful well," she said. "Like something out of a fairy story. I'd stay to lend a hand with the garden, Jack, but I don't like to leave Henry alone in the tearoom for too long. Henry's my fiancé," she explained to Jack. "He used to be an entertainer on a cruise ship. His jokes make me laugh, but not everyone appreciates them."

"Hello?" called a man's voice. "Anyone at home?"

"We're in here, Mr. Barlow," Sally shouted in reply.

My eyebrows rose. Mr. Barlow was a down-to-earth handyman, sexton, and retired mechanic whose work-booted feet were planted firmly on the ground. Had I made a mental list of the people least likely to test the wishing well's alleged powers, Mr. Barlow's name would have been at the very top of it. Happily, my faith in him was justified when he entered the kitchen lugging his tool kit, a bundle of hairy jute rope, and an iron-banded oak bucket with a sturdy iron handle.

"Morning, Jack," he said. "I heard you were looking to fix up your well, so I had a rummage in my shed and found these." He held up the bucket and the rope. "No point in buying new when old will do."

"No point at all," said Jack. "Much obliged, Mr. Barlow."

"Let's see if the rope's long enough," said Mr. Barlow, turning toward the back door.

"I'll give you a hand," said Jack, "as soon as I've—"

"You go ahead," Sally broke in. "I'll see myself out."

Jack followed Mr. Barlow into the garden and Sally trotted back to the tearoom to rescue her customers from her fiancé's sense of humor. Bree and I, left alone in the kitchen, paused for a meditative moment.

"Peggy's going to hit the roof when Jack cancels his order," Bree said, breaking the silence. "She'll have Mr. Barlow's guts for garters when she finds out his rummage lost her a sale, and she'll give Jack an earful."

"We can't do everything, Bree," I said philosophically. "Jack will have to learn some lessons the hard way. In the meantime . . ." I took off my sneakers and stepped into my Wellington boots. "We'd better clear the footpath to the front door. It's about to become a superhighway."

Nine

I would have added clairvoyance to my list of superpow-
ers if my prediction hadn't been so . . . predictable. Bree
and I were less than halfway through our clearance
project when Miranda Morrow arrived at Ivy Cottage, accompanied by Elspeth Binney, Selena Buxton, and Opal Taylor.

Elspeth and Opal wore their everyday tweed skirts, blouses,
cardigans, and sensible shoes, but Selena, a retired wedding planner, was dressier, in a pale pink, tailored skirt suit and pale pink
pumps enveloped in dainty, see-through galoshes. Miranda's leaf-
green gossamer gown set her apart from the older ladies, suggesting much about her lithe figure while revealing nothing.

"Where's Millicent?" I asked.

Elspeth, Opal, and Selena were rarely seen without their
friend and neighbor Millicent Scroggins. Bill had dubbed the
quartet "Father's Handmaidens" because of their devotion to
my genteel father-in-law. Willis, Sr., disliked the nickname
intensely, but his disapproval couldn't keep me from thinking
of Elspeth, Opal, Selena, and Millicent as the Handmaidens.

"Dentist," Elspeth answered. "The poor dear is having
trouble with a back tooth."

"I'm sorry to hear it," I said.

"Millicent's sorry, too," said Selena. "She wanted so much
to be with us when we welcomed Jack MacBride to Finch."

"You welcomed him on Saturday, didn't you?" Bree asked.

"Yes," said Opal, "but it was a general, community welcome. We wish to welcome him personally."

Their story would have been more credible had they looked me or Bree in the eye while they delivered it. Instead, they scanned every inch of the front garden and peered voraciously at the cottage, as if they hoped to see through it to the miraculous well that had, I strongly suspected, been described to them in loving detail by Peggy Taxman.

Miranda's pagan beliefs allowed her to come straight to the point.

"Thanks for the sunshine, Lori," she said cheerfully. The sunlight glinted in her strawberry-blond hair, as if to underscore the efficacy of my wish. "I hope Jack won't mind if I put his well to therapeutic use." She held up her wicker basket to display a half dozen glass bottles stoppered with corks. "My rheumatic patients might benefit from a dose of his well water."

"It hasn't been tested yet," I said quickly. "A dose might give your patients something worse than rheumatism."

"I'll use the first batch for external applications only," said Miranda. "But I'll be back for more if the tests—and Jack—give me the all-clear."

 The Handmaidens chuckled tolerantly.

"Such an imagination," said Elspeth.

"So entertaining," said Selena.

"You'll be taking Henry Cook's place soon, Miranda," said Opal.

"I'm not telling a funny story," Miranda protested. "It's common knowledge that sacred wells have healing powers. Lori used Jack's well to heal the weather. I'll use the water to heal the infirm."

Elspeth gave Miranda a condescending smile, then turned to me, saying, "*My* interest in the well is purely historical. The discovery of a traditional water source in our village should be recorded for posterity."

"Oh, I *so* agree," Selena chimed in sincerely. "It's an architectural find of great distinction."

"An artistic one, as well," Elspeth asserted. "I've heard it's lovely. Like something out of a fairy tale."

"Is Jack at home?" Opal inquired. "Will he mind showing us his well?"

"While we welcome him to Finch," Selena added hurriedly.

Bree couldn't restrain a snigger as she sliced through a mass of weeds with her brush hook, but I maintained a straight face and led the ladies through the cottage to see the architectural find of great distinction.

"Jack," I sang from the kitchen doorway as the Handmaidens spilled past me and into the back garden. "You have visitors."

The sound of high-pitched twittering filled the air as Elspeth, Selena, and Opal surged forward to greet Jack, to cluck over the state of the garden, and to admire the well, which was now equipped with an appropriately aged bucket dangling from a suitably rough-hewn rope. Miranda waited for the chatter to subside, then explained her mission to Jack.

"You're welcome to fill your bottles," he said, "as long as you—"

"Don't let anyone drink from them," Miranda broke in, nodding. "I won't. I'll use the water in massages until I know it's safe for human consumption."

"In that case . . ." Jack wheeled around and held an arm out, as if he were an impresario presenting Mr. Barlow to an audience. "Mr. Barlow? If you please?"

Mr. Barlow employed the freshly oiled crank to lower the bucket soundlessly into the well and to bring it up again, brimming with water. Elspeth, Selena, and Opal applauded and Jack pulled the bucket over to rest on the wellhead. Miranda filled her bottles, thanked her host, and departed.

"I'll be off, too," Mr. Barlow announced. "My job's done."

Jack demonstrated great tact by waiting until he and Mr. Barlow were in the kitchen before bringing up the delicate subject of payment. Mr. Barlow didn't mind discussing money matters in front of me, but he thought it unwise to mention them within earshot of the Handmaidens.

"Make it a tenner for the bucket and twenty for the rope," said Mr. Barlow.

"And your labor?" asked Jack.

"Tuppence," said Mr. Barlow, with a wry smile.

"Wait here," said Jack. "My cash stash is upstairs."

He left to fetch the money and Mr. Barlow wandered over to stand beside me in the doorway.

"Daft old biddies," he said scathingly, observing the Handmaidens. "Look at them, pretending to take an interest in the trellis and the pergola, when they know very well why they're here. Each one's making a wish as soon as the others' backs are turned."

"Did you make a wish?" I asked.

"Do I look daft to you?" he retorted.

"No," I said. "But if you were daft enough to make a wish, what would it be?"

"I wouldn't say no to a Jaguar," Mr. Barlow replied after a moment's thought. "Not to own—the maintenance is too dear—but I wouldn't say no to working on a Jaguar. A classic E-Type, for preference. Not likely to get my hands on one in Finch, but if I believed in all this make-a-wish malarkey, I'd ask the old well to bring one to me."

"Here you are, Mr. Barlow," said Jack, striding into the kitchen.

Mr. Barlow took the bills Jack offered, counted them, and tried unsuccessfully to return a few. Jack adamantly refused to take them back, saying that Mr. Barlow had earned every pence.

"A fool and his money are soon parted," Mr. Barlow said gruffly.

"A fair day's wages for a fair day's work," Jack countered, grinning.

Mr. Barlow glanced over his shoulder, saw an incoming tide of Handmaidens, said a hasty good-bye to Jack and me, and made his way rapidly to the front door, his tool kit clinking as he ran. Elspeth, Opal, and Serena swept in and allowed

Jack to sweep them out with admirable dexterity. I savored the silence for a few seconds, then headed outdoors.

I found Jack leaning against the front gate to catch his breath while Bree continued to wield her brush hook.

"It's like being swarmed by a flock of budgies," he marveled.

For the second time in two days I resisted the temptation to say "I told you so," but Bree was merciless.

"You can't say you weren't warned," she said. "I told you yesterday that Peggy Taxman was indiscreet, but did you listen?"

"Stone the crows," Jack said incredulously as a gray Land Rover pulled up behind Bree's car. "Here comes another one."

"You're in luck, my friend," I said. "It's not another one. It's Emma Harris, who bears no resemblance whatsoever to a budgie. I promised her a cup of tea, by the way."

"I could do with one myself," said Bree, wiping her sweaty brow with the hem of her T-shirt.

"I'll lock the gate behind Emma," Jack proposed, "and we'll all take a lunch break."

"At last!" Bree exclaimed. "The boy's talking sense!"

Emma Harris was the most capable woman I knew. She could knit a sweater, tend a garden, train a horse, write a computer program, and run a business without ever seeming overwhelmed or frantic. She was the kind of woman I would have aspired to be if I'd aspired to fight a losing battle. As it was, our friendship proved that, as with Jack's parents, opposites attract.

She arrived at Ivy Cottage with a digital camera, a notebook, and a laser tape measure tucked into a canvas tote. She'd drawn her graying, dishwater blond hair back into a neat ponytail and dressed with equal simplicity, in blue jeans, a lightweight, long-sleeved jersey, and black Wellington boots. She greeted Jack cordially, apologized for missing his uncle's funeral, and welcomed his invitation to sit down to lunch.

"I eat most of my meals at my desk," she explained. "A dining table will be a great luxury."

While Emma, Bree, and I put a sizable dent in Jack's casserole collection, he explained that he'd applied to Lilian Bunting for help in finding a lab to test the well water and that he'd used a sterilized milk bottle and a length of his late uncle's fishing line to retrieve the sample.

He then went on to discuss horticultural matters with Bree and Emma. Since I had nothing worthwhile to contribute, I allowed my gaze to wander around the room and noticed almost immediately that something new had appeared in it. A slightly squashed reddish-brown kangaroo—a soft toy, not a product of taxidermy—sat atop the bookcase. I waited for a break in the conversation to mention it.

"Is the kangaroo yours, Jack?" I asked, pointing to the bookcase.

"He is," Jack replied. "His name is Joey—it's what baby roos are called—and I've had him since I was an ankle biter. He'd've ended up in an op shop if I'd left him at home, so I brought him along with me on my travels. Joey's been from the Snowy Mountains to the Kimberly, from Sydney to Perth, from the Great Barrier Reef to the great hunk of rock known as Uluru." He sat back, folded his arms, and regarded Bree resignedly. "Go ahead, take the piss. Ask why a bloke has a kid's toy in his rucksack."

"I don't have to ask," said Bree. "I get it. It's no fun to travel alone. It's better to have a mate with you."

Jack seemed taken aback by her respectful response. I wasn't, because I knew something he didn't. I knew about Ruru, a small and very tattered brown owl Bree had carried with her on an epic journey that had taken her from New Zealand to her great-grandaunts' house. By sheer luck, Jack had confessed his eccentricity to three people who wouldn't find it risible. Although Emma didn't have a Reginald or a Ruru or a Joey of her own, she was far too open-minded to ridicule those of us who did.

"I'd love to sit around and chat," said Emma, pushing her chair away from the table, "but I have to be back to the manor by two, so I'd better get to work. I'll take measurements, notes, and photographs today, Jack, and use them to draw up a preliminary plan."

"I'll be in the front garden if anyone needs me," said Bree, getting to her feet.

"I'll join you after I've cleared the table," Jack told her.

"I'll be in the back garden," I announced, "clearing the path from the kitchen door to the well." I gazed at Jack with feigned innocence. "Millicent Scroggins will make her wish as soon as she's back from the dentist's. You wouldn't want her to turn an ankle, would you?"

Jack threw his napkin at me, laughed, and began to stack the dishes.

I caught Emma's eye, and with a small jerk of my head directed her to meet me in the back garden. She responded with a mildly puzzled look, but I found her waiting for me by the well when I emerged from the kitchen armed with a rake.

"I presume you're scheming," she said quietly.

"Don't be so suspicious," I scolded, raking up the strands of ivy strewn about the well. "I simply think it would be nice if the young'uns spent some time together. On their own. Without older folk around to cramp their style."

"Matchmaking," said Emma, gazing heavenward. "I should have known."

"There's nothing wrong with giving natural impulses a gentle shove in the right direction," I said.

"I'll leave the shoving to you," said Emma. She rested a hand on one of the well's sturdy posts and scanned our surroundings. "I've almost forgotten how much I enjoy gardening."

"You've been too wrapped up in the riding school," I told her, bending to my task. "You should take a break once in a while. Grow a prize-winning eggplant, knit a circus tent, invent the cure for the common cold."

"There's no room for a break in my schedule," she said. "I couldn't ask for better partners than Nell and Kit, but they can't run the school by themselves and Derek has his own business to manage."

Emma's husband, Derek, owned a construction business specializing in restoration work. His daughter Nell—Emma's stepdaughter—and her husband, Kit, lived with them at Anscombe Manor and worked full-time at the Anscombe Riding Center.

"They look after the horses and the students beautifully," Emma went on, "but the rest of it—the business end of it—is my responsibility." She heaved a small sigh. "These days I spend more time behind a desk than on a horse. I hardly ever get to teach a class anymore. I'm too busy managing schedules, accounts, supplies, maintenance, personnel . . . I do everything but climb into a saddle. When I started the school, I didn't envision myself shuffling paperwork, but the paperwork must be shuffled and I'm good at that sort of thing." She gave another little sigh. "I wish . . ."

I leaned on my rake and asked curiously, "What do you wish?"

"I wish the perfect someone would appear on my doorstep and manage the riding school for me," she exclaimed. "I'd offer room and board if I thought it would attract the right person. Heaven knows we have rooms to spare at the manor."

I stared at her, speechless. Emma was used to my passionate outbursts, but I seldom heard one from her, and I'd never before heard her utter a negative word about her beloved riding school. I wasn't quite sure what to say.

"You could advertise for a manager," I suggested cautiously.

"No, I couldn't," Emma said. "There's no such thing as a perfect someone, and besides, I don't really want a stranger stepping into my boots." She smiled wanly. "Pay no attention to me, Lori. I'm tired and when I'm tired I get fed up with unblocking blocked drainage ditches and listening to parents complain because their little darling's lesson was canceled." Her gaze drifted from the pergola to the stone wall to the rose-covered ruin of a trellis. "I won't let it spoil my time here, though. An hour or two spent up to my knees in green stuff will put me right." She bent to examine the feathery leaf of an otherwise nondescript plant, murmuring, "Interesting, very interesting . . ."

I left her to her green stuff and went back to work, wishing a knight in shining armor would ride over the horizon to slay my friend's paperwork dragons.

Ten

Emma's initial survey of the gardens at Ivy Cottage had unexpected results. Jack, Bree, and I had finished liberating the brick paths from the undergrowth and were in the kitchen sipping tea and comparing blisters when Emma asked us to join her near the old wishing well. Her face was flushed, her hair was falling out of its ponytail, and her voice trembled with excitement as she made her surprising announcement.

"All work in the gardens must stop," she declared. "Right now. Immediately. No more cutting, slashing, or uprooting until I've created a comprehensive garden plan."

"Why?" Jack asked. "I didn't notice any endangered species when I looked 'round the other day. Nothing out of the ordinary."

"It's not about protecting endangered species. It's about . . ." Emma paused to regroup, then continued urgently, "I realize that your uncle's property looks like a neglected mess, Jack, but it isn't. He knew exactly what he was doing with it and he did it brilliantly."

"I didn't think he'd done anything with it," said Jack, perplexed. "How could he? He didn't even own a spade."

"Have you looked in the shed?" Emma asked, waving a hand in the direction of the ramshackle garage.

"Not yet," said Jack. "The doors are jammed."

"Ask Mr. Barlow to open them for you," said Emma. "I think you'll find a full complement of gardening tools inside. Your uncle couldn't have done what he did without them. He must have been a great nature lover."

"He was," Jack confirmed. "He used to sit at his windows with his binoculars and take notes on whatever caught his eye."

"I knew it!" Emma said triumphantly. "Don't you see? He designed his gardens to attract wildlife—birds, bees, butterflies, bugs. Look . . ." She strode away from us, pointing to her finds as she passed them. "Bee balm, butterfly bush, yellow hyssop, witch hazel, milkweed, yarrow, cosmos, hollyhocks, globe thistles, blackberries, clematis, alyssum, sunflowers, calendula, . . ." She returned to the well, saying, "I could go on, but I'll put the rest of it down on paper."

"I don't see hollyhocks," said Bree. "Or sunflowers. Or—"

"They haven't come up, yet," Emma cut in, "but I found last summer's leaves and stalks, so I know they're here. I found four birdbaths, too, and a pair of bird tables for winter feeding. They're falling apart, but they could be repaired or replaced." She clasped her notebook to her chest and peered up at Jack hopefully. "Your uncle created gardens that celebrate and support life, Jack. It would be a crime to destroy them."

Jack rubbed the back of his neck, looking doubtful. "Can they be simplified? I've got to sell the place, you see, and I'm not sure anyone but Uncle Hector would enjoy living in the middle of a nature reserve."

"Once we tidy them up, they'll have excellent eye-appeal," Emma assured him. "Not everyone wants a lawn," she added encouragingly. "All I ask is that you leave the gardens alone until you've seen my plan. I'll bring it to you tomorrow—Thursday at the latest. There is one thing you can do, though, and I suggest you start doing it as soon as possible."

"What's that?" Jack asked.

"Examine the cottage's external walls," Emma replied. "If they're in good condition, the ivy won't hurt them. If they're deteriorating—if the mortar's loose, for example—the ivy will hasten their decay, in which case you'll have to strip the vines and make the necessary repairs. While you're up there, make sure the vines haven't gone under the roof slates or taken root in the gutters and downspouts. If they have, prune them with a firm hand. Bees love ivy and it provides shelter for small birds, but it has to be kept under control."

"Why not remove the ivy entirely?" I asked. "Doesn't it make little holes in the walls?"

"Contrary to popular belief," said Emma, "ivy *protects* stone buildings. It regulates temperature and moisture and it guards walls from pollutants that damage stone."

"If the walls are in bad shape, though, I'll need to find a stonemason," Jack said with a sigh. "Can you recommend one?"

When Emma hesitated, I jumped in.

"Emma's too modest to say it, so I'll speak for her," I said. "Her husband is the man you want. Derek Harris is a builder who specializes in restoration work. He's a brilliant stone-

mason. If the ivy has damaged your walls, he'll be able to repair them."

Jack folded his arms and gazed thoughtfully at the garden,
then turned to study the cottage's ivy-cloaked walls.

"Done," he said decisively, extending a hand to shake Emma's. "No point in asking for expert advice if I'm not going to
take it. I'll hold off on the gardens for now and start in on the
cottage walls. If I don't find a ladder in the garage, I expect I
can borrow one from Mr. Barlow."

"I suggest you borrow three ladders," I said.

"Lori and I aren't afraid of heights," said Bree, catching my
drift. "We'll be back here tomorrow, same time."

"Beaut," said Jack, gazing gratefully at us.

"Hello? Is anyone at home?" cried a voice all but one of us
recognized.

"Millicent Scroggins," said Emma, cocking an ear toward
the front door.

"Fresh from the dentist's," said Bree.

"I told you so," I said at last, wagging a finger at Jack.

My friends and I escorted him to the front porch to greet
the missing Handmaiden, whose right cheek was as swollen as
a chipmunk's. We commiserated with her on her ordeal, suggested remedies ranging from oil of cloves to ice packs, then
left her to Jack's ministrations and took off, Emma in her Land
Rover, Bree in her small sedan, and me on Betsy.

Riding a bicycle after a good night's sleep is one thing. Riding one after a day's hard labor is another. Fond thoughts of

the internal combustion engine's many charms filled my head as I pedaled home and I spent the evening hobbling gingerly from room to room.

Bill was an old hand at cycling. He rode to and from his office on the village green as often as his schedule and the weight of his briefcase would allow. He informed me during dinner that my homeward journey had been hampered not only by muscle fatigue but by topography.

"Finch is at the bottom of a river valley," he reminded me. "We're higher up the valley. You don't notice the gradual slope in a car, but you do on a bicycle. The return journey is an up-hill battle. Literally."

"We should install a tow bar," I said.

"Whit Kerby's mum has a mountain bike," said Rob. "She won a race in the Cairngorms last summer."

"The Cairngorms are mountains," Will explained, making peaks in his mashed potatoes. "They're in Scotland."

"Mrs. Kerby went straight up them," said Rob. "On a dirt course."

"She got a medal," said Will.

"For best in her age group," Rob concluded.

"Thanks, boys," I said, leaning my chin on my hand. "I feel much better now."

The twins smiled smugly at each other, pleased with themselves for comforting their mother, and Bill very wisely hid his grin behind his napkin.

After the boys had gone to bed, Bill again displayed his

wisdom by inviting me to stretch out on the sofa with my feet in his lap so he could massage them. His tender treatment of my aching arches rendered me incapable of retaliating when he offered to teach me the correct way to use hand brakes.

"Sally Pyne tattled," I murmured, slurring my words drunkenly.

"You didn't expect her to keep your death-defying maneuver to herself, did you?" said Bill.

"Not for one second," I said.

"I'm glad you wore your helmet," said Bill, working his way up to my calves.

"I'm glad I landed in the hedge," I said.

"Now, about the weather . . ." he went on. "Should I bring an umbrella to work tomorrow or did you wish for a prolonged dry spell?"

"Very funny," I retorted as forcefully as I could under the circumstances. "Unfortunately, people are taking the joke seriously."

"What people?" Bill asked.

"The good people of Finch," I replied. "Jack told Peggy Taxman about my wish coming true, and she must have bellowed the news to everyone who set foot in the Emporium because Sally Pyne and the Handmaidens showed up at Ivy Cottage to make their own wishes. Miranda Morrow was there, too. She claims well water has healing powers, but you'd expect her to have oddball ideas."

"I'd expect Sally and the Handmaidens to have oddball

ideas, too," said Bill. "I hear them at the tearoom, discussing their horoscopes as if their lives depended on them, and Sally will read tea leaves for anyone who asks."

"Mr. Barlow thinks they're balmy, too," I said, "which is too bad, because he could make a really cool wish if he wanted to."

"Such as?" asked Bill.

"He'd like to work on a classic Jaguar," I replied.

Bill threw back his head and laughed. "Good old Mr. Barlow. Give him a wrench and a banged-up car and he's a happy man. I wonder what Sally and the Handmaidens wished for?"

"Heaven knows," I said. "Youth? Wealth? Your father's hand in marriage?"

"Hope springs eternal," said Bill, chuckling.

"For the Handmaidens, maybe," I said. "Sally's heart belongs to Henry." I closed my eyes blissfully and asked, "What would you wish for?"

The soothing pressure Bill was exerting on my calf slackened infinitesimally. I peeked at him through my eyelashes and saw a shadow cross his face, but it was gone in an instant and he answered my question in his usual, playful manner.

"I'd wish for a wonderful family," he said. "Oh, wait, I already have one. I guess I'll give the wishing well a miss."

I blew a lazy kiss at him, then said with a sigh, "If only Emma were as pleased with her life as you are with yours."

"What's wrong with Emma?" Bill asked.

"She's not a happy camper at the moment," I said. "Too much office work, not enough horsey fun. Or gardening fun.

Or any kind of fun. I'd offer to help her, but if I did her accounting, she'd be bankrupt in five minutes. I'm hopeless with numbers."

"Be a sounding board, then," said Bill. "Be the one person who lets her vent whenever she feels the need."

"I will," I said, "but I wish I could do more."

"Speak to the well. It seems to like the sound of your voice." Bill laughed at his own joke, then shifted my legs from his lap to the sofa as he stood. "Sorry, love, but I brought work home with me. I must commune with my laptop."

"No worries," I said, sitting up with a groan. "I've got some communing of my own to do." I let Bill pull me gently to my feet and continued the upward motion until our lips met in a soft but thorough kiss.

"I'll be ready for bed when you are," he said when we came up for air.

"Good," I said. "Because you may have to carry me upstairs."

Bill took his laptop from the coffee table and began the unenviable task of evicting Stanley from his armchair. I limped into the study. I couldn't bear the thought of kneeling to light a fire, so I lit the mantel lights, took the blue journal from its shelf, lowered myself laboriously onto one of the tall leather armchairs before the hearth, and looked up at Reginald, who peered down at me from his special niche on the bookshelves.

"Guess what, mate?" I said. "Jack MacBride has a buddy like you, only his buddy is a baby kangaroo named Joey. I knew I liked that boy."

The gleam in Reginald's black button eyes seemed to suggest that he was predisposed to like Jack MacBride, too. I leaned back in the chair, rested my creaky legs on the ottoman, and opened the blue journal.

"Dimity?" I said. I smiled wryly as the graceful lines of royal-blue ink began to loop and curl across the page.

Good evening, my dear. Congratulations on the fine weather. You are undoubtedly a meteorological magician. With one wish, you kept the river from overflowing and made a pleasant outing on your new bicycle possible.

"You and Bill should form a comedy team," I said. "You could be his ghostwriter."

You were rather full of yourself last night.

"I was joking," I said. "I didn't expect the rain to end because I told it to. Unfortunately . . ."

I spent the next half hour repeating to Aunt Dimity everything I'd said to Bill. I gave her a more detailed account than I'd given him and I saved the best bit for last.

"I've detected signs of softening in Bree," I announced.

Clear signs?

"You be the judge," I said. "She arrived at Ivy Cottage twenty minutes before I did. She didn't tease Jack about Joey. I didn't hear any explosions coming from the front garden when I cleverly arranged for them to spend time there together. And she volunteered to help Jack again tomorrow."

The signs are promising, very promising. The relationship presents certain difficulties, of course. For example, they'll have to decide whether to live in England or in Australia. It won't be easy for Bree to abandon the house she inherited from Ruth and Louise.

"Slow down, Dimity," I said, amused by her musings. "Jack and Bree met yesterday. They have a long way to go before they face problems like deciding where to live."

I know, but I can't help wishing them well, can I?

"Wish them well by all means," I said, "but try not to get too far ahead of yourself. I'm the one who jumps to conclusions, not you."

True. There are some situations, however, that beg one to jump. With your permission, I shall jump to a conclusion about just such a situation: There is a great deal of silliness abroad in Finch.

"Permission granted," I said, "if you're referring to the wishing well silliness."

I am, of course, referring to the wishing well silliness. I'm at a loss to understand why six grown women would go out of their way to make cakes of themselves. Sally, Miranda, Elspeth, Selena, Opal, and Millicent should know better than to believe in such childish nonsense.

"I agree," I said. "And I'm afraid it won't stop with six grown women. Christine Peacock will probably be there as soon as the pub closes and I wouldn't count on Charles Bellingham, Henry Cook, or George Wetherhead to stay away."

I expect the excitement will die down when none of the wishes come true. Until then, we can rely on Lilian and Theodore Bunting to behave like adults. It wouldn't do for the vicar and his wife to replace prayers with wishes. We can rely on Emma, too. She's far too rational to make use of the wishing well.

"You can add Bill to your list of abstainers," I said. "He places wishing wells in the same category as horoscopes and tea leaves."

Good for Bill! A father should set a sensible example for his children.

A strange feeling of unease came over me as I read the word *children.*

"Bill's a brilliant father," I said slowly. "He reacted oddly, though, when I asked him what his wish would be. He didn't know I was looking at him, but I was, and his face looked kind of . . . sad. He perked up right away and said he'd wish for a wonderful family if he didn't have one already, but I wonder . . ."

What do you wonder?

"I wonder if he'd wish for a *bigger* family," I said, gazing pensively into the empty grate. "It's not as though we haven't tried, Dimity, but nothing's happened. I thought he—I thought *we*—had given up on the idea, but maybe he hasn't."

Why would you give up on the idea of expanding your family?

"It took us forever to get the twins started," I reminded her, "and I'm not getting any younger. I don't have a lot of confidence in my reproductive system."

Go upstairs this instant, Lori, and look at your beautiful boys. They should give you all the confidence you need.

I smiled at Aunt Dimity's bracing words, but the fact that my sons were eight years old told me everything I needed to know about my ability to have more children. Thankfully, I was quite content with the children I had, despite their gratu-itous praise of mountain-biking Mrs. Kerby. And I was sure—almost sure—that Bill felt the same way.

Before you go, however, please tell me how you and Betsy fared on your first outing. I presume you took advantage of the glorious weather to put her through her paces.

"I put her through her paces," I said, groaning, "and she put me through the wringer. My thighs feel as if they'd been clawed by a mountain lion and my calves scream every time I flex my feet. I'm not sure I'll be able to climb the stairs when we finish here. I may have to sleep on the sofa."

Of course you'll be able to climb the stairs. Your sons are up there. Look at Will and Rob, Lori, and be hopeful. Sleep well, my dear.

"I will, Dimity," I said. "Believe me, I will!"

I waited until the curving lines of elegant copperplate had faded from the page, then returned the blue journal to its shelf, said good night to Reginald, turned out the lights, and with Bill's help, went up to bed. I didn't stop at the boys' room. Though I appreciated Aunt Dimity's advice, I'd run out of hope a long time ago.

Eleven

I could have used Wednesday's blue skies to solidify my status as a meteorological magician. Since I wasn't quite as silly as some of my neighbors, however, it was the boring old weather report that allowed me to drive Will and Rob to school secure in the knowledge that they wouldn't be soaked to the skin when I picked them up because there would be no puddles in the school yard to tempt them.

Pride—and the thought of Bill's teasing—prevented me from leaving Betsy at home on such a fine day. When I returned from the school run, I strapped on my helmet and cycled to Ivy Cottage, appeasing my irate tendons by taking full advantage of the downward slope and pedaling only when necessary.

I still didn't know what to do with the gears, but I tested the hand brakes as I coasted along and through trial and error learned how to stop my forward motion while remaining in an upright position. Tragically, no one but a chattering squirrel was on hand to witness my graceful dismount at journey's end.

Bree had again arrived at Ivy Cottage before me. Her car was parked in its accustomed place on Willis, Sr.'s verge and she was already in the front garden when I wheeled my trusty bicycle up the brick path. She and Jack stood across from each other, looking down at the three wooden extension ladders that

lay on the ground between them. Bree's arms were folded—
never a good sign—and Jack appeared to be lost in deeply unpleasant thoughts.

"Good morning?" I said, when the pair failed to greet me.

"Morning," Bree said with a brief nod.

"G'day," said Jack, adding almost as an afterthought, "Garage door's open. Mr. Barlow's crowbar did the trick. Bung
your bike in there or she'll end up buried in ivy."

"Okay," I said equably and wheeled Betsy toward the rick-
ety shed, wondering if Bree had found a way to argue with
Jack about ladders.

As Emma had predicted, Hector Huggins had stored his
gardening implements in the garage. It was well organized and
much cleaner than I'd expected it to be, and it had room to
spare for my bicycle.

"Well?" I said, returning to Jack and Bree. "What are we
waiting for?"

"Jack doesn't trust the ladders," said Bree, sounding exasperated. "He's afraid they'll collapse under us."

"Whose are they?" I asked.

"One was Uncle Hector's," Jack replied, "and the other
two belong to Mr. Barlow." He prodded the ladder closest to
him with his toe. "Mr. B. said they were pukka, but I reckon
they belong in a museum."

"If Mr. Barlow gave them his stamp of approval," I said,
"you have nothing to worry about. He wouldn't let us use
them if they weren't, uh, pukka."

"Satisfied?" Bree demanded.

"Not very." Jack raised his head to look at her. "You're doing me a favor. How do you think I'd feel if you broke your neck doing me a favor?"

Jack was clearly more focused on Bree's neck than on mine, but I didn't mind. His concern for Bree's welfare would, I knew, please Aunt Dimity, though it had quite the opposite effect on Bree.

"Oh, for pity's sake," she muttered impatiently and without further ado, she picked up a ladder, leaned it against the cottage, extended it to roof height, and scrambled up it as nimbly as a gymnast.

"See?" she shouted down to us. "Solid as a rock. Stop fussing, Jack, and get up here!"

"If she does fall," I murmured, hoping to allay Jack's fears, "she'll land on a three-foot cushion of weeds."

"If she misses the bricks," said Jack, peering anxiously at Bree.

"She'll miss the bricks," I elaborated, "because she'll slow her fall by grabbing onto the ivy. That'll give her enough time to *aim* for the weeds."

"The vines are like a backup ladder." Jack's sunny smile returned. "She'll be right."

"Bring secateurs with you," Bree hollered, brandishing her own pair. "The ivy's sneaking under the slates. It must be pruned with a firm hand!"

Jack laughed. "She's something, isn't she?"

"She's a pistol," I agreed.

The words had scarcely left my lips when a sound louder than a hundred pistol shots rent the air. I jumped in alarm and Jack sprang toward the cottage with his arms outstretched, as if he expected Bree to plummet from on high. She kept her balance, but descended the ladder rapidly, looking rattled.

"What on earth . . . ?" I said.

"It's coming from the village," said Bree. "It sounds like a plane crash-landed on the green."

"Let's find out," said Jack.

With my husband in apparent danger, I didn't need Jack's advice to race toward the village green. I outsprinted him and Bree to the top of the humpbacked bridge, where a singular sight met my eyes.

The green lay before me, a long, oval island of tussocky grass encircled by a cobbled lane. The lane was lined with venerable buildings—businesses as well as residences—made of the same golden stone as my cottage and Ivy Cottage. The mellow melding of green and gold gave the village a timeless air of unruffled tranquility.

On that glorious May morning, however, Finch looked distinctly ruffled. Villagers leaned out of open windows or spilled through doorways or stood like statues on the green, their hands pressed to their ears as they glared at the source of the appalling din.

The sound wasn't coming from a doomed airliner, but from a red two-seater sports car. The deafening roar it emitted was out of all proportion to its size. Three village dogs slipped their leashes and tore after it, barking like mad, as it crawled past the vicarage, the schoolmaster's house, and the old school-house before coming to rest directly in front of my husband's place of work, Wysteria Lodge, whereupon the roar ceased, though the dogs kept barking.

Bill strode forth from Wysteria Lodge, caught the overex-cited pups by their collars, and returned them to their grateful owners. Only then did the hapless driver get out of the car, doff his suede driving cap, and engage my helpful husband in conversation.

The driver was a short, stout man with a bald head and a very pink face. He wore horn-rimmed spectacles, leather driv-ing gloves, and a loden-green tweed suit, and he made small, fussy gestures as he spoke, as if he were picking lint from the air.

I arrived on the scene in time to hear him utter the last word of the first question I would have asked, had I been in his situation.

". . . mechanic?"

"We have an excellent mechanic in Finch," Bill assured him. "His name is—Ah! Here he is now. Mr. Barlow?"

Mr. Barlow approached the red sports car with a dream-like expression on his grizzled face. Bill had to call his name twice before he came out of his trance and strolled over to meet the bespectacled stranger.

"Dabney Holdstrom," said the man, extending his gloved hand to our sexton.

"Billy Barlow," said Mr. Barlow. He shook the little man's hand, but his gaze remained fixed on the car. "Pretty motor you have there, Mr. Holdstrom. A 1964 Jaguar XK-E, unless I'm mistaken."

"You're not mistaken, Mr. Barlow," said Mr. Holdstrom. "And she certainly doesn't *sound* very pretty. I was tootling along one of your deliciously twisty lanes when she had a fit of some sort. I can't think what's ailing her."

"I can," said Mr. Barlow.

"Can you really?" said Mr. Holdstrom, sounding impressed. "I say, Mr., er, Barlow, is it?" He glanced at Bill for confirmation, then continued, "I realize that it would be a frightful imposition, Mr. Barlow, but do you suppose you could take a look at her? If you have the time," he added diffidently.

"I have the time," said Mr. Barlow. He was almost crooning. "I have all the time in the world for a beauty like her. The most beautiful car ever made, Mr. Ferrari called her, and Mr. Ferrari knew a thing or two about beautiful cars. Four-point-two-liter engine, all-syncromesh four-speed gearbox . . . Detachable hardtop?" he asked, with a sidelong glance at Mr. Holdstrom.

"Yes, but I left it at home," Mr. Holdstrom replied. "No need for it on such a scrumptious day."

Mr. Barlow heaved a tremulous sigh, took the ignition key from Mr. Holdstrom, and looked into the crowd of villagers who'd drifted over to enjoy the commotion. "Henry! Dick! Lend us a hand, will you?"

Mr. Barlow slid into the driver's seat while Henry Cook

and Dick Peacock put their considerable weight to use, pushing Mr. Holdstrom's stricken vehicle to Mr. Barlow's garage.

"Stranded," said Mr. Holdstrom with a heavy sigh.

"The tearoom is next door," Bill informed him. "And the pub is across the green."

"Tea is best when bracing oneself for catastrophic news," said Mr. Holdstrom, "and when one owns a classic motor, catastrophic news is the only news one ever hears." He nodded at Bill. "Thank you. I shall repair to the tearoom, there to await my fate."

The crowd parted and Mr. Holdstrom entered the tearoom, mopping his glistening pate with a large silk handkerchief. Half the crowd followed him—in hopes, no doubt, of gathering gossip fodder—but Sally Pyne trotted over to speak with me.

"Do you know who that man is?" she asked in an urgent undertone.

"Dabney Holdstrom?" I ventured.

"Yes, but do you know who *Dabney Holdstrom* is?" she asked, her face flushed with suppressed excitement.

"No," I said. "Is he someone?"

"Is he *someone*?" Sally repeated incredulously. "He's only the editor-in-chief of *Cozy Cookery* magazine! A good word from him will put my tearoom on the map!" She raised a plump hand to pat my cheek, then wheeled around, saying as she departed, "The well brought him here, Lori! The well brought him!"

I stared at her retreating back while my brain began to fizz.

Bill seized my arm, pulled me into his office, and closed the door behind him.

"Sit," he said, directing me to the leather sofa upon which he took power naps and, on rare occasions, interviewed clients.

I sank onto the sofa, feeling as though I'd stumbled through the looking glass. Bill sat beside me and put his hand on my knee, as if to anchor me in reality. It didn't work.

"Lori," he began, but I cut him off.

"Is a Jaguar XK-E the same thing as a Jaguar E-Type?" I asked.

"Yes," said Bill, "but—"

"Mr. Barlow wished for a Jaguar E-Type," I interrupted, "not to own, but to work on."

"I know, but—"

"He didn't speak to the well," I said, "but he spoke within earshot of it."

"Within *earshot*?" Bill sputtered. "Of a *well*?"

"And now there's a Jaguar E-Type *in his garage*," I marveled, gazing blindly into the middle distance. "Mr. Barlow's wish came true and so did Sally's. Sally must have wished for a visit from Dabney Holdstrom—or someone *like* Dabney Holdstrom. She makes fabulous pastries and he's the editor-in-chief of *Cozy Cookery* magazine, so it stands to reason—"

"No, it doesn't," Bill broke in, raising his voice to be heard above my babbling. "It *does not* stand to reason. *Reason* has nothing to do with it." He took a breath and continued quietly but firmly, "Coincidences happen, Lori. I'll admit that a Jaguar arriving in Finch the day after Mr. Barlow mentioned one to you is an extraordinary coincidence, but I refuse to accept any other explanation. Once you start believing in things like wishing wells, all bets are off. You may as well make decisions by ripping a chicken open and consulting its oozing entrails."

The grisly image brought me back down to earth with a thud. I blanched, then put my head in my hands and chuckled ruefully.

"Thanks," I said. "I think I was becoming hysterical."

"I'm afraid the whole village is about to become hysterical," said Bill. He gazed speculatively toward the green, where those who'd failed to nab a table in the tearoom were busily conferring on recent events.

"Maybe so," I said, "but I won't. When I'm in my right mind, I don't believe in wishing wells any more than I believe in the predictive power of chicken gizzards." I hesitated, then said, "I do believe in Aunt Dimity, though, and you have to admit that she's not your average houseguest."

"We have concrete proof that Aunt Dimity exists," Bill pointed out. "She may not exist on the same plane as we do, but the blue journal proves she's out there somewhere. If you can prove to me that Jack's well converted an offhand comment into a malfunctioning car, I'll eat my words."

"It's weird, though, isn't it?" I said. "First, the rain. Then the Jaguar. Then Mr. *Cozy Cookery*."

"Coincidences are weird," Bill conceded, "but a wishing well that actually worked would be a whole lot weirder."

"As always, you are correct, my best beloved. And on that somewhat sickening and technically inaccurate note," I said, rising, "I'll return to the sensible activity of pruning ivy. Hard work will clear the cobwebs of superstition from my tiny brain. But I'll probably need a hand massage this evening."

"Your wish is my command," said Bill. "As the wishing well said to the Handmaidens."

I laughed, but as I left Wysteria Lodge I couldn't help wondering if we'd seen the last of Finch's flurry of weird coincidences.

Twelve

I didn't go straight back to Ivy Cottage. I stopped at the tearoom to pick up a fresh loaf of bread for dinner and some strawberry jam drops for the twins' after-school snack. Henry Cook was so busy waiting on seated customers that I was still there—purely by accident—when Mr. Barlow came in to report his findings to Dabney Holdstrom. The low hum of conversation ceased abruptly as all ears, including mine, were cocked in their direction.

"Disconnected exhaust pipe," said Mr. Barlow.

"Can you mend the dratted thing?" Mr. Holdstrom asked, licking chocolate ganache delicately from his fingertips.

"Already have." Mr. Barlow held the ignition key out to him.

Mr. Holdstrom seemed disconcerted. He looked mournfully from the dangling key to the array of delectable pastries Sally had placed before him, then appeared to reach a decision.

"Would it be asking too much, Mr. Barlow, if I asked you to take the Jag for a test drive?" he said. "A good, long one. We want to be sure your repair holds, don't we?"

"It'll hold," said Mr. Barlow, "but I'll take the Jag for a spin, if you really want me to."

"I do, my good fellow, I most certainly do," said Mr. Holdstrom. "And take your time. I'm in no hurry."

Mr. Barlow left the room with a bounce in his step, looking as though every wish he'd ever made had come true. I paid for my bread and my strawberry jam drops and returned to Ivy Cottage, where I studiously ignored the wishing well.

Six days passed and nothing remarkable happened. My sillier neighbors regarded eight sunny days in a row—in May, in England—as miraculous, but the farmers and the forecasters blamed the dry spell on an immobile dome of high pressure, and so did I.

One pleasant thing seemed to lead to another after Dabney Holdstrom's visit, but I could account for all of them without resorting to supernatural explanations. The little editor had been so impressed by Mr. Barlow's repair work that he'd driven several other treasures from his classic car collection to Finch for tune-ups and sent friends along as well. I couldn't tell one sports car from another, but Bill reported sightings of a 1962 Austin Healey Sprite, a 1969 MGB-GT, and a 1965 Lotus Seven, each of which, according to Bill, would gladden a retired mechanic's heart. Mr. Barlow gave the automotive gems his undivided attention and floated through each day in a happy haze.

Mr. Holdstrom didn't return to Finch for car maintenance alone. He came back to conduct vital research. Sally Pyne's exceptional skills as a pastry chef had inspired him to write a feature article about her for an upcoming issue of *Cozy Cookery* magazine. He observed Sally in her kitchen, interviewed her suppliers, conversed with her customers, pigged out on her pastries, and promised to arrange a photo shoot, as Sally and her summer pudding were to grace the cover. When Sally asked him why he'd chosen such a commonplace confection over her more complex compositions, he'd replied simply: "It's the summer issue."

Opal Taylor would share Sally's spotlight. Opal had worked for many years as a cook for a wealthy family in Gloucester. Since her retirement, she'd padded her modest pension by selling her homemade jams and marmalades through Peggy Taxman's Emporium. When Peggy brought the jewel-like jars to Mr. Holdstrom's attention, he agreed to highlight their contents in what the villagers had taken to calling "the tea-room issue" of *Cozy Cookery*. Opal, who'd always looked down on Sally Pyne as a mere baker, became the tearoom owner's best friend overnight.

Like Sally, Opal was convinced that the wishing well had orchestrated her good fortune. I put it down to a combination of Peggy's business acumen and Mr. Holdstrom's fondness for jams and marmalades.

Millicent Scroggins's good fortune owed nothing to Dabney Holdstrom. Her dental martyrdom ended the day after her visit to Ivy Cottage, and though she ascribed her swift recovery to the wishing well, I credited it to oil of cloves, ice packs, the healing power of nature, and the wonders of modern dentistry.

Nothing extraordinary happened to Selena Buxton or to Elspeth Binney, but their eyes remained bright with anticipation, as if they believed the well would grant their wishes as soon as it found the time.

A steady stream of villagers came to Ivy Cottage to pick up an empty casserole dish or to drop off a full one. Jack felt obliged to give each helpful neighbor a guided tour of his late uncle's property and each found a reason to linger in the back garden.

Noises in the back garden roused Jack from his slumbers several nights in a row, but he wasn't sure what had made them. It was always too dark to see what was going on from his bedroom window and by the time he went downstairs with a flashlight, there was nothing to see. He blamed a neighboring badger, but Bree and I blamed our neighbors, some of whom, we were certain, would prefer to keep their visits to the well under wraps.

No one but Sally, Opal, and Millicent would admit to making a wish, and even they spoke of it in hushed voices. When I reminded Mr. Barlow of our conversation about the Jaguar E-Type, he simply laughed and said it was a funny old world. Nearly everyone in the village discussed the well with an air of amused tolerance, yet nearly everyone visited it.

Aunt Dimity endorsed Bill's opinion of the wishing well and she helped me to remain levelheaded by offering reasonable explanations for everything that happened in the wake of my wish for dry weather. Lilian Bunting looked upon the frenzy of well wishing as a passing fad and the vicar's Sunday sermon reminded everyone to "put away childish things."

I spent five of the six days toiling with Bree and Jack at Ivy Cottage. It took us two full days to trim the vines around the roof, the windows, the doors, the gutters, and the downspouts, and a further four to conduct what I thought was an excessively painstaking examination of its exterior walls. Following Jack's lead, Bree and I lifted each fluttering leaf to search for damaged stonework, but we found none. The mortar was solid, the stones were unblemished, and Jack had no need of Derek Harris's services.

Our minute examination of the cottage's walls was undeniably tedious, but it was better than a gym workout for whipping me into shape. A stiff regimen of ladder climbing was exactly what I needed to strengthen my lungs as well as my legs. I wasn't ready to sign up for a mountain bike race, but by the sixth day I could keep up with Bree, who'd begun riding her own bicycle to Ivy Cottage.

Bree continued to spar with Jack and he continued to absorb her verbal punches. My conversations with Jack were as interesting as they were informative. Though he'd spent most of his life in Australia, his work had taken him to New Zealand as well. I learned that he'd built wooden walkways to protect the fragile terrain in the Waipoua Kauri Forest, done trail maintenance work on the active Tongariro volcano, counted whales off the Kaikoura coast, and taken ice cores from the Fox Glacier. Whether by accident or design, Jack emphasized his familiarity with New Zealand whenever Bree was within earshot. I thought he was playing his cards brilliantly.

The Oxford lab gave the well a clean bill of health and Miranda Morrow returned to refill her bottles. I dropped Will and Rob off at Anscombe Manor for their riding lessons on Saturday, spent Sunday with them and Bill at Willis, Sr.'s, and regarded my neighbors' shenanigans with silent amusement.

The one truly remarkable feature of the six-day span was Emma's failure to keep her word. Though she'd promised to deliver her garden plan to Jack by "Thursday at the latest," we didn't see her or her plan until the following Wednesday. Bree, Jack, and I were too busy snipping ivy and studying stonework to let the delay worry us, but by Wednesday morning, we'd run out of things to do.

We were standing in the front garden, admiring the cottage's neat appearance and comparing calluses, when Emma arrived with a three-ring binder containing her master plan for the gardens' restoration. The binder's thickness seemed to explain why she'd taken so long to deliver it.

Emma had created a fifty-page opus that included plant lists, diagrams, instructions, general layouts, detailed layouts, and thumbnail photographs of each plant she hoped to preserve. She'd also made a series of technical drawings to show how the pergola, the trellis, the birdbaths, the bird tables, and the old stone wall would look once they were repaired. Jack seemed to be stunned by the sheer weight of the tome and Emma was clearly embarrassed by it.

"I'm sorry," she said. "It's overkill, I know, but once I got started, I couldn't stop."

"Don't apologize," said Jack. "You've put in the hard yards and I'm grateful." He leafed through the binder, then closed it with a snap. "Tell you what. I'll read it today and figure out how much of it I can handle."

"You don't have to handle it on your own," said Bree. "Lori and I aren't going anywhere."

"We wouldn't dream of letting you have all the fun," I chimed in.

"I wish I could help, too," said Emma. "But I've already fallen behind on my own work."

"You've done your part," said Jack. "We'll take it from here."

"Okay," said Emma. "If you have any questions, feel free to call me. Or send an e-mail. Or a text. Or a note. My contact information is inside the front cover." She looked regretfully from the three-ring binder to the three-ring circus of greenery bordering the brick paths and said with a valiant attempt at cheerfulness, "Well. I'd better be going. Insurance forms wait for no woman."

It pained me to watch her drag herself reluctantly from the garden because I knew how badly she wanted to stay behind.

"Let's pack it in," said Jack, after she'd gone. "It'll take me all day to digest Emma's scheme and I'll need to speak with Aldous Winterbottom about it before I decide whether or not to go ahead with it."

"Why?" I asked.

"He'll know if there's enough money in Uncle Hector's estate to pay for the scheme," said Jack. "I want to do right by Uncle Hector, but if the dosh isn't there, I may have to take some shortcuts."

"Tell Mr. Winterbottom you're getting the labor for free," said Bree.

"You're not cheap labor," Jack protested. "We're a team."

"Team Ivy," I suggested.

"Team Ivy," chorused Jack and Bree, laughing.

After an exuberant round of high-fives, Bree and I collected our bicycles from the garage and rode side by side up the lane. I'd so far resisted the almost irresistible urge to plumb the depths of Bree's feelings for Jack and she'd given me no access to her thoughts. Observation told me that Jack was besotted with her, but she was less easy to read.

I listened to her intently as we climbed the gentle slope, in part because I didn't want to miss any hints she might drop about the state of her heart, but mainly because I didn't yet have the lung power to conduct a conversation and cycle uphill with her at the same time.

She rattled on about Sally's summer pudding, Opal's jams and marmalades, Millicent's tooth, and Mr. Barlow's love affair with Dabney Holdstrom's classic cars. She invented wishes for the rest of our neighbors and laughed at them for their naiveté, but the only time Jack's name came up was when she guessed at the identities of his night callers.

"Peggy Taxman is at the top of my list," she said. "She's spent the past week laughing at anyone who mentions the well. She'd lose face if anyone saw her talking to it in broad daylight."

"What . . . wish?" I gasped.

"To buy another business," Bree said promptly. "She may

be queen of the Emporium, the post office, and the greengrocer's, but she won't rest until she's conquered every shop in
Finch. Henry Cook is high on my list of suspects, too."

"Why . . . Henry?" I wheezed.

"He used to be a star," said Bree. "He used to entertain
hundreds of people on cruise ships. He must miss it, don't you
think? He must be longing for the limelight now that Sally's
taken center stage, but he can't say it out loud because she's his
fiancée."

"Anyone . . . else?" I panted.

"Charles Bellingham," Bree replied. "He's always talking
about what a great eye he has. He'd love to find an undiscovered
masterpiece, but he wouldn't want to be seen wishing for one.
He'd want everyone—Grant especially—to think he could
spot a long-lost Rembrandt without the well's assistance."

Bree's comments were cruel, but accurate. She'd lived in
Finch long enough to know her neighbors' foibles better than
she knew her own. I had no trouble picturing Peggy or Henry
or Charles sneaking into the back garden to commune with
the wishing well privately. Pride would motivate them to con-
ceal their activities and girth—they were not the daintiest of
creatures—would prevent them from sneaking stealthily.
They could very well be responsible for the noises that had
disturbed Jack's sleep.

"Too bad you have no proof," I said, dismounting for a
breather at Bree's house. "I'd give my eyeteeth to have a photograph of Peggy sticking her head down the well."

"So would I," said Bree. "Too late, though. If I'm right—which I am—she's already been and gone."

"I'd better be gone, too," I said. "I've been a bit lax with the laundry lately. It's time to catch up."

"You really know how to enjoy a day off," Bree said with a wry smile. "Hug the boys for me."

"Will do," I said. "See you tomorrow!"

I had something more enjoyable than laundry to contemplate as I pedaled toward home. I intended to share Bree's educated guesswork with Aunt Dimity. She would, I knew, be as tickled as I was by the thought of Peggy Taxman, Charles Bellingham, and Henry Cook whispering sweet nothings to the well in the dead of night.

I turned into our graveled driveway, stowed Betsy in the garage, and threw a greeting to Stanley as I sailed through the front door and up the hallway to the study. I was in the midst of giving Reginald's pink flannel ears a fond twiddle when the doorbell rang, not once, but five times in a row.

"I'm coming!" I called, shooting a querying glance at my bunny.

Neither Reginald nor I could have known it at the time, but the five rings heralded a small avalanche of weird coincidences.

Thirteen

I found Emma waiting for me on the doorstep, her finger poised to ring the bell a sixth time. She brushed past me when I opened the door and whirled around to face me when I closed it, but she didn't speak. Instead, she bounced up and down on the balls of her feet, clasped her hands under her chin, and let loose a gurgle of laughter.

"Emma?" I said gently. "Have you been drinking?"

"Not yet," she replied, "but Derek and I may break open a bottle of bubbly later. Oh, Lori, we've had the most wonderful news! Wonderful! You'll never guess what it is."

"Tell me, then," I demanded as dozens of guesses darted through my mind. "Is it Nell? Is she preg—"

"It's not Nell!" Emma exclaimed. "It's Peter!"

"Peter's pregnant?" I said doubtfully.

Emma giggled like a five-year-old, cleared her throat, and announced exultantly, "Peter's coming home!"

My jaw dropped. Peter Harris was Derek's son, Emma's stepson, and Nell's only sibling. Though the Harrises were a close-knit family, Peter wasn't a homebody. He and his wife, Cassandra, had spent the past five years monitoring wildlife in remote outposts all over the United Kingdom. They'd made a brief appearance at Nell's wedding and taken off again almost immediately for another assignment. It was the last time any of us had seen them at Anscombe Manor.

I couldn't concentrate with Emma bouncing and giggling, so I whisked her into the living room, forced her to sit on the couch, and seated myself on the coffee table, facing her.

"Is Peter coming home to visit?" I probed. "Or is he coming home to stay?"

"To stay!" Emma crowed, bouncing up and down on the couch.

"Would you please sit still?" I said. "You're frightening Stanley."

It would have taken more than a bouncing Emma to drive Stanley from the comfort of Bill's armchair, but my ploy worked. Emma contained her delirium for the cat's sake.

"Now," I said, "tell me everything."

"Derek's phone rang two minutes after I got back from Ivy Cottage," she began. "It was Peter, calling to ask if he and Cassie could move in with us. They've had their fill of traveling and they want to start a family and they can't think of a better place to raise children than Anscombe Manor."

"I can't think of one, either," I said.

"It's such a relief," Emma went on. "Derek and I were afraid our first grandchild would be born in a stone hut in the Hebrides or in a cave halfway up Mount Snowdon or somewhere else equally rustic. But common sense prevailed in the end."

"Funny how common sense prevails when one is contemplating childbirth," I observed.

"Peter wanted us to take our time, thinking it over," said Emma, "but we didn't need to think it over. They'll be here tomorrow!"

"Short notice," I said. "Where will you put them?"

"In Peter's old room, for the time being," said Emma. "Derek is already drawing up plans for the self-contained apartment he'll build for them in the south wing." An enchanting smile wreathed her face. "It'll have a nursery."

The word *nursery* sparked memories of rocking my boys to sleep when they were small enough to hold in the crook of my arm. I could almost smell the talcum powder and the sweet, indefinable baby scent that has nothing to do with diapers. An unexpected twinge of envy assailed me when I thought of Emma and Derek singing lullabies to their grandchild-to-be.

"Have you told Nell and Kit?" I asked.

"Yes, and they're as happy as we are," said Emma. "Peter and Cassie have always been a bit of a mystery to Kit, and vice versa. They'll finally have a chance to get to know one another, living and working together under one roof."

"Working together?" I said. "Will they be working together?"

"It was Derek's idea," said Emma. "Peter told Derek that he and Cassie wouldn't be comfortable living at the manor unless they could pay their own way, so Derek suggested they work for me. And they agreed!"

"Do they ride?" I asked.

"Like the wind," said Emma, "but they'd rather ride for pleasure than give lessons. You won't believe it, Lori, but they *asked* if they could run the office! It should be a good fit. They're tactful and they're well organized—you have to be when you live out of a duffel bag—and they've handled budgets and bills and schedules for their research projects. It'll take me a couple of days to bring them up to speed, but once I do . . ." She caught her breath, then continued with a faraway look in her gray eyes, "I'll never have to look at another piece of paperwork again. I'll be able to—"

"Grow a prize-winning eggplant, knit a circus tent, and invent the cure for the common cold," I broke in cheerily.

"I don't know about curing the common cold," said Emma, laughing, "but I will be able to spend as much time as I like in Mr. Huggins's gardens!"

"Jack will be delighted," I said. "I should warn you, though, that Mr. Huggins's estate may not have sufficient funds to pay for your plan as written."

"We'll do what we can with what we have," said Emma, undaunted. She glanced at her wristwatch, then jumped to her feet. "I'd better get moving. I have a to-do list as long as my arm, but I couldn't do anything until I'd shared my wonderful news with you."

"I'm glad you did," I said, getting up to give her a hug. "It really is wonderful news."

"It is, isn't it?" She returned my hug, then broke free, saying, "Derek and I will throw a welcome-home party for Cassie and Peter at some point, but I'm not sure when. You and Bill will come, won't you? And you'll bring the twins? Peter's dying to see Will and Rob."

"We wouldn't miss it for the world," I assured her.

I walked Emma to the front door and waved her on her way, then made a mad dash for the study. My brain had begun to fizz again. I hoped Aunt Dimity would offer me a reasonable explanation for what had just happened because I couldn't think of one myself.

I'd seen Emma beside the wishing well. I'd heard her wish for the perfect someone to appear on her doorstep and manage the riding school for her. By her own testimony, her wish had come true. On Thursday, Peter and Cassie would appear on her doorstep, and in two days, after she'd brought them up to speed, they would manage the riding school for her.

"Weird coincidence, my foot," I muttered to Reginald when I entered the study. "Let's see if Dimity can reason her way out of this one."

I actually had my hand on the blue journal when the doorbell rang again. Urgently.

"Are you kidding me?" I groaned and Reginald's pink ears seemed to droop with frustration.

I released the journal and returned to the front door in a testy mood. Had my visitor been a salesman, he would have regretted ringing my bell urgently. I must have looked out of sorts because when I flung the door wide, Elspeth Binney fell back a step.

"Have I come at a bad time?" she asked meekly.

"No, not at all. Please, come in," I said, too surprised to remain irritated. To see Elspeth unaccompanied by her cronies was unusual. To see her alone on my doorstep in the middle of the day was unprecedented. "Shall I put the kettle on?"

"No, no," she said. "I can't stay long—so much to do!—but I simply had to tell you my wonderful news!"

"More wonderful news," I murmured weakly, wondering if another weird coincidence was about to land in my lap.

Elspeth followed me into the living room and sat in the same spot Emma had so recently occupied. Her posture was what one would expect from a retired schoolteacher and I found myself pulling my shoulders back as I lowered myself into my armchair.

"I wouldn't trouble you, Lori," Elspeth began, "if we didn't have two very special things in common."

"We have two things in common?" I said, baffled. "What would they be?"

"The wishing well," she said, "and a deep appreciation of my niece's artistic gifts. Do you remember my niece?"

"The niece who lives in Yorkshire?" I said. "The photographer?"

"That's right," said Elspeth. "Her name is Jemima, but we've always called her Jemma. Jemma Renshawe is her married name. You've never met Jemma, of course," Elspeth went on, "but you admired her photographs when you came to my cottage last year."

"They're beautiful photographs," I said, recalling the evocative black-and-white landscapes hanging on the walls in Elspeth's sunny parlor. "Your niece is a gifted photographer."

"Thank you," said Elspeth. "Selena, Opal, and Millicent may take painting classes from Mr. Shuttleworth in Upper Deeping, but they lack the capacity to appreciate fine art.

They think I'm proud of Jemma simply because she's my niece. They're incapable of recognizing her unique talent, but you aren't."

"Have you heard from your niece?" I asked, wishing she would get to the point.

"I have," Elspeth said, her eyes shining. "She rang this morning to tell me that she's been given a commission! A London firm is publishing a book about English villages and the book's editor commissioned Jemma to photograph the people in a Cotswold village. Naturally, Jemma thought of Finch."

"Naturally," I said.

"She rang yesterday to tell me about the project," said Elspeth, "and I invited her at once to stay with me. I'll have to prepare the guest room and get in some extra groceries today because she'll be here tomorrow!" Elspeth clasped her hands together in her lap. "Isn't it marvelous?"

"It is," I said. "It's completely marvelous, Elspeth, and I look forward to meeting your niece, but I'm a little confused. Why would the firm hire her to take pictures in the Cotswolds when she lives in Yorkshire?"

"Because *I* live in the Cotswolds," Elspeth declared.

"Really?" I said uncomprehendingly. "I'm not quite sure I see the connection between—"

"Of course you don't see the connection," she interrupted. "I haven't revealed it to you yet." She looked demurely down at her clasped hands. "I've often wondered what it would be like to live with an artist."

"Have you?" I said, leaning forward.

"Not in sin, mind you," she said hastily. "It would be a platonic relationship based on a mutual passion for art."

"Of course it would be," I said, leaning back.

"I'm not creative myself," Elspeth continued, "but I appreciate creativity in others, and I've often yearned for the opportunity to observe the intricacies of the creative process firsthand. Recently . . ." She hesitated before plunging on. "Recently I did more than *yearn* for it. I *wished* for it."

"Did you?" I said, trying to sound surprised.

"You may remember seeing me at Ivy Cottage last week," she said. "Selena, Opal, and I went there to welcome Jack MacBride to the village. Welcoming Jack was our *primary* goal, but I confess I had a secondary goal in mind."

"Peggy Taxman told you I'd stopped the rain by making a wish in the wishing well," I said, abandoning pretense, "so you thought you'd give it a try."

"I did!" said Elspeth. "And it worked! Jemma received her commission only a few days after I spoke to the well. Ergo, the well must have granted my wish. There's no other explanation!"

"There doesn't seem to be," I said, sighing.

"I hope you'll keep my confession *entre nous,*" she said. "As a former schoolteacher, I have a reputation to uphold."

"I understand," I said. "You wouldn't want to be mistaken for Miranda Morrow."

"Certainly not," said Elspeth, sniffing derisively. "Miranda

Morrow believes in *witchcraft*, a pseudoscience with no observable basis in fact."

"Whereas you've drawn a logical conclusion based on the wishing well's response to your wish," I said.

"Exactly," said Elspeth. She rose and smoothed her tweed skirt. "I must be on my way—so much to do! Thank you for listening, Lori. I'm sure you and Jemma will get along famously."

I escorted Elspeth to the front door, down the flagstone path, and all the way to the end of the driveway, where she'd left her bicycle—an old black three-speed that must have outweighed Betsy by at least forty pounds.

She glided gracefully down the lane and I looked left and right like a hunted mouse, to see if anyone else was approaching the cottage.

Charles Bellingham was. His mauve Honda Civic was unmistakable and it was heading straight for me.

Fourteen

Charles Bellingham was tall, portly, balding, and excitable. Though he was a night owl by nature, he was wide-awake when he pulled into my driveway.

"Lori!" he called, hauling his large frame out of his compact vehicle. "I'm glad I caught you!"

He strode to the rear of the car, popped the trunk, and removed from it something that looked suspiciously like a small, framed painting wrapped in brown paper.

"Don't tell me," I said under my breath. "You have wonderful news."

"I have the most wonderful news!" Charles announced, holding the parcel next to his smiling face.

"Come in," I said dazedly, "and tell me all about it."

I felt as if I were caught in a recurring dream as I led Charles into the living room and watched him sit in what was swiftly becoming the most sat upon spot on the couch.

"Tea?" I said automatically.

"No, thank you," he replied. "No fiddling with the teapot. No cups, saucers, sugar bowls, or cream jugs. Sit! Listen!"

I sank onto my armchair to await yet another revelation. Charles placed his parcel on the coffee table, spread his hands upon his knees, and glanced furtively over his shoulder.

"Are we alone?" he asked.

"There's Stanley," I said, nodding at the cat, who betrayed not the slightest sign of interest in our guest. "But he's not a big talker."

Charles gazed benevolently at Stanley, then turned his attention to me.

"I believe I've told you about Grant's disposables," he began.

"You've told everyone in Finch about Grant's disposables," I said tiredly. "It's your favorite prank. You fool people into thinking you're talking about adult diapers and only then do you tell them what Grant's disposables really are. I'm not sure Grant appreciates it. For a long time, old Mrs. Wyn was convinced that he was incontinent."

Charles sniggered. "I must remember to speak more loudly to Mrs. Wyn. Her hearing isn't what it used to be."

"It's okay," I said. "When she asked me in hushed tones about Grant's unfortunate condition, I explained to her that his disposables aren't personal hygiene products. They're the ugly paintings he stashes in your shed."

Charles Bellingham and Grant Tavistock bought and sold artwork as a hobby, but they earned their daily bread by appraising, restoring, and repairing paintings for well-to-do clients. Charles carried out the appraisals and Grant was the repair and restoration expert.

"Disposables" were the cheap and dreadful paintings Grant purchased at charity shops, car boot sales, and flea markets. He used disposables to test new products, techniques, and tools before disposing of them in his recycling bin, where, he claimed, they brought more joy to humankind than they had ever brought before.

"Why do you do it?" I asked. "Why make a joke at Grant's expense?"

"Why do I do it?" Charles echoed indignantly. "I'll tell you why! Grant rummages through his disposables after he buys them to make sure there isn't a gem hidden among them. He then tosses them into the shed higgledy-piggledy and waits for me to organize his mess for him. He does it *on purpose*, Lori, because he knows how intensely I detest chaos. He knows I'll eventually grit my teeth and sort the horrors—"

"You sort them?" I broke in.

"Yes," said Charles. "By size, shape, and medium."

"Medium?" I queried.

"Oil, acrylic, watercolor, tempera, et cetera," Charles clarified. "I'm certain I found a still life done in gravy once, but Grant insists it was a thick impasto. At any rate, I carry out the unenviable tasks of sorting Grant's disposables and placing them in their assigned racks in his workroom, and what thanks do I get?"

"The satisfaction of a job well done?" I ventured.

"Lori," Charles said gravely, "there is no satisfaction to be had from handling botched paintings of clowns, cheetahs, bananas, and sunsets."

"Someone must have loved them once," I pointed out.

"Once was more than they deserved," he retorted. "Yes, I have my little joke at Grant's expense, but it's not enough, not nearly enough, to make up for the hours I spend knee-deep in dregs. I've often longed to exact a sweeter revenge, and yesterday afternoon the means to achieve the ultimate retaliation fell into my hands. At long last, I discovered a hidden gem Grant overlooked, a grain of wheat he failed to separate from the chaff, the swan in the flock of ugly ducklings—"

"You found an undiscovered masterpiece," I interrupted, repeating the words Bree had used to describe Charles's wildest dream, "a long-lost Rembrandt."

"Not a Rembrandt," he said, "but a masterpiece nonetheless." He smiled smugly and took the wrapped parcel from the coffee table. He carefully removed the brown paper and set it aside, then held the masterpiece out for me to see.

It was an ink wash painting. Will and Rob had introduced me to ink wash painting as part of a classroom project on Japan. I doubted that I would ever forget the evening we'd spent at the kitchen table, practicing brushstrokes and learning how to remove ink stains from hands and faces.

The painting Charles held was framed in black bamboo. A vertical line of delicately scribed Japanese calligraphy seemed to float in the empty space to the right of the central image, followed by a tiny red box enclosing yet another Japanese character. The red stamp was, I recalled, the artist's personal seal or chop, used in lieu of or in addition to a signature. Will and Rob had made their own, slightly less elegant, chops by carving their initials into raw potatoes.

I studied the main image in silence, then said tentatively, "Is it a koi?"

"Very good!" Charles replied, nodding his approval. "It's a koi—a Japanese carp—pirouetting through fronds of swaying seaweed. Moreover, it's an original Asazuki"—his finger traced the line of calligraphy leading to the tiny red box—"signed and stamped by the great Asazuki herself." When I looked blank, he explained, "Chiaki Asazuki is a contemporary artist who creates miniature homages to the magnificent koi artists of the late Edo and the early Meiji periods. A piece like the one you see before you can fetch hundreds of pounds at the right auction and *Grant missed it!*"

"It's pretty small," I said reasonably.

"Its diminutive size was Grant's downfall," said Charles. "It was jammed between a paint-by-number landscape and a stupendously malformed nude. I can't fault Grant for skipping over them, but he'll tear his hair out when I show him what was hidden between them!"

"Haven't you shown it to him already?" I asked, surprised.

"Revenge is a dish best served cold," said Charles, "preferably after one has established one's facts. I spent yesterday evening telephoning collectors and double-checking the attribution online. I would have sprung the painting on him after breakfast, but he ran off to an estate sale in Cheltenham before I'd finished my toast. I've been dying to show my Asazuki to someone, but to whom could I show it? Who would recognize its beauty? Who?"

"I give up," I said.

"Bill would, but I couldn't interrupt him at work," Charles continued, as if I hadn't spoken. "Lilian Bunting was a possibility, but she's busy with meals-on-wheels, and William and Amelia are off on one of their nature walks. The disposable artists"—his unkind but apt name for the Handmaidens—"were out of the question. They may take painting lessons, but the lessons they take haven't taken. Finally, I thought of you! You, Lori, are neither a Philistine nor a pretender. You have a natural affinity for the finer things in life. And, of course, you were at home."

"Thank you," I said. Charles would have been horrified if I'd told him that I thought his precious Asazuki koi was a bug-eyed, flabby-lipped, overfed, and decidedly unattractive specimen, so I kept my opinion to myself. "And congratulations. Lady Luck has dealt you a winning hand."

"To be perfectly honest," said Charles, smiling coyly, "it wasn't all luck."

"Wasn't it?" I said and the old wishing well rose before my mind's eye like a genie emerging from a magic lantern.

"Lori," Charles said, hunching forward and fixing me with a beady stare, "if you repeat a single syllable of what I'm about to tell you, I'll deny saying it. What's said between us, stays between us."

"Understood," I said. "But I'll have to tell Bill. It's a spousal requirement."

"Allowed," he said. He placed the painting on the table and hunched over even further, assuming a posture I associated with confidential disclosures. "You may think me foolish, but I spoke to the wishing well last week."

"Did you speak to it at night?" I asked.

"Yes," Charles replied, frowning slightly. "How did you know?"

"Jack heard noises in the back garden," I explained. "Did you bump into anyone else while you were there?"

"I did not," said Charles. "I went at night for the express purpose of *avoiding* other people and I succeeded. The well alone heard my wish. And the well made it come true. It gave me exactly what I needed to punish Grant for leaving all the dirty work to me."

"You honestly believe that an old well made a valuable painting appear out of nowhere," I said.

"What else can I believe?" said Charles. "I've been sorting Grant's disposables for years, but it wasn't until after the well heard my wish that I struck gold." He drew back from me and said incredulously, "Don't tell me you're a skeptic. How can you doubt the well after it granted your wish for sunshine?"

"I, uh, there's this, um, dome of high pressure," I faltered.

"Pshaw!" Charles waved a hand at me dismissively. "Did a dome of high pressure grant Sally's wish? Or Opal's? Or Mr. Barlow's, despite his repeated assertions that he made no wish? It's the well, Lori. It has to be. I feel as if I should drop a gold coin in it, but the engraving says nothing about tangible tributes. Words of praise may be enough."

"If you praise it at night," I said, "try not to wake Jack up again."

"I'll do my best," said Charles, "but it's not easy to reach the well. Jack's garden is a botanical obstacle course."

"We're working on it," I told him.

"In that case, I'll wait until after you're done to praise the well," said Charles. "And now, if you'll forgive me, I really should be getting back. It's been a pleasure to share my Asazuki with you, Lori. I wish you could be there to see Grant's face at the unveiling, but I'll have a camera handy, to catch his expression. It should be priceless."

Charles lifted the framed painting from the table and paused to admire it before rewrapping it in the brown paper and getting to his feet. I walked him to his car, waved him off, and lurked in the driveway for a little while, watching and waiting for Henry Cook or Peggy Taxman or God alone knew who else to bring wonderful news to me. When the coast remained clear, I went back inside and strode purposefully into the study.

"Reginald," I said, "something strange is going on in Finch."

My pink bunny chose to remain silent, so I took the blue journal from its shelf and sat with it in one of the tall leather armchairs before the hearth. I felt an urgent need to immerse myself in cool reasoning and flawless logic and, fortunately, I knew where to find both.

Fifteen

"Dimity?" I said, opening the journal. "Have I got news for you!"

The familiar lines of royal-blue ink began to loop and curl across the page as soon as I finished speaking.

I presume you haven't turned the wishing well's water into wine.

"If I'd *walked* on the wishing well's water, it still wouldn't be the day's banner headline," I told her. "Something strange is going on in Finch."

Something stranger than usual?

"You be the judge," I replied.

I leaned back in my chair and recounted the series of extraordinary conversations that had prevented me from doing the laundry. I described Emma Harris's longing for the perfect office manager, Elspeth Binney's curiosity about the creative life, and Charles Bellingham's thirst for revenge. I tried to sound matter-of-fact as I discussed Peter and Cassie's unexpected return to Anscombe Manor, Jemma Renshawe's out-of-the-blue commission to photograph a Cotswold village, and Chiaki Asazuki's rediscovered masterpiece, but I didn't succeed.

"For pity's sake, Dimity," I said, "Peter and Cassie are coming home to run the office for Emma! Elspeth's photographer niece arrives in Finch tomorrow! The odds of Charles finding an original Asazuki in a pile of junk must be astronomical!" I thumped the arm of the chair emphatically. "It can't be a flurry of coincidences, Dimity. The things that are happening in Emma's and Elspeth's and Charles's lives are way too specific to be written off as mere serendipity. Each of them made a wish in or near the wishing well and—*voila!*—their wishes came true! It makes me think twice about explaining away everyone else's wishes. I hope you can offer me a rational explanation because superstitious nonsense is beginning to look pretty plausible to me."

Could someone—a human being, that is, not a leprechaun or a pixie or the fairy at the bottom of Jack's garden—have overheard any of the wishes?

I mulled over the question, calling to mind everything I'd seen and heard at Ivy Cottage since Jack, Bree, and I had uncovered the well.

"No," I said, shaking my head. "Sally Pyne had the back garden to herself. So did Millicent Scroggins. Elspeth, Opal, and Selena were out there together, but they each made a wish when the others' backs were turned."

I doubt if those three ladies would grant one another's wishes even if they had overheard them.

"Sad, but true," I agreed and went on. "I was the only one to hear Mr. Barlow and Emma express their wishes and Jack was too far away to see who was sneaking up to the well in the middle of the night or to hear what they said to it. It doesn't matter, though, does it?"

What doesn't matter?

"Let's assume for the sake of argument that someone did overhear the wishes," I said. "How in heaven's name could he or she make them come true? How could I, for instance, arrange for a publisher to give Jemma Renshawe an assignment that would lead her straight to her aunt's guest room? How could I arrange for Dabney Holdstrom to drive into Finch with a disconnected exhaust pipe? How could I bring Peter and Cassie Harris back to Anscombe Manor? The answer is: I couldn't."

You underrate your scheming skills, Lori, but I take your point. I'm afraid I can't offer you a rational explanation, my dear, but I remain convinced that a rational explanation exists. You simply haven't discovered it yet. I'm not even certain it's worth discovering. Not now, at any rate.

"Why not?" I asked.

At the moment, everyone seems to be happy. The time to look for an explanation will come when the moment of happiness passes.

"Why should it pass?" I asked.

Wishes can backfire, Lori. They sometimes backfire spectacularly. A child may wish with all her heart to eat a whole chocolate cake without pausing to consider how sick she would be afterward. A greedy man may wish for a pile of gold, but if the gold came from your pocket, you might object. One person's dream-come-true can be another person's worst nightmare.

"I see what you mean," I said, nodding thoughtfully. "I wanted it to stop raining, but if the rain stops for too long, crops die."

When the drought begins, you'll have to find a rational explanation for the strange things that are happening in Finch. Otherwise, you won't be able to stop it. And it will be essential to stop it. If you don't, crops will die. I speak metaphorically, of course. You and I both know that you aren't responsible for the weather.

"What should I do in the meantime?" I asked.

In the meantime, let your neighbors enjoy their apparent good fortune. It would be cruel to intercede too soon. It would also be use-less. Most people refuse to accept reality until it jumps up and hits them on the nose.

"Let me get this straight," I said slowly. "It's my job to fig-ure out what's really going on in Finch, but not until some sort of crisis occurs?"

An admirable summation. I suspect you won't have long to wait. As I said before, Lori, wishes can backfire.

I spent the rest of the day racing from one neglected chore to another. I cobbled together a beef stew for dinner and made a (small) chocolate cake for dessert in between catching up with the laundry, the vacuuming, the dusting, the scrubbing, and the straightening. I paused at odd intervals to scan the drive-way from the window seat in the living room or to glance expectantly at the telephone in the kitchen, but to my relief, neither the doorbell nor the telephone rang.

I'd had all the good news I could stand.

Will and Rob provided a welcome distraction from the weird goings-on in Finch. I picked the boys up from school and played cricket with them in our back meadow until I ran out of breath and traded chasing down balls for cheering from the sidelines. I called them in to wash their hands and to set the table shortly before Bill came home from work.

I was putting the finishing touches on a green salad when my husband strode into the kitchen, with Stanley padding faithfully at his heels.

"What smells so good?" Bill asked.

"I'd like to think I do," I said, batting my eyelashes at him, "but it's probably the beef stew."

Bill gave me an absentminded kiss on the cheek, then lifted the lid from the dutch oven and inhaled deeply.

"Will it be ready soon?" he asked. "I'm *starving*."

"Dinner will be served in two shakes of a kitten's tail," I assured him, giving the salad a final toss. "Why are you so hungry, anyway? Hard day at the office?"

"It was a hard day at the office," he acknowledged, "but I'm hungry because I didn't have my three o'clock doughnut to sustain me. Sally closed the tearoom all day to get ready for the photo shoot tomorrow."

"She closed the tearoom?" I said, astonished. "Sally never closes the tearoom during regular working hours. She can't afford to shut it down."

"She shut it down today," said Bill, moving to the kitchen counter to examine the chocolate cake. "The Handmaidens had a fit because they missed their daily tea-and-backstabbing session. Lilian Bunting ran out of bread and had to settle for the plastic-wrapped stuff Peggy sells at the Emporium. And Henry . . ." Bill sighed. "Poor Henry was banished to the pub."

"Why?" I exclaimed.

"Sally didn't want him to distract her with his jokes and his funny stories," said Bill. "She's taking the whole thing very seriously."

"I suppose it's understandable," I said. "I doubt she'll have another chance to appear on the cover of a national magazine."

"Good God, I hope not," Bill said vehemently as he went off to round up the boys. "I *need* my three o'clock doughnut."

A small ripple of apprehension fluttered through me as I ladled the stew into a tureen. Bill was whining and Bill *never* whined. The Handmaidens were fuming, Lilian Bunting was spreading butter on inferior bread, and Henry Cook was wondering why his fiancée no longer cared for his sense of humor. Sally's wish for fame appeared to be having unintended and rather unpleasant consequences.

"Wishes can backfire," I murmured. "I wonder if Sally's wish will explode in her face?"

The phone rang and I nearly dropped the ladle. I managed to lower it into the dutch oven without splashing stew all over the stove, but I was still a bit jumpy when I picked up the receiver.

"Hello?" I said uneasily.

"Lori?"

I heard Emma's voice and relaxed. She couldn't have more wonderful news to pass along, I told myself. Nothing could be more wonderful than Peter's return.

"I know it's dinnertime," she said, "so I'll keep it short. Would you please let Jack know that I'll be volunteering my services at Ivy Cottage on Friday?"

"Friday?" I said, surprised. "You said you'd need a few days to bring Peter and Cassie up to speed."

"I know," said Emma, "but I didn't take into account how bright and eager Peter and Cassie are. They won't need more than a day to learn the ropes."

"Great," I said. "What do you suggest Jack and Bree and I do tomorrow? We don't want to spoil your big plans."

"You can make a start on fixing or replacing the bird tables and the birdbaths," Emma replied decisively. "I'd rather you didn't touch the greenery until I'm on hand to supervise."

"We won't pluck a blade of grass without you," I said, smiling.

"Did you hear about the tearoom?" she asked.

"Bill told me," I replied. "What a kerfuffle."

"Derek was bitterly disappointed," said Emma. "He'd counted on having a custard tart after lunch. He nearly wept when I told him the tearoom would be closed again tomorrow, for the photo shoot."

"Bill's displaying withdrawal symptoms, too," I said.

"Do not come between a man and his pastries," Emma intoned and we both chuckled. "Did Bill tell you about George Wetherhead?"

"No," I said, my smile fading. "What about George Wetherhead?"

"Christmas came early for him," Emma said. "Derek ran into him during his failed quest for custard tarts and heard the whole story firsthand. You know how passionate George is about his train collection."

"It's the only thing he talks about voluntarily," I said. George Wetherhead was the most bashful man in Finch, but he was a rabid model railway enthusiast.

"Well," said Emma, "George spotted an ad for a rare antique brass locomotive in one of his newsletters last week. The seller had placed a ridiculously low price on it and George snapped it up. It arrived in the mail today and George swears it's worth ten times what he paid for it. Derek said he looked as if he were walking on air."

"I'll bet he did," I said in a hollow voice. "Does Derek happen to know whether or not George visited Ivy Cottage recently?"

"Derek doesn't," Emma replied, "but I do. I saw George there last Thursday evening, when I dropped in to take more photographs. He was chatting with Jack about a long-distance passenger train in Australia called the Ghan. I thought it was very bold of George to strike up a conversation with a total stranger."

"Did George look around the back garden?" I asked.

"He and Jack were *in* the back garden," said Emma. "That's where I found them."

"Of course you did," I said faintly. "Listen, Emma, I have to go."

"I know and I'm sorry," said Emma. "I didn't mean to keep you so long. Go. Feed your family. I'll see you on Friday!"

"See you then," I said.

I hung up the phone and wobbled unsteadily to the kitchen table, where I sank onto the nearest chair and stared anxiously into the middle distance.

"Pixies and leprechauns and fairies aren't real," I said to the thin air. "But I'm not so sure about wishing wells."

Sixteen

I spent most of the night tossing and turning and asking myself what would happen next. Would Finch crumble beneath the weight of its good fortune, as Aunt Dimity had predicted? A trickle of discontent was already seeping through the village and I didn't have the faintest notion of how to stop it. What little sleep I did get was disrupted by dreams of Finch being pulverized by a gargantuan tidal wave. I woke feeling seasick, but a cup of strong, sweet tea and yet another sun-filled morning restored my faith in my village's ability to survive whatever maelstrom Fate had in store for it.

I made breakfast for Bill and the boys, drove Will and Rob to school, and rode Betsy to Ivy Cottage, allowing the gentle downhill slope to do most of the work for me. Bree and Jack were sitting on the front doorstep when I rolled Betsy into the driveway. I tried not to smile when Jack slid closer to Bree to make room for me.

"Good news," he announced. "Aldous Winterbottom has given Emma's master plan his blessing."

"That's great," I said, "because the master planner herself will be yours to command as of tomorrow."

"Beauty!" Jack exclaimed. "But I think Emma will do most of the commanding. At least, I bloody well hope she will. Her diagrams are beyond me."

"Who'll manage the riding school while Emma's here?" Bree asked.

I quickly recounted the Peter and Cassie story, leaving out all references to the wishing well allegedly overhearing my conversation with Emma, then moved on to Team Ivy's assignment for the day.

"Bird tables and birdbaths," I said. "Emma doesn't trust us with pruning shears."

"Fair enough," said Jack. "The tables can be repaired, but the baths are beyond redemption."

"The garden center in Upper Deeping has birdbaths," said Bree.

"And Mr. Barlow will help us with the bird tables," I said.

"No, he won't," said Bree, frowning. "I asked him this morning and he said he'd be up to elbows in a Frogeye Sprite all day."

"I beg your pardon?" I said, certain I'd misheard her.

"He'll be working on another car belonging to another one of Dabney Holdstrom's flash friends," Bree explained grumpily. "He let me borrow some tools, though."

She gestured to the tarpaulin-covered patch of driveway, which had been transformed into an alfresco carpenter's workshop. Saws, hammers, nails, planes, and other tools of the woodworking trade had been arranged neatly on three planks laid side by side across a pair of sawhorses. The broken-down bird tables lay in a heap beside the sawhorses.

Though I knew next to nothing about carpentry, the correct

course of action was plain to me. It was more important for Bree and Jack to spend time together than it was for me to spend time alone with either one of them, so I feigned an expertise I did not possess.

"Okay," I said. "I'll have a stab at the tables while you two tackle the garden center."

"You'll repair the bird tables?" Bree said doubtfully.

"Of course I will," I said, jumping to my feet and rubbing my palms together energetically. "How hard can it be?"

"Famous last words," Bree said.

"Hello?" said a timid voice.

Theodore Bunting stood in the gateway between the towering hedges, gazing inquisitively at us. Jack and Bree rose from the doorstep and strode forward with me to greet him.

"G'day, Vicar," said Jack. "What brings you to Ivy Cottage?"

"Dear me," said the vicar, surveying the garden with something akin to horror in his mild gray eyes. "Rumors have been flying about for many days, but I placed little faith in their accuracy. I can see now that I was mistaken. The rumors were all too true." He shook his head. "I blame myself. Poor Mr. Huggins. I should have tried harder to—"

"He wouldn't have let you," Jack said swiftly.

"And it's not as bad as it seems," said Bree, who was very fond of the vicar. "Emma believes he planted it this way on purpose."

"On purpose?" The vicar stared at Bree in disbelief.

"Ask Emma," Bree said. "She can explain it better than I can."

"By the time we've finished pulling it back a bit," said Jack, "it'll be fit for the Chelsea Flower Show."

"May the Lord bless all the work of your hand," said the vicar. "By the looks of it, your hands will be fully occupied for some time." He sighed. "I'm afraid I've come on a fool's errand."

"I doubt it," said Jack.

"I was hoping to prevail upon one of you to mow the cemetery," the vicar confessed apologetically. "I'd do it myself, but my wife thinks it might kill me. I don't know why. I'm in excellent health for a man of my age."

I agreed wholeheartedly with Lilian. Theodore Bunting was tall, but as spare as a scarecrow and though he might be in good health for his age, he was too old to be pushing a lawn mower.

"Mr. Barlow's the sexton," said Bree, scowling. "It's his job to mow the cemetery. He should have done it last Saturday."

"I'm afraid he didn't," the vicar replied. "He's been rather tied up with the magnificent motors people keep bringing to him. I couldn't in good conscience divert him from a pursuit that gives him pleasure as well as a fine income, but there's no denying that the cemetery is starting to look"—he cast a mournful glance at the overgrown greenery edging the brick path—"rather forlorn."

"I'll tell you what, Vicar," said Jack. "I'm on my way to Upper Deeping just now, but I'll mow the cemetery for you this afternoon."

"Will you really?" said the vicar, sounding cautiously optimistic. "I don't wish to interrupt——"

"You're not interrupting anything that can't be interrupted," Jack assured him. "I'll see you after lunch."

"God bless you," said the vicar, smiling beatifically as he wrung Jack's hand. "Lilian will be delighted when I tell her——"

"Good morning!" said Elspeth Binney.

Elspeth walked into the front garden accompanied by a woman who would never be mistaken for a Handmaiden. The stranger was tall and lean, but curvy, and her legs seemed to go on forever. She had pale blue eyes, high cheekbones, lustrous honey-blond hair that flowed down her back in gleaming waves, and a tan that rivaled Jack's. She wore a khaki vest dotted with pockets over a formfitting white tank top and she'd pulled a pair of scuffed cowboy boots over her skintight blue jeans.

It was hard to guess her age—older than Jack, I thought, and younger than me—but in her case, age was irrelevant. She was certifiably gorgeous, and though I'd never seen her before, I knew who she was. The three cameras hanging from straps around her neck were a dead giveaway.

"May I introduce my niece?" Elspeth said brightly. "Jemima——"

"Jemma Renshawe," the gorgeous woman interrupted gruffly, raising one of the cameras to her eye. "Pretend I'm not here."

It was impossible to comply with her request as she writhed

around us, snapping photographs of our startled faces from every conceivable angle, but I pretended, for Elspeth's sake, to take her niece's uncouth behavior in stride.

"Pleased to meet you, Jemma," I said.

Jemma grunted.

"Yes, er, welcome to the village, um, Jemma," said the vicar, looking both uncomfortable and bewildered. "If you'll forgive me, I must return to the vicarage to, um, to revise my sermon." He sidled awkwardly toward the lane in a bid to escape the slinking shutterbug. "I'll say good-bye for now, then, shall I? I look forward to seeing you this afternoon, Jack."

"Count on it, Vicar," said Jack, who appeared to be vastly amused by the situation.

Bree was not amused. She waited until the vicar was gone, then strode up to Jemma and cupped her hand over the camera lens. Jemma rose from a contorted crouch and looked at Bree in surprise.

"Problem?" Jemma asked.

"Yes," Bree snapped, squaring her shoulders. "I don't recall giving you my permission to take my photograph."

"Oh." Jemma's puzzled expression vanished. "Sorry. Forgot. Get carried away sometimes."

"Jemma is working on a book about Cotswold villages," Elspeth intervened hastily. "She's been commissioned to take photographs of villagers."

"I'm not a villager," said Jack. "I'm not even English, so you may as well delete my photos, Jemma. Bree and Lori aren't English, either, but they live here, as does Mr. Bunting, who's English to the bone. I'm sure he won't mind being in your book."

"It's okay with me, too," I said. I wasn't wildly enthused about having my left nostril immortalized in print, but I didn't want to upset Elspeth by opting out.

"What about you?" Jemma asked Bree.

"Yes, all right, I suppose you can use my photographs, too," Bree said with ungracious reluctance. "Come on, Jack. If we keep hanging about, the garden center will be closed before we get there."

Bree marched off to climb into Jack's car and Jack ran after her, calling cheery good-byes to Elspeth and to Jemma. Jemma grunted at me and left the front garden. Elspeth watched her go, then turned to me.

"Your niece is very . . . interesting," I observed.

"She has an artistic temperament," said Elspeth. "When she has a camera in her hands, she becomes obsessed." Elspeth's brow furrowed worriedly as she gazed toward the empty gateway. "She didn't even want a cup of tea after her long drive down from Yorkshire. She preferred to get straight to business."

"She's certainly not a time waster," I said encouragingly. "She swept in and out of here like a real pro."

"Yes," Elspeth said without conviction. "She doesn't approve of posed photos, you see. She prefers to capture images fleetingly, in unstructured environments. She believes impromptu photos give a more accurate reflection of human nature."

"Fascinating," I said dutifully.

"She's brought an awful lot of equipment with her," Elspeth said, and the creases in her forehead deepened. "Two computers, a printer, and all sorts of paraphernalia. It wouldn't fit on the desk in the guest room, so Jemma spread it out on my dining room table."

"A small sacrifice," I said, "when you consider the end result."

"Indeed," said Elspeth. "It will be worth it in the end. And it's all very . . . interesting. If you'll excuse me, I should probably go after her."

Elspeth pressed two fingers to her temple, as if she had a headache coming on, and hurried away to search for her artistic niece.

I didn't envy her the task of reining in such an intense character and I wasn't at all sure how my neighbors would react to having a camera thrust at them in an impromptu manner by a monosyllabic goddess. It seemed likely that the men would comb their hair, pull in their tummies, and compete for the chance to pose for her, but I doubted the women would. Opal, Millicent, and Selena wouldn't hesitate for a moment to tell their dear friend exactly what they thought of her niece, and if Jemma shoved a camera under Peggy Taxman's nose, the camera—and quite possibly Jemma—would end up in pieces.

I moseyed over to the driveway to examine the broken bird tables, but I was still thinking about Elspeth. Her wish to observe the creative mind at work had already lost her a dining room table. Would it lose her a few friendships as well?

"Then there's Mr. Barlow," I murmured fretfully.

If Mr. Barlow's infatuation with classic cars had ended when he'd fixed Dabney Holdstrom's precious Jaguar, all would have been well. He would have had his fun and Finch would have had its sexton-handyman back. But the cars wouldn't stop coming and Mr. Barlow wouldn't stop working on them and the things he was supposed to be doing weren't getting done.

"He's not himself," I said to a foraging robin.

Mr. Barlow believed in old-fashioned virtues like doing one's duty and keeping one's promises, yet he'd failed signally to do his duty as a sexton and he'd gone back on his promise to lend a hand, if needed, with Ivy Cottage. I didn't want to imagine what Finch would be like without its hardworking handyman, but as I hefted a hammer it dawned on me that I might have to.

I gave myself a preview of the apocalypse by attempting to do what Mr. Barlow should have done. After twenty minutes or so of banging nails every which way but straight into the wood, the inevitable happened. I whacked my left thumb so hard with the hammer that the wave of pain nearly knocked me off my feet. I dropped the hammer, grasped my wrist, and did a little dance of agony, during which I cursed every Jaguar E-Type ever made.

I was on my way into the cottage to find ice for my throbbing digit when the sound of raised voices reached my ears. Alarmed, I forgot my injury and raced toward the village, arriving atop the humpbacked bridge in time to watch the first act of Finch's final downfall.

Seventeen

I wasn't alone in witnessing doomsday. The curious leaned from windows or stood in doorways or froze in their tracks all up and down the village green. Mr. Barlow emerged from his garage near the bottom of the bridge, spotted me, and climbed up to share my grandstand view.

"'Morning, Lori," he said, as if the end of the world weren't nigh. "What did you do to your thumb?"

"We'll talk about it later," I responded distractedly.

He slipped a socket wrench into his tool belt and wiped his greasy hands on a grimy rag, which he stowed in the back pocket of his grubby coveralls. The oily stench he brought with him made me feel sick to my stomach, but I swallowed hard and forced myself to focus on the matter at hand.

"What's going on?" I asked.

"Grant and Charles are having a tiff, I reckon," he replied.

I reckoned he was right. Grant Tavistock and Charles Bellingham were bellowing at each other over their white picket gate. Grant was on the outside, glaring up at Charles, and Charles was on the inside, glaring down at Grant while waving a horribly familiar, small, framed painting in Grant's face. They were arguing so loudly that it was impossible not to eavesdrop.

"It's an Asazuki!" Charles crowed. "An original Asazuki!"

"I *know* it's an Asazuki!" Grant shouted. "I can *see* it's an Asazuki! I don't need *you* to tell me what an Asazuki looks like!"

"Apparently, you do," Charles said gleefully. "Because it was right under your nose and you missed it!"

"If you don't get it away from my nose," Grant said, shoving Charles's arm aside, "I'll punch you on yours!"

"I'd like to see you try," said Charles.

"I don't think you would," said Grant, raising a clenched fist.

"Who do you reckon would win if they had a dustup?" Mr. Barlow asked conversationally. "Charles has the height, the weight, and the reach, but Grant's kept himself in better shape."

"I sincerely hope they *won't* have a dustup," I said, appalled by the thought of either man sprawled across the cobbles in my peaceful village.

"Suit yourself," Mr. Barlow said equably. "I'd back Grant. Quicker, lighter on his feet, more stamina. It's the wiry ones you have to watch out for."

Charles apparently decided to watch out for the wiry one standing within arm's reach of his nose because he clutched the painting to his chest, withdrew to a safe distance, and changed tactics.

"It's not about the Asazuki," he was saying. "It's about you taking advantage of my good nature."

"If you didn't *want* to sort the disposables, why didn't you *say so?*" Grant exploded. "I didn't force them on you! I didn't lock you in the shed!"

"No, but you left the shed all topsy-turvy because you knew you could rely on me to organize it for you!" Charles retorted.

"I'm sick to death of you organizing things!" said Grant. "I'm sick of you nagging and fussing and hoovering and polishing and making me feel like a guest in my own home!"

"You," said Charles, "are an ungrateful swine."

"And you," Grant snarled, "are a paranoid neat freak with delusions of grandeur. And *I've* had *enough!*"

Grant spun on his heel, got into his car, and sped off in the direction of Upper Deeping. Charles frowned ferociously, stomped into the cottage, and slammed the door so hard that the sound reverberated from one end of the village to the other.

"They've lost their minds," I said.

"Who's the boa constrictor?" Mr. Barlow asked.

"Who's the what?" I asked, staring at him.

"The bendy beauty with the cameras," he replied.

He gestured toward Jemma Renshawe, who'd wrapped her gorgeous self around the war memorial, presumably to capture artistic images of Grant and Charles yelling at each other. Her aunt stood in the memorial's shadow, looking as if she'd rather be anywhere else.

"It's Elspeth's niece," I said. "She's taking photographs for a book about Cotswold villages."

Mr. Barlow burst out laughing. "Charles and Grant will be well pleased to have their bickering beaks put in a book for all the world to see."

"Pleased?" I said, sagging against the bridge's low stone wall. "They're the vainest men in Finch. They'll have six fits when they find out what she's done."

"I wouldn't get comfortable just yet, Lori," Mr. Barlow advised. "There's more to come."

"Where?" I asked, pushing myself upright.

Mr. Barlow's pointing finger followed Peggy Taxman as she exited her general store and sailed majestically across the green to enter the tearoom.

"I've seen this one coming," said Mr. Barlow, folding his arms.

"What have you seen coming?" I asked.

"The clash of the titans," he replied. "Peggy's been pea-green with envy ever since Sally had her lucky break with Dabney Holdstrom, and Sally's bragging hasn't helped. Always has to have the upper hand, does Peggy, and she hasn't had it lately. Looks as if she's geared herself up to bring Sally down a peg."

If anyone could deflate an overblown ego, it was Peggy Taxman. Peggy was a force to be reckoned with. Grown men ran for cover when her pointy, rhinestone-studded glasses came into view and grown women generally did whatever she told them to do.

Sally Pyne didn't appear to be in an overly submissive state of mind as she chased Peggy out of the tearoom. Sally's round face was screwed up and beet-red with rage, while Henry Cook, who trailed after her, looked as though he had one foot hovering precariously over a land mine. I couldn't blame him. Both women looked as if they were ready to explode.

"What sort of getup is Sally wearing?" Mr. Barlow asked.

His perplexity was understandable. Short, plump, white-haired Sally Pyne usually wore stretch pants, a loose-fitting blouse, and sneakers to work. It took me a full five seconds to figure out why she'd replaced her customary attire with a flouncy, full-skirted, green gingham dress, a frilly pink apron, and lavender satin slippers.

"It must be for the photo shoot," I said as the penny dropped. "The photo shoot for the *Cozy Cookery* magazine cover."

"She looks like an angry Easter egg," Mr. Barlow said, chuckling.

I couldn't laugh along with him. I felt as if I were witnessing the collision of two mighty tectonic plates. My sense of dread increased exponentially when Jemma Renshawe released her hold on the war memorial and made a beeline for the villagers who'd gathered on the green to watch Peggy and Sally face off. I doubted that my neighbors would look kindly upon Jemma if she blocked their view of what promised to be a highly entertaining confrontation.

Peggy stopped halfway across the green and swung around to make a stand. Sally came to a halt a few feet away from her and Henry hung back a few more steps.

"Wise of them to keep their distance," Mr. Barlow commented. "Henry's beefy and Sally's plucky, but Peggy could fell an oak tree with one slap."

I whimpered.

"How dare you interrupt my photo shoot?" Sally roared.

"You may as well cancel your photo shoot," Peggy thundered, "because the tearoom won't be yours for much longer." She pointed a finger at Sally. "I've told you once, but I'll say it again. I'm buying up your lease!"

"My lease isn't for sale!" Sally bellowed.

"So you say, but I know better," Peggy said, with a self-satisfied smirk. "You may be able to find your way around a kitchen, Sally Pyne, but you've no head for business."

"No head for *business*?" Sally echoed, her voice rising along with her blood pressure.

"An experienced businesswoman doesn't shut up shop for two days running," said Peggy. "She doesn't leave paying customers out in the cold while she swans about, acting like the queen of the May."

"*The queen of the May?*" Sally screeched, her ruffles trembling.

"There goes the boa," Mr. Barlow observed.

Jemma Renshawe was wriggling through the grass on her belly with her trim backside in the air, pausing every few feet to roll onto her side and photograph the villagers from below. The women who were wearing skirts looked scandalized and those who were wearing trousers scowled at her, but the men followed her progress avidly, elbowing one another in the ribs and waggling their eyebrows expressively.

"Jemma, *please*," Elspeth whispered piercingly as she wound her way through the assembled throng.

Her niece ignored her plaintive hiss and continued crawling.

"Cats and clowns," said Mr. Barlow.

"Hmmm?" I said, too absorbed in the drama to spare him a glance.

"Cats and clowns," Mr. Barlow repeated, gesturing toward the onlookers. "The women want to scratch her eyes out and the men look like village idiots. And she's getting it all on film." He chuckled happily. "I reckon Charles and Grant won't be the only ones having fits when her book comes out."

I shushed him and bent my ear toward the green.

"I am not swanning about," Sally protested. "Haven't you heard of publicity? It's the way an *experienced businesswoman* attracts new customers. My media exposure will reach a much larger demographic than your poxy shop windows."

"Media exposure? Demographic?" Peggy scoffed. "Don't wave your fancy words in my face until you know what they mean. And there's nothing wrong with my shop windows."

"There's an inch of dust on those rusty old tins of beans," Sally retorted, "and the *C* fell off of your crumpets sign two months ago. Having a sale on *rumpets*, are we?"

The villagers tittered cautiously, acknowledging Sally's wit while at the same time respecting Peggy's power.

"Ow!" cried Jemma Renshawe.

"Did I tread on you, dear?" Millicent Scroggins inquired. "So sorry."

"I think it might have been my fault," said Opal Taylor. "I didn't mean to kick you, dear."

"Jemma," said Elspeth, looking mortified. *"Please . . ."*

Jemma sat up with a pained grimace and rubbed her reddened shoulder vigorously, then scrambled to her feet and began creeping through the crowd, aiming her camera at random villagers.

"We aren't having a sale on anything," Peggy bellowed, ignoring the sideshow, "because *I'm* about to buy your building. Once I have your lease in my hand, the tearoom will be mine!"

"B-but I live above the tearoom," Sally stammered, looking thunderstruck. "If you buy the building, you'll be my *landlady*."

"I'll be your boss as well," Peggy said smugly.

"Over my dead body," Sally shot back.

"Suit yourself," said Peggy. "I wouldn't have kept you on anyway. The amount of money you throw away on flour and sugar and cream and eggs is disgraceful. I know a supplier who'll give them to me for half the price."

"They'll have half the quality, too, I'll wager," Sally said doggedly. "Cheap ingredients taste cheap. Not that you'd know the difference."

A chorus of gasps rose from the onlookers.

"She insulted Peggy," I said, awestruck. "No one insults Peggy Taxman."

"Not to her face, they don't," said Mr. Barlow.

"When I'm running the tearoom," said Peggy, "I'll turn a pretty profit."

"You? Run the tearoom?" Sally laughed derisively. "Your

cakes fall, your lemon curd tastes like soap, and you've never baked a loaf of bread you haven't burnt."

"I don't intend to waste my valuable time slaving over a hot oven," said Peggy. "I plan to hire a *real* baker."

"Is your husband a real baker, then?" Sally taunted. "He'd better be, because you won't find anyone else willing to work for you."

"You're sacked!" bellowed Peggy.

"You can't sack me because I don't work for you and I never will," Sally hollered. "For your information, Mistress High-and-Mighty, I don't need to work at all." She reached behind her, pulled Henry Cook forward, and linked arms with him. "My Henry will support me."

"How will Henry support you?" Peggy demanded. "He works for you!"

"Not anymore," said Sally. She drew herself up and surveyed her audience with an air of great satisfaction, then dropped her bombshell. "Henry is going back into show business!"

The villagers emitted a collective and deeply impressed, "Oooooh!"

"Sally dear," Henry began, but he had no chance of interrupting Sally, who was in full flow.

"My Henry is too humble to toot his own horn, so I'll toot it for him," said Sally. "One of Dabney's motoring friends is a theatrical agent. His name is Arty Barnes—"

"The scrawny little chap with the big nose?" Dick Peacock

asked. "He was in my pub last week. Likes his lager, does Arty. Good storyteller, too."

"Arty has an eye for talent as well as a way with words," Sally said, beaming at Dick. "He thinks Henry is the next big thing. Thanks to Arty, my husband-to-be will make his return to the stage at a comedy club in Bristol on Tuesday night."

"It's just one gig," said Henry, looking very uncomfortable.

"One gig leads to another," said Sally, patting his arm. "After he finishes his run in Bristol, Henry will take his show on the road and who knows what will happen next? His own television series? A lead role in a movie? Anything's possible! When my Henry hits the big time, we won't have to live in a pokey little flat above a shop. We'll buy a proper house as far away from the *Grand Poohbah*"—she pointed at Peggy—"as we can get!"

"You're getting a little ahead of yourself, aren't you?" Peggy asked.

"I have complete faith in my Henry," Sally replied. She whipped off her frilly pink apron and threw it at Peggy's feet. "Go ahead. Buy the building. The tearoom is all yours. Let's see what a dog's dinner you make of it." She turned to the villagers. "The rest of you are invited to see Henry perform at the Lots O' Laughs club in Bristol on Tuesday night at seven o'clock. There'll be free jelly doughnuts to celebrate the stellar occasion—and *my* jelly doughnuts won't *poison* you!"

While Peggy prepared a rejoinder, Elspeth's niece received another lesson in good manners.

"Oof!" Jemma grunted as she bent double and clutched her side.

"Were those your ribs, dear?" said Opal. "I'm afraid I caught you with my elbow. Do forgive me. I didn't see you creeping up behind me."

Elspeth's jaw was set and her face was crimson as she hurried forward, put an arm around Jemma's waist, and hustled her toward the safety of her cottage. As they departed, a stocky, bearded man in blue jeans, a button-down shirt, and tasseled loafers put his head out of the tearoom, caught sight of Sally, and strode across the green to address her.

"Mrs. Pyne?" he said, tapping his wristwatch impatiently. "We really must be getting on. Mr. Holdstrom will want at least ten more shots of you and your summer pudding. As I explained earlier, he likes to choose from a variety of images when it comes time for him to make his final selection."

"Sorry, Rick," said Sally. "I've been replaced. If you want to photograph the tearoom's owner, you'll have to deal with the dragon lady." She bent her head toward Peggy, then clapped Rick on the shoulder. "Good luck, young man. You'll need it."

"Pah!" Peggy said scornfully. She flicked a hand at Sally, as if she were shooing away a gnat, then wheeled around and sailed majestically toward the Emporium.

"Er, Mrs. Pyne?" said Rick, looking utterly befuddled. "We can't change course in the middle of a shoot."

"You'll have to," said Sally.

"What about my jams and marmalades?" said Opal Taylor, stepping forward. "You could photograph them."

"I'm not here to photograph jams and marmalades," Rick said curtly. "I'm here to photograph Mrs. Pyne and her summer pudding."

"Sally and her pudding are no prettier than me and my marmalades," Opal said obstinately.

"It's not a matter of prettiness," Rick informed her, sounding exasperated. "An assignment is an assignment."

"Change the assignment," Opal commanded. "I can be ready for you in two ticks."

"Come, Henry," said Sally. "I need to speak with my solicitor."

"Mrs. Pyne!" Rick said, stretching his arms toward her beseechingly. "You can't walk out in the middle of a shoot."

"Watch me," said Sally.

She and Henry hotfooted it to my husband's office, Sally bouncing on her toes like a boxer, Henry dawdling behind her with his head bowed. Opal attempted to pursue her argument with the hapless Rick, but he ignored her, pulled a cell phone from his pocket, and spoke into it rapidly as he retreated to the tearoom.

"Is Bill Sally's solicitor?" Mr. Barlow asked as the villagers dispersed.

"I hope not," I said fervently. "Can you imagine him brokering a truce between Sally Pyne and Peggy Taxman?"

"Rock and a hard place," said Mr. Barlow. He took the socket wrench from his pocket and spun it between his fingers. "Show's over. Guess I'll get back to work. Nice talking with you, Lori. I'd have a doctor take a look at that thumb, if I were you. It's gone a funny color."

I was too worn out to tell him that he was responsible for my injury. I felt as battered as Jemma Renshawe, as if each harsh word, each angry look that had passed between my neighbors had left a bruise on my heart. I leaned on the low stone wall and stared blindly into the river while my thumb throbbed and my overloaded brain spun in circles.

A vehicle stopped behind me on the bridge and I turned to see Jack MacBride peering at me through the open window of his rental car. Bree was in the passenger seat and the backseat was filled with birdbaths.

"Are you okay, Lori?" Jack asked. "You look a bit crook."

I understood his meaning and went along with it. I needed time to process the day's kaleidoscopic events before I could explain them to my young friends.

"I don't feel at all well," I admitted.

"It's my fault," Jack said contritely. "You've been putting in too many hours at Uncle Hector's."

"Wait here," Bree called across him. "We'll unload the car, bung Betsy in the boot, and come back for you. You're not cycling home today."

"Thanks," I said.

"What happened to your thumb?" Jack asked.

"What can I say?" I replied with a tired shrug. "I'm not a carpenter."

"My fault again," said Jack, rapping himself on the forehead with his fist.

"Don't move, Lori," said Bree. "We'll be right back."

They drove off and I turned to gaze at my beloved village. Finch looked tranquil, but I knew in my bruised heart that it was crumbling beneath the weight of its good fortune.

Eighteen

ack and Bree returned with a makeshift ice pack—six ice cubes wrapped in a clean tea towel—and let me nurse my thumb in silence all the way home. While Jack stashed Betsy in the garage, Bree walked with me into the cottage. She offered to telephone Bill, but I declined, telling myself that, if Bill were Sally Pyne's solicitor, he wouldn't be able to leave his office until she'd had her say, which could take quite some time.

"Don't be such a mother hen," I chided Bree gently. "You should know by now that I can look after myself. Run along. I'll be fine."

"Okay," Bree said reluctantly. "But if you need anything, ring me."

"I will," I said, forcing a smile. "Go!"

Bree and Jack departed and I dragged myself to the study. The room was blissfully still and silent and the ivy leaves cloaking the diamond-paned windows filtered the bright sunlight that had beaten down upon me atop the humpbacked bridge. I approached Reginald wordlessly, took him from his niche, and held him to my cheek, taking comfort, as I had done throughout my life, from the touch of his soft pink flannel. If my thumb hadn't been as big as a bloated sausage, I would have sucked it.

With a sigh, I returned Reginald to his niche and took the blue journal with me to a tall leather armchair near the hearth. I leaned back in the chair, put my feet on the ottoman, propped the journal on my knees, opened it clumsily with one hand, and began to cry.

Lori, my child, what's wrong?

"Everything," I sobbed, looking down at the familiar handwriting through a flood of tears. "Mr. Barlow didn't mow the cemetery and he didn't help us fix the bird tables and Charles is mad at Grant and Grant is mad at Charles and Jemma embarrassed Elspeth and Rick won't shoot Opal's marmalades and Peggy's buying the tearoom and Sally's moving away because Henry's going to be a big star and . . . and . . . and *my thumb hurts*," I howled.

Why does your thumb hurt?

"I h-hit it with a h-hammer," I replied tremulously.

I see. Have you had anything to eat or drink since breakfast?

"N-no," I quavered miserably. "I didn't sleep very well last night, either. T-tidal waves."

Tidal waves disrupted your sleep? You poor thing. All right, my dear, here's what you're going to do. You will ring Bill and tell him to come home. I don't care if he's writing the Duke of Northumberland's last will and testament, he's to come home AT ONCE. While you're waiting for him, you'll reheat a cup of the chicken broth you made last week.

"B-broth," I hiccuped, nodding docilely.

A hot, nourishing drink will lessen the effects of shock.

"Am I in shock?" I asked, vaguely surprised.

You're dehydrated, malnourished, exhausted, injured, and, yes, you're in shock. You may have a touch of sunstroke as well, if your tidal wave comment is anything to go by. Which is why, after you've swallowed every last drop of the broth, Bill will take you directly to the hospital in Upper Deeping.

"I don't *want* to go to the hospital," I wailed.

Of course you shall go to hospital. Your thumb may be broken. If it becomes infected, you could lose your entire hand.

The dire prognosis brought me up short. I stopped crying and stared at my distended digit in disbelief.

"But Dimity," I said faintly, "I have so much to tell you."

You can tell me later. I'm not going anywhere. But you are. Ring Bill now.

Bill found me at the kitchen table, crying into my chicken broth. He didn't reproach me for not calling him sooner or scold me for ogling my neighbors when I should have been taking care of myself. He simply wrapped me in a blanket and drove me straight to the hospital.

After a few X-rays, blood tests, and antibiotic injections, the attending physician informed Bill that my thumb was badly contused rather than broken and that I'd probably lose the nail, which struck me as a better deal than losing a whole hand. The doctor agreed with Aunt Dimity's diagnosis of dehydration and put me on an IV drip before sending me home with three kinds of prescription medications and a thumb that resembled an itty-bitty mummy.

One of the drugs was a sedative, but Bill didn't need to administer it because I was fast asleep before we reached the cottage. He carried me upstairs and put me to bed and I awoke briefly as he was tucking me in.

"The boys," I murmured drowsily.

"They're spending the night at Father's," he said. "Deirdre will take them to school tomorrow morning."

"Good old Deirdre," I said, closing my eyes. "Are you Sally Pyne's solicitor?"

"I'll tell you tomorrow," said Bill.

He smoothed my hair back from my forehead, kissed me tenderly on the lips, and sat with me until I dropped off to sleep again.

I awoke at half past nine on Friday morning, feeling ravenous. Bill was seated in the armchair near the sliding glass door to the deck, tapping away at his laptop's keyboard, and Stanley was asleep in the pool of sunlight next to Bill's chair. When I raised my head from the pillows, Bill closed the laptop and came to sit beside me on the bed.

"Are you Sally Pyne's solicitor?" I asked.

"Excellent," said Bill. "The medication hasn't affected the gossip quadrant of your brain." He kissed the tip of my nose. "No, I'm not Sally's solicitor. She came to me for advice on managing Henry's career and I referred her to a colleague in London."

"Thank heavens," I said.

"How are you feeling?" he asked.

"Not bad," I said.

"Good," he said. "The painkiller the doctor gave you must still be working."

"It hasn't killed my appetite," I said. "I could chase a horse and eat the jockey."

"Would a bowl of porridge do?" Bill asked.

"I'd prefer a full fry-up with a large glass of orange juice and a pot of tea," I said. "I haven't had anything to eat since the IV drip."

"A full fry-up it is, then," said Bill. "I'll prop you up on your pillows and you can have breakfast in bed."

"I'll sit at the kitchen table, thank you," I said. "I didn't break a leg, Bill. I can manage the stairs."

"Okay," he said brightly. "Let's see you sit up."

I used my right arm to push myself into an upright position, watched the room tilt alarmingly, and slumped back onto my pillows.

"Breakfast in bed might not be a bad idea," I conceded.

I felt steady enough after breakfast to take a shower, get dressed, and descend to the living room under Bill's close supervision. I stretched out on the couch, but Bill wouldn't sit still until he'd arranged my medications on the coffee table, placed two pillows at my back, thrown a quilt across my legs, and put a cushion in my lap to elevate my left hand, as per doctor's orders. He adjusted pillows, quilt, and cushion repeatedly, until they met his specifications for my comfort, then sat in his armchair and stroked Stanley, who'd hopped into his lap.

"Thanks, dear," I said. "You can go to the office now."

"No, I can't," he said, frowning.

"Yes, you can," I said. "I promise to take it easy for the rest of the day. I have everything I need down here, so I won't have to tackle the stairs, and I won't leave the cottage unless it catches fire. You can bring Will and Rob home from school and I'll even let you make dinner."

"Dinner shouldn't be too difficult," he said. "The casserole parade should begin around noon."

My neighbors brought casseroles to invalids as well as to those grieving for a lost loved one. They believed—quite soundly, in my opinion—that grief, illness, and injury were equally incapacitating and did what they could to make life easier for the stricken.

"There you are," I said. "I won't have to lift a finger, much less a thumb, for the rest of the day."

"Lori," Bill began, but I cut him off.

"I'll go crazy if you sit there and stare at me," I said. "And I'll feel terrible if my inability to swing a hammer screws up your work schedule. You have the conference call with your new Polish client this afternoon, don't you? The call you've had to reschedule three times already because of the dotty uncle?"

"I can reschedule it again," said Bill.

"If you do, I'll feel even worse," I said. "I'll come down with a raging fever and my arm will fall off and it'll be your fault." I smiled coaxingly. "Go to work, Bill. I *promise* to behave myself."

Bill eyed me doubtfully, but he shifted Stanley from his lap to the floor, stood, and disappeared up the hall. He returned a moment later to place Reginald and the blue journal on the coffee table.

"Thought I'd save you a trip to the study," he said.

"You really are the most perfect of perfect husbands," I told him.

"I'll be gone for a couple of hours, three at the most," he said sternly. "If I come home and find you doing handsprings—"

"I've sworn off handsprings." I held up my mini-mummy. "And carpentry."

Bill gave a grudging laugh, collected his laptop and his briefcase, kissed me good-bye, and left the cottage. Stanley jumped onto the armchair, snuggled into the indentation Bill had made in the seat cushion, and went to sleep.

"My husband really is perfect," I said to Reginald and he didn't disagree. I reached for the blue journal, propped it in front of my elevated hand, opened it, and said, "Dimity?"

A short but elegant line of copperplate appeared on the blank page.

Is it broken?

"No," I said. "Just smashed. I can hardly feel it at the moment. I'm on drugs."

Drugs have their uses.

"Now, about yesterday's news," I began, but I got no further.

Conserve your energy, Lori. I've had almost twenty-four hours to analyze your semi-incoherent outburst and I believe I understand most of it. I'll give you my impressions and you can stop me if I go wrong.

"Fire away," I said.

Mr. Barlow didn't mow the cemetery and he didn't help you fix the bird tables because he's been too busy working on the classic cars brought to him by Dabney Holdstrom and Mr. Holdstrom's friends, classic cars that appear to be related to a wish Mr. Barlow made near the wishing well.

"Correct," I said.

You attempted to repair the bird tables without Mr. Barlow's help and your attempt ended when you hurt yourself. It could be argued that Mr. Barlow is indirectly responsible for your accident.

"I blame Dabney Holdstrom," I said. "His cars lured Mr. Barlow away from his proper jobs."

Why didn't you attend to your thumb immediately? You must have known it was damaged.

"I meant to put ice on it," I said, "but I heard Charles and Grant yelling at each other and I had to find out what was going on."

Ah, yes, I remember: Charles is mad at Grant and Grant is mad at Charles. I can't say I'm surprised. Did Charles use the Asazuki painting as an excuse to air an assortment of grievances against Grant?

"Mostly he accused Grant of taking him for granted," I said.

"Grant aired a few grievances, too, before he drove off in a huff. It was an old-fashioned, no-holds-barred shouting match."

Prompted by the masterpiece Charles wished to find.

"Exactly," I said.

Charles used an exquisite work of art as a weapon in a childish argument. It was bound to end in tears. Let us move on to Elspeth's embarrassment. Jemma is the photographer-niece whose mission it is to photograph Cotswold villagers.

"She is," I said.

Did her manner embarrass Elspeth?

"She has no manners," I said. "That's what embarrassed Elspeth. It's as if Jemma doesn't realize she's photographing real, live human beings. She just barges in and starts snapping away, regardless of whether her subjects wish to be photographed or not."

Artists can be self-absorbed.

"Then Jemma's a true artist," I said. "She dumped her gear all over Elspeth's cottage, refused the cup of tea Elspeth offered her, and offended Elspeth's friends. If Elspeth hadn't dragged her away, Opal and Millicent would have made mincemeat of her. I don't think her kind of creative energy is the kind Elspeth had in mind when she made her wish."

Creative energy is not to be taken lightly. It isn't like fairy dust, gilding all it touches. It's like a bulldozer, knocking down whatever gets in its way.

"By now, Elspeth probably agrees with you," I said.

I confess that I reached an impasse when I came to "Rick won't shoot Opal's marmalades." Who is Rick and why would Opal want him to shoot her marmalades?

I spent the next fifteen minutes telling Aunt Dimity the intertwined stories of Peggy, Sally, Henry, Rick, and Opal.

"In short," I concluded, "it's a big mess."

Rick's conflict with Opal seems unremarkable. As he said, an assignment is an assignment. Opal can bark orders at him until she's blue in the face, but it will make no difference. Rick needs his employer's permission, not hers, to alter a photo shoot.

"What about Peggy and Henry, though?" I asked. "Bree's guesses about them were spot on. No one saw them visit the wishing well, so they must have gone there at night, as Charles did. Peggy's wish must have been to own the tearoom and Henry's must have been to take his act on stage again. And their wishes, like everyone else's, came true."

With catastrophic consequences. Sally's taste of Cozy Cookery *fame went straight to her head. Her arrogance goaded Peggy into buying a business she doesn't need and won't be able to run. Furthermore, Sally is delusional if she believes that Henry's comedic gifts will catapult him—and by extension, her—into the stratosphere of stardom.*

"Henry is pretty funny," I reminded her.

Henry Cook tells humorous anecdotes in a tearoom. I'm not convinced that he has the drive to claw his way to the top of the entertainment industry. He may have given in to Arty Barnes's blandishments as a lark, but I doubt very much that he yearns for the high-powered career Sally envisions.

"He didn't seem to be as excited as Sally was about the gig

at the comedy club," I said reflectively. "He looked kind of gloomy when she started boasting about his big break."

Of course he did. He knows that Peggy's purchase of the tearoom will end the comfortable life he and Sally have fashioned for themselves in Finch. He also knows that he will be unable to support himself and Sally with his modest talents. He must feel as if his world is caving in on him.

"He's not alone," I said. "Peggy can't bake and no competent baker will work for her because she's such a bossy-boots. Once she buys the tearoom, Finch's supply of jelly doughnuts and custard tarts will dry up. I know of at least two grown men—namely, Derek Harris and my own sweet Bill—who will become extremely cranky without their daily pastry fix."

Peggy, too, will become disagreeable when her new venture fails, as it inevitably will.

"And she'll take it out on the rest of us," I said, adding darkly. "The wishing well has a lot to answer for."

The wishing well. Yes. It does seem to be at the center of Finch's recent spate of disasters.

"People have gotten what they wished for," I said, "but it hasn't made all of them happy. Sally's smugness, Peggy's lust for power, Elspeth's naiveté, and Charles's thirst for revenge made their wishes backfire. Mr. Barlow's wish hasn't backfired on him, but it has backfired on the vicar, not to mention my thumb. I suppose my own wish backfired on me. I wished the rain would stop and ended up dehydrated."

It's not hard to understand why so many wishes have failed, Lori.

The real mystery is why so many came true in the first place. There's something unreal about what's happening in Finch, something contrived, as if a mastermind were at work behind the scenes, as if a puppeteer were pulling the villagers' strings.

"He'd have to pull some pretty long strings to control the rain," I said.

Let's set aside the rain for the moment and focus on the more terrestrial wishes. Who could the mastermind be? Jack is the most likely suspect, of course. He discovered the well. He's allowed all and sundry to visit it. Finch was a relatively peaceful community until he arrived.

"Jack MacBride? A conniving meddler?" I said, laughing. "Impossible. He was nowhere near the wishing well when the wishes were made."

One needn't be near the well to learn who made which wishes. Remember, Lori, there are no secrets in Finch. I suspect Sally and the others couldn't keep themselves from divulging their wishes to someone who in turn mentioned them to someone else and so on, until everyone in Finch knew of everyone else's wishes. The puppeteer could get wind of them quite easily.

"It still can't be Jack," I argued. "It would take someone with power and influence to grant so many wishes. A guy with power and influence doesn't live out of a backpack. Our puppeteer would also have to know a lot of people—Jemma's editor, for instance, and Arty Barnes the talent agent—and Jack doesn't know anyone outside of Finch. How could he? He hasn't been in England since he was six."

Dabney Holdstrom has power, influence, and a wide circle of friends, and his arrival in Finch precipitated a number of unfortunate events. Perhaps he's pulling the strings.

"Why would Dabney Holdstrom make the villagers' wishes come true?" I asked. "Why would he care about them at all?"

I don't know, but someone might. It's time for you to take action, Lori.

"Is it?" I said weakly. The burst of energy that had brought me downstairs was beginning to dissipate and the painkiller was wearing off. The mere thought of taking any kind of action made my thumb throb. "What did you have in mind?"

I suggest you start with a bit of investigative work. Look into Dabney Holdstrom's background. Is he distantly related to someone in Finch? Was a family member evacuated to Finch during the war? Could he feel a debt of gratitude to a villager for a long-forgotten favor? Find out about his connections. Does he know the editor who gave Jemma Renshawe her commission? Does he publish the newsletter through which George Wetherhead found his rare locomotive? Is he familiar with the estate agent who listed the tearoom's sale? Could he somehow be responsible for sending Peter and Cassie Harris back to Anscombe Manor? Is Arty Barnes really impressed by Henry's talent or is he acting at the behest of his old friend, Dabney Holdstrom? Get out there, Lori! Ask questions! Collect facts!

"Okay," I said meekly. "But may I have a cup of tea first?"

I don't expect you to start until you feel up to it, my dear. Pain can be quite exhausting.

"In that case, I'll have a cup of tea and a nap," I said.

An excellent notion. Sleep is the best medicine. May your nap be undisturbed by tidal waves.

"Thanks, Dimity," I said, smiling.

The curving lines of royal-blue ink faded from the page and I laid my head against the pillows, but before I could close my eyes, the doorbell rang.

"The casserole parade begins," I murmured.

I stashed the blue journal behind my pillows, tucked Reginald beneath the quilt, and thought about standing until a searing pain in my thumb changed my mind.

Fortunately, Bill was as lax as a villager when it came to locking up.

"It's open!" I called. "Come in!"

Nineteen

I sat up and peered over the back of the couch, expecting to see Sally Pyne or Peggy Taxman or one of the Handmaidens kick off the casserole parade. Instead, Mr. Barlow shuffled into the room, holding one of the cellophane-wrapped boxes of chocolates Peggy sold at the Emporium.

To my relief, Mr. Barlow had exchanged his grubby coveralls for a short-sleeved cotton shirt and twill trousers, neither of which reeked of motor oil. His hands and his face were spotless and it looked as though he'd run a wet comb through his short, grizzled hair.

"'Morning, Lori," he said, coming around the couch to offer the box to me. "How're you feeling?"

"Better than I felt yesterday," I said. "I always feel better when a gentleman brings me chocolates. Thank you."

"You're welcome." He remained on his feet, with his hands stuffed into his pockets and his head bowed. "Bill came by my place on his way to the office and told me how you busted up your thumb."

I frowned. "Bill shouldn't have—"

"Yes, he should," Mr. Barlow interrupted. "Nothing wrong with a man speaking up for his wife. Nothing wrong with a man speaking the truth to a friend, either, and Bill brought a few truths home to me this morning." He rubbed the back of his neck and sighed heavily. "I reckon I owe you a whole bar-

row full of apologies, Lori. I'm sorry I didn't fix the bird tables. I'm sorry you got hurt using one of my hammers. And
I'm sorry I stood there like a half-wit yesterday and told you to
see a doctor when you wouldn't have had to see a doctor if I'd
kept my promise to Jack."

"Apologies accepted," I said gently. I flapped my good hand
at him peremptorily. "Now, sit down and make yourself comfortable or I'll have a stiff neck to go along with my stiff
thumb."

Mr. Barlow glanced at the sleeping Stanley, then took a
seat in my armchair. He leaned toward me, his hands loosely
clasped between his knees.

"You're not the only one I've wronged," he said. "The vicar
had to ask Jack MacBride to do the work I should've done in
the churchyard last Saturday. The grass was halfway up Heze-
kiah Tansy's marble angel by the time Jack got there. He had
to go over it with the string trimmer and the rake before he
could do the mowing. Took him the best part of the afternoon
to finish." He shook his head. "I felt about two inches tall when
Bill told me. The vicar asking a stranger to do my job . . ." He
peered earnestly at me. "I'll apologize to Jack and the vicar
after I'm done here. I wanted to say sorry to you first, because
you paid the biggest price for my malingering."

"You weren't malingering," I protested. "You were working."

"I was having the time of my life," he countered. "Never
thought I'd get to touch a Jag E-Type or '65 Lotus, not if I lived
to be a hundred, and there I was, tinkering with them, driving

them, putting them through their paces. It was a dream come true right enough, but dreaming don't mend bird tables or mow lawns."

I shifted my aching hand to a less agonizing position and decided to make the most of Mr. Barlow's visit by asking him about Dabney Holdstrom. The thought of commencing my investigation without leaving the couch appealed to me greatly.

"Do you and Mr. Holdstrom chat much?" I asked.

"What would we chat about?" asked Mr. Barlow, looking puzzled.

"The usual things," I said. "His family, his friends . . ."

"Why would I want to know about his family or his friends?" Mr. Barlow asked. "We aren't mates, Lori. I'm grateful to him for steering his friends my way, but we don't have anything in common, apart from the cars."

"Do his friends talk about him?" I asked.

"Not much," said Mr. Barlow, "except to say how surprised they are to see him in a quiet little place like Finch. One of them—I think it was Arty Barnes, the theatrical chap—said Mr. Holdstrom was reliving his childhood."

"Did he grow up in Finch?" I asked eagerly.

"No," said Mr. Barlow. "He grew up the other side of Upper Deeping, in a little place called Skeaping. The village with the weird museum your lads are so fond of."

"Skeaping Manor," I said, with a pang of disappointment.

"Mr. Holdstrom went to London as soon as he left school, but he still has family back in Skeaping," said Mr. Barlow.

"That's what the Barnes chap told me." Mr. Barlow regarded me questioningly. "What made you think Mr. Holdstrom might've grown up in Finch?"

"He's been extremely kind to you and to Sally and to Opal," I said, "and he introduced Henry to Arty Barnes."

"And you reckon . . . what?" said Mr. Barlow, looking perplexed. "He's been nice to us because he has fond memories of his boyhood home?" He shrugged. "Makes sense, I suppose, except for the part about him not growing up in Finch."

"Yes," I agreed dryly, "that does put a dent in my theory."

"I should be going, Lori," said Mr. Barlow, getting to his feet. "Mr. Holdstrom will be coming to pick up his Morris this afternoon and I want to make sure it's humming. I hope he won't take it too hard when I tell him I'm done with classic cars."

"You're done with them?" I said. "I thought you were having the time of your life, fiddling with those fancy engines."

"I was fiddling while Finch burned," said Mr. Barlow. "No more. I've had my fun. It's time I got back to my proper jobs. Anything need doing around here, Lori? Squeaky hinge? Loose floorboard?"

"You could give me a painkiller," I said. "I'm not sure I can open the childproof lid."

Mr. Barlow was pleased to be of service. He bustled off to the kitchen and returned with a glass of water and a sandwich consisting of a slab of cheese between two thick slices of bread.

"It says on the label 'to be taken with food,'" he pointed out.

I was still full from breakfast, but I dutifully ate a few bites of the sandwich before taking the tablet Mr. Barlow placed in my palm. He unwrapped the box of chocolates, too, and apologized to me once more before letting himself out of the cottage.

I rested my head against the pillows and wondered how long it would take for the drug to start working, but my reverie was interrupted by the crunch of tires on gravel. Groaning, I sat up, looked through the bay window, and saw Selena Buxton walking up my flagstone path. She was dressed as neatly as ever, in a baby-blue skirt and blazer, with matching pumps, and she was carrying a baby-blue casserole dish. The casserole parade had begun.

I counted to three, then hollered, "Come in! It's open!"

The front door opened and closed. Selena put her head into the living room and held the dish up for me to see.

"Chicken Divan," she said. "I'll pop it in the fridge, shall I?"

"Yes, thank you," I said. "Then come back and keep me company."

I wanted nothing more than to sink into a deep and dreamless sleep, but I couldn't let Selena go without interrogating her. As a Handmaiden, she was honor bound to stay up-to-date on the latest gossip. I could count on her to pass along anything that had been said by or about Dabney Holdstrom since his arrival in Finch.

I smiled up at her as she returned to the living room and took a seat in my armchair.

"Will and Rob adore your Chicken Divan," I said, "and so does Bill. Thank you for making one of their favorite dishes."

"It's nothing, really," she said. "As soon as I heard about your accident I realized that you'd need help feeding your family." She pursed her lips primly and smoothed her skirt as she continued, "I'm afraid your other neighbors are far too busy with their own affairs to give your suffering a second thought."

"Maybe they haven't heard about my suffering," I said.

Selena eyed me incredulously.

"You can't imagine that a mad dash to hospital would go unnoticed in Finch," she said. "Your poor thumb has been the talk of the village. By rights, your fridge should be full by now, but it appears that neighborliness has gone by the wayside in our little community."

I shrugged. "If people are busy——"

"Oh, yes, people are busy, busy, busy," Selena broke in sourly. "Miranda is dosing her patients with bottles of well water, Sally is sewing a striped waistcoat for Henry to wear on stage, Peggy is taking an inventory of the tearoom's furnishings, and Emma is closeted with Peter and Cassie at Anscombe Manor. Even my closest friends . . ." She faltered, then straightened her shoulders and continued spiritedly, "Even my closest friends are too busy to give you the attention you deserve. Elspeth is running around after that dreadful niece of hers and Opal asked Millicent to help her set up a mail-order business for her jams and marmalades."

"A mail-order business?" I repeated. "What's wrong with selling her wares through the Emporium?"

"Opal doesn't feel the Emporium will be able to handle the volume of sales that will come in once her products appear in

Cozy Cookery," Selena replied, her voice heavy with sarcasm. "She has no idea what she's getting herself into, of course. I told her that increased production will mean increased costs for supplies, equipment, packaging, postage, publicity, licenses, health inspections, and so on, and she called me—" Selena's nostrils flared with indignation. "She called me an interfering know-it-all, told me to mind my own business, and asked Millicent to help her instead of me."

"Ouch," I said. "That must have hurt."

"What *hurts*," Selena said angrily, "is that I have no business to mind! I went to the wishing well, just like everyone else, but has my wish been granted? No! It has been snatched away from me, ruined, annihilated!"

"What did you wish for?" I asked, wondering what kind of wish could provoke such strong emotions.

Selena took a few calming breaths and folded her well-manicured hands in her lap.

"Last year, after Sally and Henry became engaged," she began, "I offered my services to Sally. As you know, I spent twenty-five years as a professional wedding planner and I thought my knowledge and experience would be useful to her."

"Have they picked a date for the wedding?" I asked, my gossip's antennae quivering.

"They're leaning toward August," she replied.

"A year after they became engaged," I said, smiling. "How romantic."

"I leave romance to the bride and groom," said Selena.

"And they leave the wedding to me. A lot of groundwork can be laid before a specific date is selected. I offered to lay the groundwork."

"Did Sally accept?" I asked.

"She did," said Selena. "She's a marvelous seamstress, so she'll make her own gown, but I've sketched age-appropriate gowns for the bridesmaids and the matron of honor and lined up morning suits for the groom, the best man, and the groomsmen at a rental shop in Upper Deeping."

"I'll bet Sally makes her own cake, too," I put in.

"Naturally," said Selena, "but I've selected the invitations, the flowers, the music, the reception hall, the band, and the caterers, as well as the gifts for the wedding party. I've also devised a tasteful decorative scheme for St. George's, and I've kept overall expenses within Sally's declared budget." Selena's eyes gleamed with pleasure, as if the lovingly orchestrated spectacle were unfolding in her imagination.

"It sounds as though you've put a lot of work into planning the wedding," I said.

"I have," Selena agreed. "I wanted Sally and Henry's wedding day to go off without a hitch. That was my wish, Lori. No sudden rain showers, no embarrassing speeches, no broken zippers, no quarrels, no drunks, everyone arriving on time and having a splendid time. I asked the wishing well for a perfect wedding."

"It's a beautiful wish," I said.

The gleam in Selena's eyes went out.

"Beautiful, yes, but it won't come true!" she cried. "Sally has thrown my plans back in my face." Selena made a noise like a growl in the back of her throat. "She's decided to be married in a *registry office* without attendants or guests or music or anything."

"Why?" I asked, though I thought I knew the answer.

"It's this ridiculous notion she has about the rebirth of Henry's career," Selena said fretfully. "She wants to get the wedding over and done with before the bookings start to pour in. She's talking about buying a *caravan* to live in while they're 'on the road.'"

"What about *Cozy Cookery*?" I asked. "Dabney Holdstrom is writing a feature article about her. Is she going to leave him in the lurch?"

"Haven't you heard?" Selena's look of astonishment quickly turned into one of pity. "Of course you haven't. You've been out of circulation since yesterday afternoon."

"What's happened?" I demanded.

Selena sounded like her old gossipmongering self as she leaned forward to impart her news.

"Sally won't allow Mr. Holdstrom to publish the article," she said. "She won't be on the cover, either. Sally says it's because she lost the tearoom, but rumor has it that Mr. Holdstrom offended her by objecting to the green gingham monstrosity she wore for the photo shoot."

"Her outfit was a bit much," I conceded, "but I don't think it would have mattered if she'd held on to the tearoom. After all, the article was as much about the tearoom as it was about her. I'm sure she's trying to do the honorable thing by letting Dabney Holdstrom off the hook, but she must be incredibly disappointed."

"She's not half as disappointed as Mr. Holdstrom," Selena said. "I saw him leave Sally's flat and he looked devastated. I felt for him, poor man. He put a lot of work into his article and Sally threw it back in his face." Selena's face darkened. "My wish won't come true and his won't, either."

I blinked. "Did Dabney Holdstrom visit the wishing well?"

"Oh, yes," said Selena. "Sally egged him on to have a go at it last week. No one knows what he wished for, of course, but if I were an editor of a magazine like *Cozy Cookery*, I'd wish for a pastry chef like Sally Pyne on my cover *if* she agreed to wear a less ridiculous costume. Wouldn't you?"

"Yes," I said thoughtfully. "I suppose I would."

"Then you'd be as devastated as Dabney Holdstrom," Selena declared, "and as disappointed as I am. Disappointment seems to be the order of the day in Finch and friendship doesn't mean what it used to mean. If you need proof, look in your fridge. Only one casserole? It's shameful." She clucked her tongue and got to her feet. "I'll let you rest, Lori. I've enjoyed our little chat. No one else seems to have time for me."

She smiled wanly and departed, leaving me to my very tangled thoughts.

Twenty

S ally Pyne had given up her church wedding and her
magazine cover in order to follow her fiancé on his dubious comeback trail. Opal Taylor was starting a mail-
order business without knowing the first thing about mail-order
businesses. Noon was approaching and I had only one casserole
in my refrigerator because friendship didn't mean what it used
to mean in Finch. Selena's best friends had abandoned her and
the wishing well had failed her. It had, apparently, failed Dabney
Holdstrom, as well.

"The world has gone mad," I muttered.

I pulled Reginald out from under the quilt and gazed into
his black button eyes while I tried to follow the various sce-
narios to their logical conclusions.

"We know the tearoom will go straight downhill after
Peggy buys it," I said, "but what will Sally do if Henry flops? A
good baker can always find a job, but will she be content to
work for someone else after she's been her own boss for so
many years? Will cookies, cakes, and summer puddings be
enough for her after she's set her sights on Hollywood? Will
the church wedding be back on again or will she and Henry be
too poor to pay for it? Or," I went on with a small gasp of dis-
may, "will she break it off with Henry because she blames him
for dashing her dreams?"

Reginald offered no answers, but I was on a roll, so I kept going.

"Opal is setting herself up for a fall, too," I told him. "Even if she does figure out how mail order works, mass-produced marmalades never taste as good as the ones made in small batches. Apart from that, she won't be able to pick enough fresh berries to fill hundreds, maybe thousands, of orders. The quality of her products will decline, orders will tail off, and she'll lose the investment she's made in expanding her business. Instead of supplementing her income by selling her homemade goodies through the Emporium, she'll drain it by wasting her hard-earned cash on a hopeless venture. What will happen to Opal when her bank account runs dry?"

I stroked Reginald's hand-sewn whiskers as I continued, but my mind was so full of calamities that I hardly saw him.

"Miranda Morrow won't poison people with her bottles of well water," I said, "but she won't heal anyone either. If her patients lose confidence in her, she'll be written off as a crackpot and no one will remember how effective her herbal ointments and poultices and tisanes are."

It took me a while to conjure a bad outcome for model railway enthusiast George Wetherhead, but I managed it.

"What if his antique locomotive turns out to be stolen property?" I said. "It would explain why such a rarity was sold for a bargain price. George would be heartbroken if his new toy was taken away from him, but he'd have a heart attack if a constable showed up on his doorstep, asking questions."

Satisfied, I moved on.

"Dabney Holdstrom's had a double disappointment," I said. "Mr. Barlow won't repair his cars and Sally won't star in his magazine. I guess I'd be pretty devastated if I granted a wish for someone who said, 'No, thank you.' But if Dabney's the wish granter, why did he make a wish? Was he trying to blend in with the villagers? When in Finch, visit the wishing well? And last but not least: Why does the wishing well grant some wishes, but not others?"

I gazed blindly at my pink bunny for several minutes before it dawned on me to share my troubled thoughts with Aunt Dimity. I was about to remove the blue journal from its pillowy hiding place when I heard the unmistakable clip-clopping sound of horses walking sedately up the lane. Reginald and I watched through the bay window as two gray mares turned into my driveway. I recognized the riders instantly, though I hadn't seen them in a long time.

Peter and Cassie Harris were the most unexpected and the most welcome visitors I'd had all morning. They dismounted, tied their steeds to the hitching post Will and Rob used for their ponies, unloaded their saddlebags, and strode up the flagstone walk with their arms full of everything, it seemed, except a casserole dish.

Peter and Cassie were in their midtwenties. His dark good looks complimented her blond prettiness and though he was slightly taller than she was, they were both tall, lean, and blessed with the healthy glow that comes from working in the great outdoors.

"It's open!" I bellowed as I tucked Reginald beneath the quilt. "Come in!"

The pair strode into the living room, deposited their offerings on the coffee table, and bent to give me kisses on both cheeks and much gentler hugs than usual, presumably out of deference to my injury.

"We come bearing gifts," Peter announced, nodding toward the coffee table. "Mum sent the lilacs, the soup, and the grapes—"

Though Emma was Peter's stepmother, he never referred to her as such. Emma had come into his life when he was a young boy and she'd been "Mum" to him ever since.

"—Dad sent the book of crossword puzzles," Peter continued, "and Kit and Nell send their love. The magazines were my idea and the eye pillow was Cassie's."

"It's made of raw silk and filled with lavender," said Cassie, "to promote relaxation and sleep."

"Thank you," I said, thinking of how little sleep I'd had since I'd sent Bill to work. "Thanks for everything."

Cassie scooped up the lilacs and the soup and carried them into the kitchen. Peter perched on the edge of the coffee table and surveyed my bandaged thumb.

"Does it feel as bad as it looks?" he asked.

"As a matter of fact, it doesn't," I said in mild surprise. "The painkiller must have kicked in."

"Dad thought you would be on pain pills," said Peter. "That's why he sent the book of crossword puzzles instead of a bottle of brandy."

"It's the thought that counts," I said, smiling.

Cassie returned with the lilacs arranged in a vase. She placed the vase on the end table nearest my head—the shortest distance between the flowers' fragrance and my nose—and sat beside Peter on the coffee table.

"The others will be along later," Peter informed me, "but Cassie and I couldn't wait to see you."

"He's right," said Cassie. "One of the advantages of living next door is that we'll be able to spend more time with our favorite people."

"It's all settled, then?" I said. "You're moving into Anscombe Manor?"

"It's all settled," Peter confirmed. "Dad hopes to have our flat fitted out by next month."

"Emma's throwing a party in our honor tomorrow night," said Cassie. "You, Bill, and the twins are invited."

"Mum would have asked you herself," said Peter, "but she left for Ivy Cottage right after breakfast."

I laughed. "If I know your mother, she'll be gone until dark."

"You know my mother," Peter agreed.

"The party starts at eight o'clock," said Cassie, "but if you're worried about the boys staying up past their bedtime, come early. Our homecoming wouldn't be complete without them."

"Your homecoming has made Emma and Derek very happy," I said.

"They've made us very happy by taking us in," said Peter.

"It'll be a big change from what you're used to," I warned. "Swapping fresh air and freedom for an office job won't be easy."

"It'll be easy for us," said Cassie. "Our funding dried up six months ago. We've been living on our savings, but they're almost gone."

"I'm so sorry," I said.

"Don't be," said Peter. "Our enforced holiday made us realize that we were ready to change gears."

"Living out of a duffel bag gets old after a while," Cassie explained, "as does living in huts, tents, and rusty old caravans. Peter and I love the wilderness, but it isn't the best place to raise a family."

"A family!" I exclaimed, putting my good hand out to Cassie. "Are you—"

"Not yet," she said, laughing, "but I hope to be, soon."

Peter gazed at his wife with such tenderness that tears sprang to my eyes even as I smiled. I might never have another child of my own, I told myself, but I'd have the infinite pleasure of pampering theirs.

"Cassie and I were ready to put down roots," said Peter, "but we didn't know where to put them until an old friend told us that Mum was getting fed up with her role at the riding school."

I blinked back my tears and went on the alert. If Peter's old friend turned out to be Dabney Holdstrom, I'd know for certain who Aunt Dimity's puppeteer was.

"Who told you about Emma?" I asked. "And when were you told?"

Peter and Cassie exchanged speculative looks.

"It must have been five, maybe six, days ago," Peter replied, "though it seems like a lifetime ago. One of Mum's horticultural chums wrote to me, to let me know about the situation at home. Her name is Beverley St. John. She lives near Upper Deeping and she was around a lot when Mum and Dad first bought Anscombe Manor. She helped Mum with the landscaping."

"Peter calls her Auntie Bev," said Cassie. "He's known her since he was a boy and they've always kept in touch."

"Did Auntie Bev mention a man named Dabney Holdstrom in her letter?" I asked.

"No," Peter answered. "Who's Dabney Holdstrom?"

"Never mind," I replied. "Tell me about the letter."

"Auntie Bev told us what Mum hadn't told us," said Peter, "because Mum never complains."

"And suddenly, the way ahead seemed clear to us," said Cassie. "We hated the thought of sponging off our families, but if we could earn our keep by taking on a job Emma detested, everyone would be happy. We wouldn't feel like parasites and Emma wouldn't be chained to a desk."

"We talked it over, rang Mum, and here we are," said Peter. "Your new old neighbors."

"I couldn't be more pleased," I said. "Will and Rob will turn cartwheels when they see you."

"We'll be there to greet them when they show up for their lessons tomorrow morning at . . . eight?" Cassie said tentatively.

"Eight it is," I said. "You've learned the schedule already. I'm impressed."

"It's a work in progress," she cautioned. "I've just about memorized Saturday, but the rest of the week is still a blur."

The horses tied to the hitching post whinnied as a car pulled into the driveway.

"Bill's home early," said Peter, turning to look through the bay window. "Our cue to leave, I think. We'll say a quick hello to him and be on our way."

"I'm so glad you came by," I said. "Thanks again for all the presents."

"We'll see you tomorrow night," said Cassie, rising. "Look after your thumb."

"I won't have to," I told her. "Bill will look after it for me."

My comment was meant to be humorous, but it proved to be an accurate description of Bill's intentions. When I told him I'd spent the morning chatting with Mr. Barlow and Selena Buxton as well as with Peter and Cassie Harris, he locked the front door, carried me upstairs, and forbade me to leave the master bedroom, regardless of how many times the doorbell rang. He made a lovely asparagus omelet for my lunch and left the room while I ate it, so I wouldn't be tempted to expend energy talking to him.

In truth, I had no energy left to expend. I finished the

omelet, pushed the tray aside, and settled down for a long-delayed, much-needed nap. Will and Rob tiptoed into the bedroom at some point and I assured them drowsily that Mummy was fine, but nothing else penetrated my overtaxed brain until morning.

Twenty-one

As usual, Aunt Dimity was right. Sleep was the best medicine. I woke at half past seven on Saturday morning, feeling almost normal. My thumb ached a little, but not enough to require medication, and the room didn't tilt when I got out of bed.

I put on my bathrobe and wandered downstairs to find a note on the kitchen table informing me that Bill had taken Rob and Will to their riding lessons and would, at their urgent request, stay to watch their jump class.

I'd planned to spend the morning in the study, giving Aunt Dimity the latest news about Finch's tumultuous affairs, but after reading Bill's note, I decided to pursue a more active agenda, one that would have won his disapproval had he known of it. My husband was the light of my life, but he could be just a tad overprotective.

I took a quick shower, downed a hurried breakfast, dressed in jeans and a T-shirt, and wrote a note on the back of Bill's, informing him that I'd gone to Finch. As I closed the front door behind me, I felt for the first time a surge of anger toward the meddlesome puppeteer. Thanks to his interference, I wouldn't be able to pedal my beautiful Betsy down the sun-dappled lane while listening to birds twitter in the hedgerows because *I couldn't work her hand brakes*. I was irked with him for throwing my village into turmoil, but I was *furious* with him for keeping me off my blue bicycle.

"When I get my hand on you, string-puller," I growled, "I'm going to smack you silly."

I had to drive Bill's Mercedes because he'd taken the Range Rover and I had to steer without the aid of my mummy thumb, but I made it to Ivy Cottage in one piece. I had no intention of engaging in manual labor, but I couldn't abandon Team Ivy without a word of explanation.

The front garden was a hive of activity. Mr. Barlow was in the driveway, measuring a trellis panel, Jack and Bree were pounding stakes into the ground, and Emma was connecting one stake to another with lengths of string. Though the sound of pounding hammers made me shudder, the absorbed expression on Emma's face delighted me. She looked like a pig in clover.

"Are you making a maze?" I asked from the gateway.

Mr. Barlow raised his hand briefly to acknowledge my presence, but the others dropped what they were doing and rushed over to greet me. I thanked Emma for the soup and the grapes and the lilacs, told her how much I'd enjoyed seeing Peter and Cassie, and assured her that my menfolk and I would be at the homecoming party. I thanked Bree and Jack, too, for driving me home from the humpbacked bridge in my hour of need.

"Bree and I swung by your place yesterday afternoon to find out how you were," Jack said, "but Bill told us you were not to be disturbed." He ducked his head guiltily. "I'm sorry we spent so much time faffing about in Upper Deeping, Lori. If we'd come back sooner—"

"You're not to blame for my lack of coordination," I interrupted. "Your mission was to find the perfect birdbaths and mine was to repair the bird tables. I hope one of us succeeded."

"Emma approves of our birdbaths," Bree informed me. "And we're not making a maze, we're marking out borders and flower beds."

"We're implementing Emma's grand design," said Jack.

I felt like a complete heel for walking out on my team when they had so much work ahead of them, so I said with as much sincerity as I could muster, "If there's anything I can do . . ."

"Bill told me you were as weak as a kitten," said Emma, eyeing me suspiciously. "Does he know you're out and about?"

"He will when he reads my note," I replied evasively.

"I thought so," said Emma. She lowered her voice. "Bill read the riot act to Mr. Barlow after you hurt yourself, and he made our young friends here feel pretty small for leaving you alone with a toolbox full of dangerous weapons. He'd drive a stake through my heart if I put you to work, so run along." She folded her arms and regarded me sternly. "You are officially relieved of duty."

"Thanks," I said. "I'll see you tonight. Good luck with the grand design."

Relieved at having been relieved, I drove Bill's car over the humpbacked bridge and parked it in front of the Emporium.

The right-hand window display, I noted, had been thoroughly dusted and the rusty cans of baked beans had been replaced by shiny new ones. Jasper Taxman, Peggy's mousy, soft-spoken husband, stood in the left-hand window, adding a new *C* to the crumpets sign.

"Thus endeth the 'rumpets' sale," I murmured, and got out of the car. I tapped on the shop window to get Jasper's attention and he motioned for me to come in. The sleigh bells affixed to the front door announced my entrance.

Finch's post office occupied a caged space at the far end of the long wooden counter that held the Emporium's old-fashioned register. The counter faced rows of shelves stocked with standard grocery items as well as such rural necessities as udder balm, baling twine, and poultry feed. A quick glance down each aisle told me that I was the only customer in the shop and that Peggy was, thankfully, elsewhere.

Jasper Taxman climbed down from the display window and regarded me politely. Like Hector Huggins, Jasper had been an accountant before his retirement and he was equally nondescript. He wore brown suits, brown ties, brown socks, and brown wingtip shoes, but beneath his mud-colored exterior beat a surprisingly passionate heart. He could silence his overbearing wife with a gentle glance when he chose to, but more often than not he stood back and admired her for imposing her will on the rest of us. Jasper understood better than anyone that Peggy was the powerhouse behind the village fete, the flower show, the harvest festival, the sheep dog trials, and myriad other events that brought neighbors together and brought Finch to life.

"I'm glad to see you looking so well, Lori," he said. "Bill gave me to understand that you would be incapacitated for several days."

"Bill worries too much," I said. "Where's Peggy?"

"She's in the kitchen at the tearoom," he replied, "attempting to make hot cross buns. I can ring her if you need to use the post office."

"Don't ring her," I said. "I'd rather speak with you alone, if you don't mind."

"It's about Peggy's purchase of the tearoom, isn't it?" he said with a faint sigh. "I don't mind telling you, Lori, that I'm not happy about it, not happy at all. We could probably afford to buy another business, but we wouldn't be able to staff it. My wife is a demanding employer. I doubt that any job applicant would meet her stringent requirements. If one did, I doubt that he or she would remain in my wife's employ for more than a week."

I couldn't agree with him without insulting his better half, so I said, "You're stretched pretty thin as it is, with this place, the greengrocer's shop, and the post office. Why would Peggy want another business?"

"My wife is, as you must know, a competitive woman," said Jasper. "It galled her to play second fiddle to an ascendant Sally Pyne. She . . ." Jasper blushed, but went on. "She asked the wishing well to provide her with the means to restore the balance of power in Finch. The estate agency's flyer arrived in the mail two days later, announcing the sale of the tearoom building. But it's not right, Lori."

"What's not right?" I asked. "Peggy's wish? Peggy's rivalry with Sally?"

"Neither," he said. "I'm talking about the estate agency's flyer. It's all wrong. Let me show you."

He went behind the counter, retrieved a sheet of glossy paper from a low shelf, and handed it to me. It came from the Troy agency in Upper Deeping and it looked like a typical real estate advertisement. The firm's name, address, and contact information were printed at the top of the page, above thumbnail photographs of various properties accompanied by brief descriptions and price estimates. Sally's building was the first property listed.

"I don't see what's wrong," I said.

"Look again," said Jasper. "Read what it says about the tearoom."

"'Prime retail space with living accommodations in charming village,'" I read aloud. I reread the words silently and shrugged. "Once a potential buyer finds out how small the charming village is, he may not rank the retail space as prime, but other than that, I don't see what the problem is."

"Where's the price for the tearoom?" Jasper asked, pointing at the entry.

I followed his pointing finger and saw that the tearoom's listing was the only one lacking a big red pound sign followed by a string of red numbers.

"I guess I missed the price because it's not there," I said.

"I believe Peggy overlooked its absence as well," said Jasper. "She's usually quite methodical in her business dealings, but her determination to gain the upper hand with Sally has made her reckless. Peggy saw the tearoom's listing and charged across the green to announce her intentions without looking into the details. I've had to do the requisite spadework for her."

"What spadework have you done?" I asked.

"I rang the agency to request a price," he said, "but no one answered. I then sent several e-mails, but I received no reply. Yesterday, I drove to Upper Deeping and discovered that the address listed on the flyer belongs to a vacant storefront. I made inquiries at neighboring shops and learned that the storefront's previous tenants included a confectioner, a candle maker, and a woman who made knitted jumpers for infants. No one recalled the Troy agency." He looked down at the flyer and shook his head. "I can only assume that a mistake has been made or that someone is playing a rather cruel joke on my wife."

"Has anyone else in Finch received a flyer?" I asked.

"No others have come through the post office," said Jasper. "To my knowledge, none have been hand-delivered. It's as if the flyer were meant for Peggy's eyes only, as though she'd been targeted by some sort of prankster."

"Have you told Peggy what you've learned?" I asked.

"Not yet," said Jasper. "She's overexcited. Until she calms

down, I won't be able to reason with her. Besides, it may be a mistake. The printer may have reversed a few numbers or printed the wrong numbers when he made the flyer."

"How will you find out if it's a mistake?" I asked.

"I'll ask Sally Pyne to find out for me," he replied. "Sally leases her building from someone. The building's owner should know whether it's for sale or not."

I blinked at him in disbelief. "Hasn't *Sally* checked with the owner?"

"Henry tells me she hasn't," said Jasper. "Sally, also, is too overwrought to think straight, but I shall ask her to speak with the leaseholder as soon as she calms down. I'm dealing with two powerful, proud, and extremely angry women, Lori. It's not an easy task."

"A rock and a hard place," I said, repeating Mr. Barlow's apt words. "May I borrow the flyer, Jasper? I'd like to have it on hand in case something similar shows up at my place."

"Yes, of course," said Jasper. "I've already made copies to show to Peggy and Sally."

I folded the glossy, professional-looking advertisement in half, slipped it into my shoulder bag, and rejoiced in having secured my first piece of hard evidence. It seemed obvious to me that the puppeteer had responded to Peggy's wish by producing a bogus flyer from a nonexistent company. I decided not to voice my suspicions to Jasper—without proof, they would seem farfetched. If I could trace the flyer back to its creator, however, I'd be able to reveal to him the identity of the prankster who'd pulled the wool over his wife's eyes.

"Did you make a wish in the wishing well?" I asked out of sheer curiosity.

"No," said Jasper, "but if I had, it would have been for my wife to be content with what she has."

I smiled sympathetically and left the Emporium. I paused to gaze across the green at the tearoom, then turned my steps toward the old schoolmaster's house at the far end of the green, where George Wetherhead lived. If the puppeteer had forged a real estate advertisement, I reasoned, he might have printed a fake newsletter, too.

I nearly ran into Christine Peacock as she stepped out of the pub she owned with her husband, Dick.

"Good morning, Lori," she said. "You're looking well, considering—"

"I *am* well," I interrupted.

I didn't intend to have a long conversation with Christine, but I couldn't resist asking her a question I'd meant to ask her for days. Christine Peacock took a keen interest in UFOs. I'd expected her to fall under the wishing well's spell faster than anyone else in the village, but I hadn't heard one word about her making a wish.

"I hope you don't mind my asking," I went on, "but have you or Dick visited the wishing well at Ivy Cottage lately?"

"Certainly not," she said loftily. "Wishing wells are for children and childish adults. Dick and I are neither."

"Right," I said. If I'd had more time I would have asked her to explain the difference between UFOs and wishing wells, but I was in a hurry, so I let sleeping dogs lie.

"Will we see you at Emma's party tonight?" she asked.

"Wouldn't miss it for the world," I told her, and continued on my way.

I was passing Crabtree Cottage when the front door opened and Charles Bellingham called out to me to wait. He hurried toward me, looking far more subdued than he had while he'd been taunting Grant Tavistock over their white picket gate.

"I didn't expect to see you in the village today," he said. "Bill told me you'd be in bed for a week." He didn't wait to hear my disclaimer, but rushed on. "Has Grant been in touch with you?"

"No," I said. "I haven't seen him since he stormed off. Why? Hasn't he come back?"

"He's been gone since Thursday," Charles said with a catch in his voice. He twisted his hands together fretfully. "I shouldn't have made such a to-do about the Asazuki. Grant swears it wasn't there when he brought the box of disposables home. He accused me of buying it, just to make a point, but I didn't, Lori, I promise you, I didn't. I found it in the shed, exactly as I said."

"Where did the painting come from?" I asked. "Did you trace its previous owners?"

"Of course I did," said Charles. "The painting's provenance was part of the case I was building against Grant. I have no idea where he acquired it because he doesn't keep track of the disposables. The box it was in could have come from a car boot sale, a charity shop, or flea market."

"Not much to go on," I said.

"Not much at all," Charles agreed. "I dug deeper, though, and I found out that the painting had been sold to a gallery in Upper Deeping some thirty years ago."

"Which gallery?" I asked.

"Selwyn's on Summer Street," Charles replied. "Old Mr. Selwyn died ten years ago, but the gallery still carries his name. I asked the current owner if he could tell me who bought the Asazuki from the gallery, but he had no idea. The relevant sales records were destroyed in a fire shortly after Mr. Selwyn's death."

"Too bad he didn't keep them on a computer," I said.

"Mr. Selwyn was too old a dog to learn new tricks," said Charles. "He preferred paper records. An unlucky preference, as it turns out."

I couldn't help but admire the energy Charles had put into his revenge plot, even though I deplored the plot itself.

"Whoever bought the painting from the gallery must have known what it was worth," I said. "Why would he shove it in a box with a bunch of worthless daubs?"

"Who knows?" said Charles. "The owner may have died without informing his relatives of the painting's value. It's the sort of thing that happens all the time in the art world. Grant insists, however, that the Asazuki was never in with the disposables."

"If it wasn't there in the first place," I said, "and you didn't put it there, how did it get there?"

"I've been mulling it over," said Charles, "and it's a funny thing, but I seem to recall hearing an odd noise in the back garden a couple of nights before I found the Asazuki. I thought it was the shed door rattling in the wind—Grant can't be bothered to latch it properly—but it could have been someone *closing* the door." He raised his hands, palms upward. "Who could it have been, though? The art fairy, leaving a treat for me because I've been a good boy?"

I laughed and said, "I doubt it."

"I do, too," said Charles. "A human being must have put the painting in the shed. I can't imagine why he would and I sincerely wish he hadn't. The Asazuki has caused nothing but strife."

"Don't blame the painting," I said severely, "or the person who gave it to you. You used a rare and wonderful work of art to score cheap points off of someone you love. If you want my honest opinion, Charles, I think you should be ashamed of yourself."

"I am," said Charles, looking crestfallen. "I behaved like a school-yard bully." He scanned the green frantically, as if he were searching for a lost puppy. "I don't know what I'll do if Grant doesn't come home."

"He'll come home," I said soothingly. "He just needs a little time to simmer down. For all you know, he could be working out a way to apologize to you. He said some pretty nasty things the other day."

"Nothing more than I deserve," Charles said ruefully. "I *am* a paranoid neat freak with delusions of grandeur."

"Nobody's perfect," I said gently. "But Grant thinks you are, most of the time."

Charles managed a small smile.

"If Grant rings you, will you tell him how sorry I am?" he asked.

"I'll tell him," I promised, "but I'm sure you'll speak with him before I do."

I reached over the white picket gate to pat Charles's shoulder, turned, and struck out once more for George Wetherhead's house. I'd taken no more than ten steps, however, when Elspeth Binney rushed up to me, looking desperate.

Twenty-two

" I 'm so glad you're fit again, dear," said Elspeth. "Bill—".

"—told you I was on my deathbed," I broke in, nodding. "Not true. I'm fine."

"I wish I were," she said. "I must apologize to you for the way Jemma behaved the other day."

"She was a tiny bit intrusive," I allowed.

"A tiny bit?" Elspeth exclaimed and the floodgates opened. "She's a barbarian! She stays up half the night, sleeps until noon, eats whenever it suits her, and leaves dirty dishes, clothes, and photographs strewn all over my cottage. I found a *brassiere* hanging on the back of my Windsor armchair this morning and a bowl of congealed porridge on my Queen Anne table. *It left a ring.*" She raised her eyes to the heavens and groaned softly. "I wondered what it would be like to live with an artist and now I know. It's like being locked in a prison cell with an ill-mannered, self-centered adolescent."

"I'm so sorry, Elspeth," I said. "Have you asked Jemma to be a little more considerate?"

"I've dropped several broad hints," said Elspeth, "but she's impervious to them. Honestly, Lori, I wouldn't mind clearing up after her if she was doing something worthwhile, but her photographs are . . . are . . ."

"Unique?" I ventured.

"They're *appalling*," Elspeth said hopelessly. "I don't know why she chose to take them at such odd angles. I suppose she considers it artistic, but the results are terribly unflattering. Everyone looks *demented*. If Jemma's photographs ever get into print, no one in Finch will ever speak to me again."

"If the publisher doesn't like them, they won't be included in the book," I said. "Who is Jemma's publisher?"

Elspeth looked chagrined.

"It's not a London house, as I thought," she said. "It's a small firm in Upper Deeping called Market Town Books. Jemma's editor is a man named Gilbert Hartley. I believe he owns the company."

"Why not give Mr. Hartley a call?" I said. "Find out if he wants unflattering portraits in his cozy little book about the Cotswolds. Jemma may be trying to impress him with her originality when he would actually prefer something more conventional." I smiled encouragingly. "Hand the problem over to Mr. Hartley, Elspeth. He's Jemma's boss. She'll listen to him. Probably."

Elspeth's expression became marginally less troubled, but before she could speak, Millicent Scroggins strolled up to us. She didn't appear to be very pleased with the world.

"You're up bright and early this morning, Lori," she said. "Bill—"

"Bill is a worry wart," I said patiently. "I'm perfectly fine. You look flustered, though."

"Blame Opal," she snapped. "If she asks you to help her

with her mail-order business, I'd advise you to run for your life."

"What has she done to upset you?" Elspeth asked eagerly.

"She's turned into Peggy Taxman," Millicent declared. "God knows I've tried to be a good friend to her, but a friend shouldn't be ordered about and barked at and told off every five seconds." Her eyes narrowed into angry slits. "She expected me to lick three hundred labels yesterday. Three hundred labels in one go! My tongue would have been rubbed raw."

"You could have used a damp sponge," I offered.

"So I told her," said Millicent. "I said licked labels were unsanitary and very probably illegal and she bit my head off!" Millicent sniffed indignantly. "It was the last straw. I told her exactly what I thought of her and her vaunting ambitions and left her to lick her wretched labels herself."

"Opal's taken on too much," said Elspeth. "She'll give herself a nervous breakdown if she's not careful."

"It would serve her right," Millicent said tartly.

"Ladies! You won't believe what I've just heard!"

Selena Buxton scurried across the cobbles to join Elspeth, Millicent, and me, and though she glanced at my bandaged thumb, she was too intent on imparting her news to inquire after my health.

"It's over," she announced dramatically. "Opal rang Dabney Holdstrom last night and told him not to print the piece about her jams and marmalades because she couldn't cope with the attention it would garner."

"Who told you about Opal?" asked Millicent.

"Opal!" Selena replied. "I just came from her cottage. I stopped there to deliver the parish newsletter and she pulled me inside to tell me I'd been right all along."

"Right about what?" Elspeth asked.

"I hinted that she might be minimizing the difficulties involved in running a mail-order business," said Selena. "She took it badly at the time, but she saw the light after she calculated how much it would cost her to purchase jam jars in bulk. She's decided to go on making small batches and selling them through the Emporium." Selena's gaze came to rest on Millicent. "Opal's sorry about mistreating you."

"She should be," Millicent said sourly.

There was a pause in which the fate of four friendships seemed to hang in the balance. Selena—the loneliest of the Handmaidens—drew a deep breath and attempted to tip the scales.

"I think we could all do with a nice cup of tea," she said brightly.

"I'm not setting a toe in the tearoom," Millicent declared. "Peggy's in there, baking hot cross buns. I expect the building to go up in flames any minute."

"I'm not suggesting that we have tea at the tearoom," said Selena. "I'm inviting you, Elspeth, and Lori to my house for tea and scones. We'll pick up Opal on the way. Now, Millicent," she went on, putting a placating hand on her friend's wrist, "I know she's tried your patience, but you can't deny that her strawberry jam is heavenly on scones."

"I'd be delighted to join you," said Elspeth. "I'd have to tiptoe around my own cottage." She exchanged expressive glances with Selena and Millicent. "Jemma's still in bed."

"Such an interesting young woman," said Selena.

"I'll come, too," Millicent said instantly, as if she'd rather lick a thousand labels than miss a conversation concerning Elspeth's "interesting" niece. "And I'll be polite to Opal as long as she's polite to me."

"Lori?" Selena said.

Since I had no desire to crash a Handmaidens' reunion, I declined the invitation. The ladies bid me good morning and went off together to call on Opal. I ran across the green to the old schoolmaster's house, looking neither left nor right for fear of being waylaid yet again.

I made it to the front step unmolested, raised my hand to knock on the door, and let it fall to my side as George Wetherhead swung the door open. The little man was wearing a light jacket and cradling a cardboard box to his narrow chest, and his comb-over was plastered to his mostly bald head. He started when he found himself standing face-to-face with me, but he quickly recovered himself.

"Hello, Lori," he said. "How are you feeling? Bill tells me——"

"I'm fine," I said, wondering if Bill had gone door to door with his thumb alert or if he'd climbed to the top of the war memorial and shouted it through a megaphone. "Are you going somewhere, George?"

"There's a model train show in Chipping Norton," he informed me. He gazed lovingly at the cardboard box. "I'm bringing my new locomotive."

"The antique, brass locomotive you bought for a bargain price through an ad in a newsletter?" I inquired.

"That's the one," George said proudly. "She's a real beauty."

"Did you wish for her?" I asked. "At the wishing well?"

George's face reddened.

"I, um, y-yes," he stammered. "As a matter of fact, I did. Everyone else was doing it, so I thought I might as well have a go." His eyes widened behind the thick lenses of his black-framed glasses. "It was quite remarkable, Lori. Two days after I visited the well, the newsletter arrived with an insert advertising the kind of locomotive I'd always dreamt of owning but could never afford. Luckily, I was the first to respond."

"Which newsletter was it?" I asked.

"*The Coneyham Express*," he replied. "A fellow enthusiast, a chap named Tim Coneyham, publishes it out of his home near Upper Deeping. I've subscribed to it for years."

It wasn't the answer I'd anticipated. I'd expected George's newsletter to be as phony as Peggy Taxman's real estate flyer. Instead, *The Coneyham Express* was as familiar to him as the daily newspaper. Moreover, it came from someone George knew.

"Does Tim Coneyham usually include inserts in his newsletter?" I asked, clutching at straws.

"Not usually," George answered. "It's something he does from time to time, when he needs to make room for a new acquisition. His own collection is enormous, Lori," George went on, his voice tinged with awe. "It takes up seven rooms in his house. When he buys a new piece, he sometimes sells an old one because he's a true enthusiast. He'd rather have his trains out in the open, where he can see them, than stored in boxes in his cellar."

"So you bought the locomotive from Mr. Coneyham," I said, nodding. "Why do you suppose he sold it for so little?"

"Tim's quite well-off," George informed me. "He can afford to be generous to collectors like me, who have to scrimp and save to add even a modest piece to our collections. I must say, though, that he's never before sold such a valuable locomotive for such a low price. The wishing well definitely came through for me." He shifted the cardboard box to one arm and pulled his car key out of his jacket pocket. "Forgive me, Lori, but I really must be going. The show starts at ten."

"Sorry," I said. "I didn't mean to hold you up. Have a great time, George. I'm sure your locomotive will knock everyone's socks off."

George ducked his head and smiled bashfully. I left his front doorstep, wandered aimlessly onto the green, and came to a standstill with names tumbling through my head—the Troy real estate agency, the Selwyn art gallery, Gilbert Hartley and Market Town Books, Tim Coneyham and *The Coneyham Express*. How did they fit together? I asked myself. How were they related to Dabney Holdstrom?

I couldn't answer my own questions. My brain felt sluggish, as if it had absorbed too much information too quickly, and my thumb was insisting that it was *not* fine. Since a pain-killer would help one and a chat with Aunt Dimity would help the other, I decided to go home.

I turned toward Bill's car, but stopped short when I noticed Henry Cook sitting all by himself on the wooden bench near the war memorial. Plump, mustachioed, wavy-haired Henry was an outgoing, gregarious man. It worried me to see him alone.

"Henry?" I called. "Are you okay?"

"I'm fine," he replied with a melancholy smile.

My thumb and I knew better than to believe him.

"Mind if I join you?" I asked.

"Not at all," he replied, moving over to make room for me on the bench.

I sat beside him in silence, surveying the tranquil scene. When he, too, remained silent, I ventured tentatively, "Nice day."

"No, Lori," he said, shaking his head. "It is not a nice day. It's a bloody awful day. I don't want to leave Finch and I don't want to live in a caravan and I don't want to marry my Sal in a registry office, but no one cares about what I want."

"I do," I said promptly. "What do you want, Henry?"

"I want everything to be back the way it was before the flipping wishing well was opened," he said vehemently. "It wasn't my idea to go there, Lori. Sally wanted me to do it, so I did it, to please her. I thought it would be a bit of a giggle."

"What wish did you make?" I asked.

"I asked the blinking thing for one more turn on stage," he replied, "one more chance to have a laugh with the punters before I hung it up for good. I didn't believe for one minute that anything would come of it, but then this bloke, this Arty Barnes, shows up at the tearoom with his chum Dabney Holdstrom. Arty listens to my patter, he likes what he hears, and before you know it, he offers me a one-nighter at the club in Bristol."

"Your wish came true," I said. "You must have been pleased."

"You'd think so, wouldn't you?" Henry said. "But I wasn't pleased. I was scared spitless."

I looked at him in surprise. "What scared you?"

"If you'd ever been a comic, you wouldn't have to ask," said Henry. He hunched forward and stared at the tussocky grass around his feet. "I began to remember what it was like to get up in front of a roomful of strangers, half of them pie-eyed and the other half yapping nonstop. I remembered the silence that crashes down like a guillotine when a joke bombs. The tension, the flop sweat, the nausea, the nerves—it all came back to me as clear as day."

He shuddered and his swarthy face turned pale. For a moment I thought he was going to be sick, but he smoothed his neat mustache, took a few breaths through his nose, and went on.

"It was too much for me," he said. "I was going to turn down Arty's offer, but then Sally and Peggy had their slanging match and Sally came up with her grand plan and all of a sudden, I not only couldn't say no to the one-nighter, I had to say yes to *years* of one-nighters." He glanced mournfully at me. "It'll never happen, Lori."

"Why not?" I asked.

"For one thing," said Henry, "Arty Barnes isn't a bona fide theatrical agent. He's the club owner's brother-in-law. He lines up acts for the club, but he doesn't have contacts anywhere else. He's strictly small potatoes."

"Bang goes the movie contract," I said, trying to lighten Henry's mood.

Henry chuckled in spite of himself.

"You're a wag, Lori," he said, elbowing me gently in the ribs. "But I'd never have gotten a movie contract. I'm not a main-stage comedian. I'm not even a small-time comic anymore. I'm the chap in the tearoom who tells funny stories and I like being that chap. I wish I'd never wished for anything more."

"Wishing isn't all it's cracked up to be," I said. "Have you told Sally that her grand plan won't work?"

"Not yet," he said. "It's not easy to tell the woman you love that you're not the leading man she thinks you are. Sally's set her heart on seeing my name in lights."

"What about the tearoom?" I asked.

"She's put it behind her," he said gloomily. "She says she won't fight for it because she has to prove to Peggy that we can get along without it."

"I haven't seen Sally this morning," I said. "Where is she?"

Henry pointed to the apartment above the tearoom.

"In her flat," he said, "making a new waistcoat for me to wear on my big night."

He sounded like a man contemplating the shroud he would wear during his funeral.

"You should be up there with her," I said. "You should be telling her what you've told me. The longer you wait, the harder it will be for both of you."

"What if she decides to go it alone?" Henry asked. "What if she doesn't want to marry a broken-down old has-been?"

"You'll never be a has-been to Sally," I said bracingly. "You're her leading man, Henry, and you always will be, no matter what happens. So stop feeling sorry for yourself and start being honest with—" I broke off as Henry stood.

"The tearoom's on fire!" he cried.

I turned my head and saw a thin stream of smoke issuing from the tearoom's front entrance. Before Henry or I could react, Sally burst through the side door that led to her upstairs apartment and ran into the tearoom, shrieking at the top of her lungs that Peggy Taxman wasn't fit to make toast.

"What are you waiting for?" I demanded, giving Henry a shove. "Rescue her!"

"I'm coming, Sal!" Henry shouted and he lumbered off to save his lady love, looking every inch the leading man.

Twenty-three

Peggy blamed Sally's oven and Sally blamed Peggy's incompetence for setting the hot cross buns alight. The two women were so busy berating each other that the entire building might have burned to the ground if Henry hadn't arrived in the nick of time. He wielded the kitchen's fire extinguisher with such dexterity that Sally hailed him as her hero and even Peggy admitted that he'd done well.

The fire brought everyone in the village running, but Henry put it out before any lasting harm was done and the onlookers soon lost interest. I held my left hand to my chest to protect my thumb as I made my way through the retreating bystanders and heaved a sigh of relief when I reached Bill's car.

"Lori!"

I looked up to see Bree Pym running toward me. She, Jack, and Emma had appeared atop the humpbacked bridge at the first cry of "Fire!" but Jack and Emma had evidently gone back to work after the initial excitement had died down.

"Hi, Bree," I said as she approached. "How's the master plan coming along?"

"Slowly," she replied. "Jack stops every five minutes to ask Emma if he's read her diagrams correctly. Then she spends twenty minutes explaining them to him. We may finish by Christmas, if we're lucky."

I laughed. "I've left you to cope with a pair of perfectionists, Bree. Sorry about that."

"No worries," she said.

Bree looked down at her hands, shuffled her feet, and chewed on her lower lip, as if she were debating how to say what she wished to say next. I wondered if yet another startling revelation was coming my way.

"Lori," she said finally. "Why didn't you change your surname when you married Bill?"

"Oh," I said, caught off guard. It was the last question I'd expected to hear from her, but I didn't mind answering it. "It's pretty simple, really. As the only child of two only children, both of whom are dead, I'm the last surviving member of my family. When I married Bill I wanted to honor my mother and father by keeping the name they gave me."

"Did Bill mind?" Bree asked.

"No," I said. "He understood. Still does."

"What about the twins?" she pressed. "Will and Rob are Willises. Have they ever asked you why you're the only Shepherd in the family?"

"They aren't confused by it because they've grown up with it," I said. "But sometimes, when a new friend is confused, they ask me to explain it again so they can pass my explanation along to their friend. They never knew my mom and dad, so it gives me an opportunity to show them photos and tell them stories about my childhood. Grandma and Grandpa Shepherd will never be as real to them as Grandpa Willis is, but I don't think my parents will be forgotten."

Bree nodded thoughtfully. I burned to ask her if she was considering a name change—from Pym to MacBride, for instance—but I held back. I was a friend, I told myself, not a nosy Handmaiden. If Bree wanted to confide in me, she would. If not, I'd respect her privacy.

"Thanks," she said. "I was just wondering because . . ." She looked away. "Well, I was just wondering."

"No problem," I said. "Would you like a lift back to Ivy Cottage?"

She grinned. "I think I can make it there on my own. See you at the party!"

"See you then," I said.

Bree ran off and I got into Bill's car. It was past noon, I was starving, I needed to pop a pill, and I had to do a little more research before I spoke with Aunt Dimity. I averted my eyes from the rearview mirror and headed straight for home.

No one but Stanley was there to greet me when I walked into the cottage and his greeting consisted of opening his eyes briefly when I put my head into the living room. The untouched note on the kitchen table suggested that Bill and the boys hadn't yet returned from Anscombe Manor. Since Bill seldom accompanied Will and Rob to their riding lessons, I suspected them of treating their father to a lengthy display of their equestrian skills.

I made a cheese and tomato sandwich and ate it at the kitchen table before taking another dose of my pain medication. The telephone rang as I was putting my solitary plate into the dishwasher. It was Bill, calling to let me know that he and the twins were at Fairworth House with his father.

"I thought you could use a little more R & R," he said. "I brought a change of clothes for Will and Rob and we'll go straight from here to the party at Anscombe Manor. I've already told Peter and Cassie not to expect you."

I gave an outraged squawk, then clamped my mouth shut. If Bill thought I was going to miss the homecoming party, he had another think coming. I decided to keep my own counsel, however, and surprise him by showing up anyway.

"Okay," I said. "I'll see you later."

"You'll be asleep by then," Bill said, laughing. "Take it easy, love. Don't try to do too much."

"I won't," I said angelically and hung up.

I smiled wickedly as I entered the study.

"My husband is a good man," I said to Reginald, "but he sometimes takes his knight in shining armor routine too far. Do I look like a wilting lily to you? I didn't think so." I touched a finger to Reginald's snout. "I can't wait to see his face when I turn up at the party, ready to dance the night away."

Reginald seemed to approve of my plan. I smiled at him, but instead of reaching automatically for the blue journal, I sat at the old oak desk and opened Bill's laptop. Will and Rob knew more about computers than I did, but I could at least search the Web.

I spent an hour tapping away at the keyboard and reading the words that appeared on the screen. I then closed the laptop, took the blue journal from its shelf, and opened it as I sat in one of the tall leather armchairs before the hearth.

"Dimity?" I said. I grimaced as the familiar lines of royal-blue ink curled across the page to form what had become an overly familiar question.

How are you feeling, my dear?

"I'm fine," I replied forcefully. "Honestly, Dimity, Bill's given everyone in Finch the impression that I'm at death's door. I've spent the entire morning contradicting him."

He cares about you, Lori.

"I know and it's lovely," I said, "but he has no right to tell Peter and Cassie that I won't be at their homecoming party because I'm too weak and feeble to totter over to Anscombe Manor."

I didn't know Peter and Cassie were having a homecoming party.

"We have tons of catching up to do, Dimity," I said. "Do you remember telling me to conduct an investigation? Well, I've been conducting one and I've collected masses of information, so get ready to be amazed."

I shall brace myself.

"First," I said, "Dabney Holdstrom is exactly who he says he is. He's the editor-in-chief of *Cozy Cookery* magazine. Second, he grew up three miles south of Upper Deeping, in Skeaping village."

Home of Skeaping Manor, the Cotswolds' most horrid museum.

"That's the place," I said. "Dabney wasn't born and raised in Finch and he wasn't evacuated here during the war, which leads me to two conclusions."

He isn't granting wishes to the villagers because he has fond memories of Finch or because he owes the village a debt of gratitude for providing him or his family with a safe haven during the war.

"Correct," I said. "People were evacuated *to* Skeaping, not *from* it. Also, Dabney Holdstrom had nothing to do with Peter and Cassie's return to Anscombe Manor. They decided to come back after they got a letter from an old friend named Beverley St. John. Aunt Bev, as they call her, lives just outside of Upper Deeping and she keeps tabs on the home front for Peter. She told him Emma was dissatisfied with her job at the riding school."

I see. Go on.

"Peter and Cassie had been out of work for six months when they received Aunt Bev's letter," I said. "They needed jobs and Emma had one she didn't want, so . . . bingo! They came home."

Beverley St. John brought Peter and Cassie home, not Dabney Holdstrom. Very well. Tell me more.

"Jasper admitted that Peggy did ask the wishing well to give her the tearoom," I said. "She thought her wish had come true, but she was wrong."

The tearoom isn't for sale?

"No," I said. "Peggy thought it was because it was listed on a flyer from the Troy real estate agency in Upper Deeping, but the Troy agency doesn't exist. Jasper drove to the address in Upper Deeping and found a vacant storefront, and I came away empty-handed when I searched for it online. The flyer's a fake, Dimity, and no one in Finch received it but Peggy. Our puppeteer used it to play a mean-spirited prank on Sally as well as Peggy."

Sally Pyne seemed to believe that the tearoom was for sale.

"Sally hasn't even spoken to her landlord about the sale," I said. "She's determined to prove to Peggy that she doesn't need the tearoom because Henry's going to be a big star. Only, Henry's not going to be a big star."

As you'll recall, I never thought he would be.

"Henry agrees with you," I said. "He has no intention of going back into show business. He wished for a last hoorah and that's what he got. Dabney Holdstrom's friend, Arty Barnes, offered Henry one performance, no more, and he didn't do it as a favor to Dabney Holdstrom, but because he's a talent scout for the comedy club's owner, who happens to be Arty's brother-in-law."

Does Arty Barnes live in Upper Deeping?

"He does," I said. "I looked him up online and he's who he says he is—a small-time talent agent who lines up acts for his brother-in-law's club. Jemma Renshawe's publisher is for real, too. Market Town Books is a vanity press located in Upper Deeping. It's owned by a guy named Gilbert Hartley, who is also editing the book about Cotswold villages."

I believe a vanity press is used by writers willing to pay to have their books published.

"That's right," I said. "Someone must be awfully fond of Cotswold villages."

Indeed. Continue to amaze me.

"The Asazuki painting was last seen hanging in the Selwyn gallery on Summer Street in Upper Deeping," I said. "Charles tried to find out who bought it from the gallery, but he was out of luck. The old owner passed away ten years ago and the sales records were destroyed in a fire. Grant swears the painting wasn't among those he put in the shed, and after much soul-searching, Charles has decided to believe him."

Good for Charles. I hoped he'd come to his senses. He should know by now that Grant wouldn't lie to him about such a thing. Can Charles explain how the painting got into the shed?

"He heard a noise in the back garden a couple of days before he found the painting," I said. "Since he doesn't believe in the art fairy, he blames a person or persons unknown for depositing the painting surreptitiously in Grant's box of disposables."

Am I remembering correctly, Lori? Is it a painting of a fish?

"It is," I said. "It's an ink wash painting of a Japanese carp, or koi, pirouetting through fronds of swaying seaweed. I think it's astoundingly ugly, but Charles regards it as a masterpiece."

Beauty is in the eye of the beholder, my dear, and occasionally in the hands of the banker. The painting is worth a great deal. What else have you discovered?

"Let me think . . ." I scoured my brain for further facts before continuing. "Oh, yes, George Wetherhead. George bought his locomotive from a train collector in Upper Deeping who publishes a newsletter called *The Coneyham Express*. I was suspicious at first because the locomotive was advertised on an insert instead of in the newsletter proper, but it seems legitimate. The seller's name is Tim Coneyham and George has known him for years."

Anything more?

"Elspeth's niece is still driving her mad," I said. "Opal Taylor changed her mind about having her jams and marmalades featured in *Cozy Cookery*. She doesn't want to turn a hobby into a full-fledged business."

Very wise.

"Opal and Millicent nearly came to blows over whether to lick or not to lick the labels for Opal's jars," I said, "but I'm pretty sure Elspeth and Selena helped them to patch things up. Selena's having a tough time. She had a romantic church wedding planned for Sally and Henry and she asked the wishing well for perfect weather, wedding guests, et cetera, but it looks as though she wasted her time as well as her wish."

Has the wedding been called off?

"Not exactly," I said. "Sally thinks her famous fiancé won't be able to fit a church wedding into his busy schedule, so she's leaning toward a quickie service in a registry office."

Oh, dear. Not a registry office.

"Again, Henry's with you," I said. "He hates the idea, so Sally may have to stick with the original plan and Selena may get her wish after all. I hope she does. I love church weddings. Speaking of which . . ." I sat up as I recalled the last morsel of news I'd gathered in Finch. "Bree asked me why I didn't change my name when I married Bill."

Did she indeed? What, I wonder, would put thoughts of marriage into her head? I wouldn't dream of matchmaking from beyond the grave, Lori, but I suspect Bree's young Australian friend might have something to do with it. Have you observed a progression in her relationship with Jack?

"I haven't seen much of them since I whacked my thumb," I admitted, "but if she's asking about name changes, it must mean something. I bow to your superior matchmaking instincts, Dimity. Sally and Henry may not be Finch's only engaged couple for much longer."

Unless something happens to drive Bree and Jack apart.

"What would drive them apart?" I asked.

Bree values honesty, Lori, and I suspect that Jack hasn't been entirely honest with her or with anyone else in Finch, for that matter.

"I don't understand," I said, frowning. "How has Jack been dishonest? You can't think he's the puppeteer. We ruled him out, remember?"

Neither one of us knows for certain whether Jack is or isn't responsible for the chaos that has engulfed Finch since the well was rediscovered. Which is why you must do a little more detective work—hands-on detective work.

"Will I need both thumbs?" I asked.

One should suffice. The handwriting paused, then began to loop and curl lazily across the page. It was as if Aunt Dimity were thinking aloud. *I find it interesting that the villagers' wishes were answered exclusively by people who live or have lived in or in the vicinity of Upper Deeping. Even the Asazuki painting was last seen in Upper Deeping.*

"At the Selwyn gallery on Summer Street," I said, nodding.

The painting's subject intrigues me as well, as does the fictional real estate agency's name.

"A koi and Troy? They rhyme, but other than that . . ." My voice trailed off because I couldn't for the life of me imagine what intrigued Aunt Dimity.

Then there's the book published by Market Town Books and paid for by an author who loves Cotswold villages.

"Everyone loves Cotswold villages," I protested, but Aunt Dimity didn't seem to be listening.

The wishing well itself rouses my curiosity. Do you recall the words carved into the plaque-like stone on the wellhead?

"Speak and your wish will be granted," I said.

I've always found it strange that one must speak to the well. Traditionally, one deposits a coin in a wishing well and keeps one's wish to one's self, much as one does when making a birthday wish. It's almost as if the wishing well at Ivy Cottage were listening.

"We've been here before," I said, smiling, "and I'm pretty sure we agreed that wells don't have ears."

The well doesn't need ears to listen, Lori. A microphone would do.

My smile vanished and I phrased my next question carefully. "Are you suggesting that the well could be wired to pick up sound?"

It could be. It would explain why so many wishes have come true.

"Are you accusing *Jack* of rigging the well?" I asked.

I won't accuse anyone of anything until after you've taken a closer look at the well. If you don't find a microphone, then we're back to square one. If you do, then it opens up a number of possibilities.

"One of which might drive a wedge between Bree and

Jack," I said. "I don't want to be the one who rains on their parade, Dimity."

It's a risk you'll have to take if you wish to know the truth. I assume, of course, that you would like Bree to know the truth as well.

I glanced at the ivy fluttering against the diamond-paned windows over the old oak desk and remembered how much fun it had been to watch Bree warming to Jack as they clipped ivy together. If he'd won her trust unfairly, he didn't deserve her. And she certainly deserved someone better.

"I'll do it," I said, returning my gaze to the journal. "I'll go to Ivy Cottage tonight, while everyone else is at the party."

Thank you, Lori. While you're waiting for darkness to fall, I suggest that you have a nice lie-down. You may not be at death's door, but you've had a busy day and you'll need your wits about you when you examine the well.

I waited for the handwriting to fade from the page, then closed the journal and attempted to gather my thoughts. It was a pointless exercise because Aunt Dimity was right—I did need a nap. I put the journal back on its shelf, patted Reginald's head, and went upstairs to stretch out on the bed for a half hour or so.

"Leave it to me, Dimity," I murmured as my head hit the pillow. "I'll get to the bottom of the well."

Twenty-four

I slept until sundown. I probably would have slept until daybreak if Stanley hadn't jumped onto the bed to demand his supper. I stumbled out of the bedroom and down to the kitchen to fill his bowl, splashed cold water on my face to wake myself up, and nearly jumped out of my skin when the telephone shattered the silence. It was Bill again, calling to make sure I hadn't concussed myself, imbibed a deadly poison, or lopped off an arm in his absence. He didn't express such fears explicitly, of course, but I knew what he was thinking.

"How are you doing?" he asked, raising his voice to be heard above the hubbub of a party in full swing.

"I just woke up," I told him. "I'm still a bit groggy."

"Go back to sleep," he shouted. "Emma made up a bed for Will and Rob in the hayloft, so I thought I'd stay on for a bit. Peter's telling us about the year he and Cassie spent in the western isles of Scotland."

"Sounds riveting," I said. "Stay as long as you like."

"Are you sure?" he asked.

"I'm positive," I said. "Stay until midnight. It's not every day that we have such a grand occasion to celebrate."

"You're right about that," said Bill. "All right, then . . . if you're sure . . . I'll see you later, possibly much later."

"Enjoy yourself," I said, and put the receiver back into its cradle.

Since I was about to embark on a search for truth, I was glad I hadn't lied to my husband. I felt a tiny bit guilty for not telling him what I was about to do—I would have felt guiltier if he hadn't been having such a good time—but I promised myself that I'd tell him the whole story as soon as I knew what the whole story was.

I put a flashlight into my shoulder bag and as an after-thought added a multi-tool, in case I had to unscrew, scrape, or pry open some part of the well. It was a cool night with a light breeze, so I pulled a woolen sweater over my T-shirt and grabbed a Windbreaker from the coat rack in the hallway on my way out of the cottage. I climbed into Bill's car, started it, and noticed for the first time how quiet the engine was. As I backed out of the driveway, I thanked Mr. Barlow silently for taking such good care of the ordinary, everyday cars his neigh-bors entrusted to him.

Anscombe Manor glowed in the distance as I passed its long, curving drive, but the lights were out in Bree Pym's redbrick house and Ivy Cottage was cloaked in darkness. I pulled into Jack's driveway, taking care not to bump into the sawhorses and the building materials Mr. Barlow had left be-hind. I took the flashlight and the multi-tool from my bag, slipped the multi-tool into my pocket, turned the flashlight on, and got out of the car. I closed the door by nudging it with my knee.

I thought I was familiar with the terrain around Ivy Cottage, but it had changed since I'd last been there. The implementation of Emma's master plan made it much easier for me to navigate the property than it had been for Peggy Taxman, Charles Bellingham, and the rest of the well's nocturnal visitors.

Staked strings lined a grassy path from the driveway to the back garden's tumbledown stone wall and colorful plastic ribbons tied to various plants and shrubs for identification purposes helped me to avoid low branches and grasping vines. The broken pergola had been removed altogether. I stepped cautiously through the gap in the stone wall where the pergola had been and followed another stake-and-string-lined path to the well.

The wishing well loomed over me, looking faintly sinister in the darkness, like something out of a ghost story instead of a fairy tale. I wanted to scold it for causing so much trouble among my generally kind and helpful neighbors, but the thought of a live microphone silenced me.

The garden wasn't silent. Leaves rustled in the breeze, an owl hooted nearby, the well's oak bucket creaked eerily as it swung from its jute rope, and a faint slithering sound in the undergrowth sent shivers down my spine. I told myself not to be a ninny, but I couldn't help wondering what kind of wildlife might be lurking in the refuge Hector Huggins had created.

I calmed my nerves by focusing on the well. I examined the wellhead's smooth river stones, the shingled roof, the crank, the spindle, the lid, and the wooden posts, but nothing obvious presented itself. I removed the lid and bent over the well, as if I were making a wish, but though I shone my light up and down inside the well, I saw nothing that looked like a recording device.

Stymied, I straightened impatiently, bashed my head on the oak bucket, and gritted my teeth to keep myself from saying words I didn't wish to have recorded. I rubbed the rising bump on my head vigorously, then froze to stare, transfixed, as the flashlight's wavering beam caught a black gleam coming from deep within a split that ran the length of the right-hand post. I steadied the flashlight, leaned closer to the post, and saw that a black-coated wire had been cunningly inserted into the split.

I placed the flashlight on the lip of the well, pulled the multi-tool from my pocket, opened its longest blade, and working my way upward, used it to tease the wire from its hiding place. When I'd loosened as much of the wire as I could reach, I pulled the rest of it free from the post with a gentle tug and watched as a microphone tumbled from a notch at the top of the post to swing like a pendulum from the end of the wire. I could hardly believe my eyes.

I left the microphone dangling and used the multi-tool's blade to chip away the mortar at the base of the post. It took me less than a minute to lay bare a tiny transmitter. My sense of disbelief gave way to outrage as one thought seared across my mind.

Jack MacBride was the puppeteer.

Jack had led Bree and me to the back garden. Jack had pulled the curtain of ivy back to reveal the wishing well to us. Jack had "accidentally" told Peggy Taxman about my wish, knowing full well that she would spread the news throughout Finch. Jack had lured the villagers to the well, listened to them, laughed at them.

I didn't care why he'd done it. I didn't care whether he'd felt an Australian's need to take a dig at the old country or whether he'd wished to punish my neighbors and me for ignoring his uncle or whether it was simply a young man's sick and twisted idea of a joke. His betrayal of our trust had been unconscionable.

I yanked the wire out of the transmitter. No longer afraid to speak, I slipped the multi-tool into my pocket, picked up the flashlight, and turned to face Ivy Cottage.

"Where there's a transmitter," I muttered, "there must be a receiver."

The back door was unlocked. I let myself into the kitchen and panned the flashlight slowly around the room. It struck me as an unlikely listening post. Sally Pyne, Miranda Morrow, Mr. Barlow, Emma Harris, Elspeth Binney, Opal Taylor, Millicent Scroggins, and Selena Buxton—each had stood in Jack's kitchen at one time or another and Bree and I had spent hours there, washing up, taking tea breaks, chatting cozily with Jack and with each other. Too many people had passed through the kitchen. It was too public a space for the kind of covert operation Jack had conducted.

The double parlor, too, was a public space, I thought as I stepped into it. It was the room one had to move through to reach the kitchen, the back door, and the wishing well. As such, it wouldn't work well as a lair. I looked into the rooms opposite the double parlor and saw that they were empty, as if Mr. Huggins, the childless bachelor, had found no use for them.

I went upstairs. I'd never before climbed the stairs in Ivy Cottage. I doubted that anyone other than Jack had gone up there since his uncle's death. The cottage's upstairs rooms were private, off limits to visitors, and at least two of them overlooked the back garden.

A narrow corridor lined with four doors, two on each side, bisected the second floor. I didn't have a good reason to look into every room, but my dander was up and I was determined to leave no stone unturned.

I opened the first door to the right and saw what amounted to a small and meticulously arranged freshwater fishing museum. The flashlight's beam illuminated fishing poles in fan-shaped racks, waders, long-handled nets, wicker creels, tackle boxes, and a workbench set up for the fine art of fly-tying. I recalled the many hours Mr. Huggins had spent fishing from atop the humpbacked bridge and closed the door gently.

The first door on the left opened into a sparely furnished bedroom. Jack's backpack stood in one corner and Joey the baby kangaroo sat on the low table beside the single bed. It hurt my heart to see Joey, because the little guy reminded me of why I'd liked Jack so much. I found it difficult to believe that a

man who cherished a bright-eyed, reddish-brown kangaroo—
an Australian Reginald—could treat decent people with such
contempt.

"Your daddy's been very naughty," I said, "but I know that
you, at least, will forgive him."

I gave Joey a wan smile and left the bedroom to continue
my search. The room next door to the fishing museum appeared to be a library, though the books were strangely uni-
form in size and identically bound in black leather. Each
volume had a different year stamped in gold on the spine. I
assumed they were records of Mr. Huggins's rod-and-reel adventures and closed the door.

The second room on the left was the room I was looking
for, though it turned out to hold more than I bargained for. I
expected to find a radio receiver and I found one amid a jum-
ble of electronic devices strewn across a long table beneath a
window that overlooked the wishing well.

I did not expect to find cork-lined walls upon which were
pinned glossy real estate flyers, copies of *The Coneyham Express*
and *Cozy Cookery*, menus from the tearoom and the pub, sale
notices from the Emporium, St. George's parish magazines,
the roster for the flower arrangements in the church, and a
multitude of flyers announcing the village fete, the flower
show, the harvest festival, the sheep dog trials, and events at
the Anscombe Riding Center.

There were photographs as well, hundreds of photographs,
taken from many angles and in every season, of the tearoom,

the Emporium, the greengrocer's shop, Mr. Barlow's garage, Peacock's pub, St. George's church, Wysteria Lodge, the war memorial, the humpbacked bridge, the Little Deeping River, Anscombe Manor, Bree's redbrick house, my father-in-law's wrought-iron gates, my honey-colored cottage, and seemingly every dwelling place in Finch.

Those photographs were vaguely unsettling, but they weren't nearly as disturbing as the slightly blurred shots of people I recognized, people I saw nearly every day of my life, not only my friends and my neighbors but my husband, my sons, and myself. My hand trembled as I moved the flashlight's beam from one shadowy image to the next and I felt a growing sense of unease that teetered perilously close to horror.

"Hello, Lori."

I wheeled around and pointed my shaking flashlight at a face that had in recent weeks become very familiar.

"Come to make another wish?" said Jack.

Twenty-five

*J*ack reached for a wall switch and turned on an overhead light. He was dressed in an open-necked white cotton shirt, his cargo trousers, and his hiking sandals. His golden hair was gorgeously tousled and his sky-blue eyes were amused.

I tightened my grip on my flashlight and stepped back, my heart pounding.

"I thought you were at the party," I said, trying to keep my voice steady.

"I was," he said. He thrust his hands in his pockets and sighed. "Bree said she was sick of the sight of me, though, so I left." He smiled. "If I'd known I'd be entertaining a guest—"

"Why is Bree sick of the sight of you?" I broke in. I gestured angrily at the cork-lined walls. "Did she find out about *this*?"

"No," said Jack. "She found out about something else. It's my own fault, really. I should've known I'd be recognized."

"Recognized?" I repeated. "What are you talking about?"

I jumped sideways as he came toward me, but he did nothing more than grab a wheeled office chair from its place near the electronics-strewn table and roll it closer to me.

"Have a seat," he said. "This could take a while."

He sat on the floor, with his back against one of the few blank spots on the walls. With his legs crossed at the ankles and his hands folded loosely in his lap, he looked as threatening as a surfer waiting for a wave. I switched off my flashlight and sank onto the office chair.

"Do you remember the first time you came to Ivy Cottage?" he asked. "I told you and Bree about Uluru and the conservation work I did there."

"You eradicated invasive plants," I said. "I remember."

"Then you probably remember the rest of it," he said, "the projects that took me to Mount Tongariro, Fox Glacier, the Waipoua Kauri Forest, and the Kaikoura coast in New Zealand."

"I haven't forgotten any of it," I said, "but I don't see what it has to do with——"

"It has to do with why Bree's brassed off with me," he interrupted. "I'm trying to explain."

"Sorry," I said. "Go ahead."

"Thanks," he said. He bent his legs, rested his wrists on his knees, and laced his fingers together. "It's all true, what I told you, but I didn't quite tell you everything. I didn't simply work on the projects I mentioned. I designed them." He ducked his head, as if he were embarrassed. "The fact is, Lori, I'm a bit of a prodigy. I could afford to leave home when Dad cut me off because I'd already received a full scholarship to university along with a generous living allowance and a research grant. By the time I was twenty, I'd earned a whole string of degrees. I've spent the past five years doing field work and making a name for myself as an eminent ecologist."

"Hold on," I said. "You told Bree and me that you were broke. You told us you were too broke to visit your uncle. Ecologists get paid, don't they?"

"Most of my personal income is tied to grants," he explained. "I can't use it for private jaunts around the globe, and I plow what I earn from writing or appearance fees back into my projects. I've never been in it for the money, Lori."

"Okay," I said. "You're a child prodigy who became an eminent ecologist. Why didn't you just say so?"

"How?" he asked in return. "What was I supposed to say? How do you do, I'm Jack MacBride, the brightest bloke on the block?" He ducked his head again and this time he was actually blushing. "I reckoned if it came up, it came up, but until then, I'd just be Jack, the bloke from Oz."

"You sound like Henry Cook," I said. "He just wants to be the chap in the tearoom who tells funny stories."

"There's a lot to be said for maintaining a low profile," said Jack. "People treat you differently when they find out you're well known."

"Was it Peter or Cassie who recognized you?" I asked and when Jack looked up in surprise, I said, "It must have been one or the other. No one else at the party knows enough about your field to pick an eminent ecologist out of a crowd."

"They both recognized me," he said. "They'd seen a documentary film I was in and they'd read articles I'd written for various academic journals. They read my blog as well." He shook his head. "Emma told me they were involved in conservation work, but if I'd known they were such big fans, I wouldn't have gone to the party."

"Why not?" I asked. "You're not ashamed of what you do, are you?"

"No," he replied, "but I would have found another way to break it to Bree. I was working my way up to it, but something kept holding me back."

"Natural diffidence," I said. "It can be a major handicap."

"You're telling me," he said feelingly. "She didn't like hearing about my achievements from someone else. She accused me of being dishonest, disingenuous, and deceitful, which mean the same thing but pack a punch when they're strung together. That's when I left the party."

"I don't blame you," I said. "But Jack . . . If Bree's upset with you for being too modest to tell her the truth about yourself, how do you think she'll feel when she finds out about . . ." I swept an arm through the air to indicate the bizarre collage surrounding us.

"No worries," he said, brightening. "Bree knows all about Uncle Hector's project. I showed it to her last week."

"Uncle Hector's project?" I echoed uncomprehendingly.

"That's right," he said and got to his feet. "Come with me."

I followed him across the corridor and into the room that resembled a library. He strode to the far end of the room and lit a lamp on a wooden desk. Apart from the lamp, the desk held a mug filled with pens and pencils, a laptop computer, the black box I'd last seen in the trunk of Jack's rental car, and a stack of typing paper covered with neat, precise handwriting.

"Uncle Hector's memoir," said Jack, placing a hand on the stack of paper. "I'm transcribing it. Market Town Books no longer accepts handwritten manuscripts."

"Market Town Books?" I said faintly.

"Uncle Hector based his memoir on forty years' worth of notes," said Jack. He pulled one of the black-leather-bound books from a shelf, and riffled through it to show me page after page filled with the same precise handwriting.

I looked from the volume in Jack's hand to the rows of books lining the walls.

"How could one man have so much to say about *fishing*?" I asked.

"The memoir isn't about fishing," said Jack. "It's about Finch." He returned the book to the shelf and half sat on the edge of the desk. "My uncle loved this village. He spent forty years watching, listening, and learning about everyone who lived here. And he wrote everything down." Jack nodded at the bookshelves. "In there you'll find the winners of every competition held in Finch over the past four decades. Uncle Hector recorded the runners-up and the losers as well, but he also described each person's reaction to triumph or failure and how those reactions rippled through the community and influenced relationships for months, sometimes years, on end."

"Good grief," I said, letting my gaze travel over the gold numbers stamped on each black-leather spine.

"He wrote about his neighbors' habits, their passions, their pet peeves," Jack went on. "He wrote miles of dialogue to capture their speech patterns. He studied the buildings, too, and he found out what he could about their histories."

"You told us he wrote about nature," I said reproachfully.

"He did," said Jack. "Almost every page contains an observation about Finch's ecosystem. You're never in doubt about the season because he wove his knowledge of nature into the ongoing narrative. He took photographs as well. You've seen a small portion of them in the other room."

"When did your uncle take the photographs?" I asked. "I don't recall ever seeing him with a camera."

Jack folded his arms and asked quietly, "How often did you see him at all?"

I dropped my gaze.

"Not often," I admitted. "Not even when he was right in front of me. Your uncle didn't stand out in a crowd, Jack. He didn't even stand out on his own." I thought of Bill's description of Mr. Huggins as a wallpaper man, but I couldn't bring myself to say the words aloud.

"You don't have to be the life of the party to have a good time," said Jack. "My uncle was too reserved to jump onto the dance floor, but he admired those who were brave enough to throw themselves into the dance."

I didn't know what to say, so I said nothing.

"Uncle Hector was afraid that Finch would one day change beyond all recognition," said Jack. "He saw it happening all over England—real communities becoming pseudo-villages for holiday makers or, worse, disappearing into the maw of bloody awful housing estates. He wanted to capture a world he loved before it vanished. He was almost relieved when he found out that the village would outlive him."

"Was he . . . ill?" I asked softly.

"A year ago, Uncle Hector was diagnosed with an inoperable brain tumor," Jack replied. "No one could tell him how long he had to live, so he got going straightaway on two new projects." Jack tapped the manuscript. "He distilled his life's work into one volume and he began to create a very special going-away gift for his neighbors. He asked me to complete both projects if he died before they were done. I promised him I would." He stood. "Let's go back to the other room, Lori."

We returned to the room with the cork-lined walls and I sat once again on the office chair, turning it to follow Jack as he crossed to the window to look down on the back garden.

"The well sparked his big idea," he said. "It had always been there, but Uncle Hector made the plaque that turned an ordinary well into a wishing well."

"Speak and your wish will be granted," I said, then listened intently while Jack described the rest of his uncle's preparations.

Mr. Huggins had used his in-depth knowledge of the villagers to make highly educated guesses about the wishes they would make, but he'd installed the listening device as a backup, in case one or two of his neighbors surprised him. He'd also installed a video camera in the well's shingled roof.

"Uncle Hector added the camera for my benefit," said Jack. "I might not recognize voices, especially if people spoke in whispers, but he was fairly sure I'd be able to put names to faces." He nodded toward the wall of photos.

"I understand the mechanics," I said, "but I don't understand how your uncle made so many wishes come true."

"He turned to his clients," said Jack, "and he asked them for a few favors."

"What clients?" I asked.

"My uncle was a senior partner in an accounting firm," Jack informed me.

"The accounting firm in Upper Deeping," I said as comprehension dawned, "whose clients lived or had lived in or in the vicinity of Upper Deeping."

"That's right." Jack returned to his spot on the floor and sat with his back to the wall. "Uncle Hector's clients trusted him, relied on him, were grateful to him. Dabney Holdstrom, Gilbert Hartley, Tim Coneyham, Arty Barnes, and Beverley St. John were more than happy to repay him for his years of faithful service, especially after they learned that he was dying."

I put a hand to my forehead as Jack reeled off the by now familiar names, then motioned for him to go on.

"When someone made a wish," he said, "I'd contact the appropriate client and he'd follow the instructions Uncle Hector had left for him."

Dabney Holdstrom had taken time off from his job at *Cozy Cookery* magazine, loosened the exhaust pipe on his Jaguar E-

Type, and driven to Finch, where he'd "discovered" Mr. Barlow, Sally Pyne, and Opal Taylor. As president and owner of Market Town Books, Gilbert Hartley had hired Jemma Renshawe to photograph the villagers for a forthcoming book. Tim Coneyham had slipped the insert into *The Coneyham Express*, Arty Barnes had offered Henry Cook a one-night stand at the comedy club, and Beverley St. John, who'd kept Hector Huggins apprised of Peter and Cassie's employment situation, had written to Peter to inform him of Emma's plight.

"When Dabney Holdstrom came here," I said suddenly, "he didn't come to make a wish in the wishing well. He came to meet you."

"He shouldn't have," said Jack. "But I'm glad he did. It was a pleasure to meet one of Uncle Hector's friends. Bree and I met Tim Coneyham, too, when we were looking for birdbaths in Upper Deeping. Uncle Hector paid him what the antique locomotive was worth, of course, so Tim could offer it to George Wetherhead at a knockdown price. As for Gilbert Hartley . . ."

Hector Huggins had paid Gilbert Hartley in advance to publish his memoir and to illustrate it with the photos Mr. Huggins had taken of Finch's environs as well as the photos Jemma Renshawe would take of the villagers.

"My uncle wasn't happy with the snaps he'd taken of his neighbors," Jack explained. "He could photograph the churchyard, the river, or the bridge at his leisure, but he had to grab his portraits on the fly. He hoped a professional photographer would do a better job."

"Have you *seen* Jemma's photographs?" I asked doubtfully.

"No, but Gilbert Hartley has," said Jack. "Apparently, Elspeth Binney rang him this afternoon to ask if her niece had understood the assignment correctly. Gilbert had a little chat with Jemma and she agreed to provide him with a set of portraits that were less, um, *experimental.*"

"Thank heavens," I said. "Elspeth would have had to leave Finch if Jemma's original shots had been published." I paused to review what Jack had told me so far and realized that he still had some explaining to do. "What about the Asazuki? I assume you put it in Charles and Grant's shed after Charles made the wish your uncle predicted he would make, but where did the painting come from?"

"It was one of Uncle Hector's most prized possessions," said Jack. "He bought it from a gallery in Upper Deeping years ago. The owner was one of his clients."

"Old Mr. Selwyn," I said, "of Selwyn's gallery on Summer Street."

Jack's eyebrows rose.

"Charles gets the credit, not me," I said quickly. "He tracked the painting to Selwyn's gallery. He's an art dealer. It's what he does."

"Uncle Hector knew Charles and Grant would appreciate the Asazuki," said Jack. "It used to hang above the fireplace downstairs. Uncle Hector said it captured the spirit of the carp."

"A painting only a fisherman could love," I murmured. I'd missed the connection between Mr. Huggins's avocation and his taste in art, but Aunt Dimity hadn't. "What about Peggy's wish? Did you make the fake real estate flyer?"

"Uncle Hector made the flyer," said Jack, "but I made sure it reached Peggy."

"Did your uncle invent the Troy real estate agency, too?" I asked.

"It was his little joke," said Jack. "Hector, the warrior prince in Greek mythology, was from Troy."

"Koi, Troy," I said under my breath. Aunt Dimity hadn't only connected the fisherman to the fish painting, she'd linked Mr. Huggins to the birthplace of his Trojan namesake as well. I suddenly felt dumber than a doorstop, which may explain why I spoke sharply to Jack. "It was a rotten trick to play on Peggy. Your uncle pretended to grant her wish when he knew all along it wouldn't come true."

"My uncle wasn't attempting to grant Peggy's wish," said Jack. "He wanted to grant Jasper's."

"I don't see how you're going to make that happen," I said. "Jasper hasn't made a wish."

"Jasper Taxman may not have spoken his wish to the wishing well," said Jack, "but he muttered it many times at the Emporium, when Peggy was out of earshot. Uncle Hector heard him."

"Wait a minute," I said slowly, as something Jasper had said returned to me. "I may have heard him, too. Jasper told me that, if he *had* made a wish, it would have been for his wife to be content with what she has."

"You and Uncle Hector heard the same thing," said Jack. "Uncle Hector decided that the only way to grant Jasper's wish was to give Peggy the tearoom so she could see for herself that it was too much for her." Jack grinned. "I have to hand it to my uncle. He knew exactly what would happen. He knew Sally's success would ruffle Peggy's feathers, just as he knew that Peggy's domineering personality would cloud her judgment."

"Peggy saw what she wanted to see on the flyer," I put in, "and Sally was too angry to double-check Peggy's so-called facts. If Sally had taken the time to make one phone call to her landlord, she would have realized that her building wasn't for sale."

"Instead, Sally stomped off in a huff, giving Peggy the chance to make a shambles of her brief tenure as a pastry chef," said Jack. "Jasper's wish has come true, by the way. I overheard him chatting with Bill tonight. Peggy has given up her expansionist dreams and will henceforth focus her energy on improving the Emporium, the greengrocer's shop, and the post office."

"Lucky old post office," I said, rolling my eyes. "But what about Sally? Has she spoken with the landlord?"

"She has," said Jack. "More importantly, she's spoken with Henry."

"And?" I said impatiently.

"And she will begin baking her fantastic pastries again as soon as the new oven is installed," said Jack. "Once Henry finishes cleaning up the mess Peggy left behind, he'll return to his role as the chap who tells funny stories in the tearoom."

"No wonder Bill sounded so happy when he called me from the party," I said. "He knows where his next jelly doughnut is coming from. Did Sally or Henry mention their wedding? Is the church wedding back on?"

"It is," said Jack. "I can't guarantee fine weather or control the guests' behavior, but after everything that's happened, I think Selena Buxton will regard a wedding at St. George's as a wish granted."

I smiled and we sat in silence until another gap in the puzzle occurred to me.

"What about Millicent's back tooth?" I said. "And my rant against the rain? Your uncle's encyclopedic knowledge of Finch wouldn't have made it possible for him to grant those wishes."

"They were the most magnificent strokes of luck," said Jack, "not least because of their timing. Your wish-come-true got the ball rolling and Millicent's helped to speed it along. No one, not even Uncle Hector, could have orchestrated it. It was luck, pure luck."

"You call it luck," I said glumly. "I call it a waste of a wish. I should have wished for . . . for . . ." My voice faded as a jolt of childish superstition overwhelmed my common sense. Since I couldn't say my real wish aloud for fear of jinxing it, I invented another one on the spot. "I should have wished for the ability to aim a hammer accurately."

I spoke lightheartedly, but Jack began to apologize all over again, so I changed the subject.

"Some villagers haven't visited the wishing well yet," I pointed out, thinking of Christine and Dick Peacock, among others.

"I know," said Jack. "Why do you think I asked you and Bree to examine the stonework so minutely? Why do you think I welcomed Emma's master plan for the gardens? I was buying time. I wanted to give everyone a chance to make a wish. If we'd finished the gardens, I would have found something wrong with the cottage. I would have stayed until the last wish was granted, because that's what Uncle Hector asked me to do." He sighed. "But I don't reckon I'll get to see his plan through to the end."

"Why not?" I asked.

"You said it yourself when I drove you home from Uncle Hector's funeral luncheon," he replied. "There are no secrets in Finch. Now that you and Bree know the truth, you won't be able to keep it to yourselves. One of you will come out with it accidentally and it'll be all over the village before you can blink. Uncle Hector warned me about the village grapevine. He described it as the most efficient mode of communication known to humankind." Jack shook his head sadly. "No, Lori, I reckon my wish-granting days are over."

"How close are you to finishing your work on the memoir?" I asked.

"Pretty close," he said.

"If I were you, I'd spin it out for as long as I could," I said. "Courtships take time, especially if a bloke is courting a girl as complicated as Bree."

Jack's mouth fell open, then curled into a sheepish grin.

"Noticed, did you?" he asked.

"I'm not blind," I retorted. "You've been courting her from day one, though I can't imagine why. I haven't forgotten the first time Bree and I came to lunch at Ivy Cottage. You laughed off her snotty comments and put up with her rudeness and turned the other cheek every time she gave you a verbal smack in the chops, despite the fact that you didn't know her well enough to see through her tough-girl act. Why were you so nice to her when she was so mean to you?"

Jack studied his hands for a moment, then gazed at me steadily.

"You're wrong when you say I didn't know Bree," he said quietly. "I've known her almost as long as you have. Uncle Hector told me about her in his letters. He told me about her drunken father and the misery he caused her. He told me how you found her in Queenstown and coaxed her into coming to England to meet her great-grandaunts before they died. He told me what it meant to her to lose them. He told me how fond she is of Mr. Barlow and how she teases Peggy Taxman and how she helped some little kids from Upper Deeping until they moved up north with their mum. Uncle Hector told me how much Bree depends on your friendship and how lonely, how very lonely she is in that big redbrick house."

I closed my eyes and smiled as the full impact of his words came home to me. "You loved Bree before you ever met her."

"It sounds crazy, I know," he began, "but—"

"It doesn't sound crazy to me," I interrupted, leaning toward him and returning his steady gaze. "I know from personal experience that it can happen. Ask Bill about it sometime. Ask him to tell you how he fell in love with me."

"I will," said Jack, looking puzzled but willing to play along.

"Did Uncle Hector tell you what wish Bree would make?" I asked. "Because if I had to hazard a guess, I'd say she'd wish to fall deeply in love with a man who loved her deeply. Simple as that. Complicated as that. Just that."

"She's bloody annoyed with me at the moment," Jack reminded me.

"It'll pass," I said. "You know as well as I do that Bree can't stay mad at you, and you know why. Take a lesson from your uncle, Jack. Reel her in slowly."

"Come to think of it," said Jack, "I'm not as far along with the memoir as I thought I was and it looks as though the roof may need some major repairs." He smiled. "I may be here for quite some time."

"Good man." I gave him an approving nod and stood. "It's time we were on our way, my friend."

"Where are we going?" he asked, getting to his feet.

"To the party at Anscombe Manor," I answered. "You're going to tell everyone there what you've told me here. Except the part about Bree. That's between you and me."

"Do you think the villagers will be brassed off?" Jack asked.

"Some of them might be, at first," I said, "but in the long run they'll be proud and pleased and grateful to you and your uncle." I nodded toward the familiar faces gracing the cork-lined walls. "It's not every village that has its own biographer."

Epilogue

My Village by Hector Huggins was published in September, to general acclaim. The acclaim could be general because instead of publishing one copy, Market Town Books published a copy for every villager mentioned in it. Jack paid for the extra volumes out of the money his uncle left him, which turned out to be quite a tidy sum.

Jemma Renshawe's photographs had improved markedly when she'd stopped ambushing her subjects and started asking them how they wished to be portrayed. Sally and Henry had posed in front of the tearoom; Mr. Barlow, in front of his garage; Peggy and Jasper, halfway between the freshly painted Emporium and the greengrocer's shop; the vicar and Lilian Bunting, on the steps of St. George's Church.

Charles and Grant had posed in front of their garden shed, with the Asazuki painting held between them, and the antique brass locomotive featured prominently in George Wetherhead's portrait. Bree had chosen to be photographed standing behind her great-grandaunts' headstone, smiling broadly, as if Ruth and Louise were standing beside her.

No one looked demented.

Much to Elspeth Binney's relief, Jemma returned to Yorkshire as soon as she completed her assignment. Elspeth spent three days restoring order to her cottage, then resumed hosting the Handmaidens' biweekly bridge nights. Though she still takes painting classes from Mr. Shuttleworth in Upper Deeping, she no longer yearns for the dubious privilege of living with an artist.

Opal Taylor added red currant jelly to her line of jams and marmalades, but she makes it only when it suits her and only when red currants are in season. Millicent forgave Opal for snapping at her during the mail-order fiasco, but when Opal offered her a selection of her sweet wares by way of an apology, Millicent refused politely, for the sake of her back tooth.

Henry Cook's one-nighter was canceled, as was Sally Pyne's appearance on the cover of *Cozy Cookery* magazine. They resumed their normal routine as if fame had never beckoned and were married in St. George's church in August. A few clouds passed overhead as they were entering the church, a toddler began to wail halfway through the ceremony, and some of the guests at the reception had a bit more to drink than was absolutely necessary, but on the whole, it was as perfect a wedding day as anyone, including Selena Buxton, could have wished for.

Miranda Morrow's bottles of well water enhanced her reputation as a healer. Bill credited the placebo effect while I gave the nod to Miranda's skills as a massage therapist. Whatever the case, the patients she treated for rheumatism, lumbago, and assorted aches and strains found relief in her ministrations.

George Wetherhead won a prize for an essay he wrote about his locomotive. Peter and Cassie moved into their flat in Anscombe Manor before the paint in the nursery was quite dry. Emma transformed Mr. Huggins's wilderness into an attractive haven for wildlife, then turned her attention to her own garden, which had suffered several years of benign neglect.

Mr. Barlow built a new pergola, a new trellis, and five new bird tables for Ivy Cottage, without hitting himself even once with a hammer. He repaired the tumbledown stone wall as well, but he didn't forget his regular duties. Despite the extra workload, he kept the church and the churchyard in tip-top shape and he responded promptly to any odd-job emergency that cropped up.

Bree admitted to duping me with her astonishingly accurate guesses about the wishes made by the wishing well's nocturnal visitors. Her guesses weren't, in retrospect, astonishing because they hadn't been guesses. Jack had taken her into his confidence by then and she'd known exactly what Charles and Peggy and Henry had said to the old well. Though she'd promised to keep Jack's secret, she'd been unable to resist having a little fun with me as we'd cycled together along the sun-dappled lane.

Bree isn't starved for companions her own age anymore. Jack, Peter, and Cassie are in and out of the redbrick house constantly, planning expeditions, having meals together, or simply hanging out. Jack has put his conservation work on hold in order to make extensive repairs to Ivy Cottage's roof.

He continues to reel Bree in with a lightness of touch that would have made Hector Huggins proud.

Mr. Huggins's grave is never without flowers.

"Mr. Huggins paid attention to his six-year-old nephew," I said, "and he paid attention to us."

The study was still and silent. A fire roared in the hearth, keeping the chill of a damp October night at bay. Bill, Will, and Rob had been asleep for hours, but I'd come downstairs for a cup of hot milk and a chat with Aunt Dimity. I smiled at Reginald, then looked down at the blue journal as the familiar lines of royal-blue ink continued to curl and loop across the page.

Hector Huggins was an extremely observant man. He watched his neighbors as closely as he watched the birds, bugs, and beasts in his gardens, and he treated them with the same respect, the same tenderness. He paid you and the rest of the villagers the profound compliment of finding you endlessly fascinating.

"Too bad his plan went so badly awry," I said.

His plan worked out perfectly, Lori. Everyone's wish was granted. It was up to each individual to determine whether a wish-come-true was a blessing or a curse.

"George's locomotive was a blessing," I said. "And Sally's brush with celebrity was definitely a curse."

Was it a curse, I wonder? Sally, Henry, and Peggy came away from the experience with a renewed appreciation of the many gifts life has bestowed upon them. The same could be said for Elspeth Binney, Opal Taylor, Charles Bellingham, and Mr. Barlow, among others. Perhaps a wish granted, whether it turns out as we expect it to or not, teaches each of us what we truly value.

"I wish we'd valued Hector Huggins while he was alive," I said. "Bree was wrong when she said he had no friends, Dimity. We were all his friends. We just didn't know it." I shifted to a more comfortable position in the chair. "Though I still find it difficult to forgive him for keeping me off Betsy. If Mr. Huggins hadn't granted Mr. Barlow's wish, I wouldn't have mashed my thumb. I lost a month's cycling, thanks to him, and I won't be allowed to ride her again until next spring."

Is Bill still wrapping you in cotton wool?

"He'd wheel me around in a wheelchair if I let him," I said. "I think he still feels guilty for keeping me in the dark after the doctor fixed my thumb. I don't blame him, though. I was so weak and woozy I wouldn't have understood what he was trying to tell me. Though my bouts of nausea should have tipped me off."

The blood tests did turn up an unanticipated result.

I put my hand on my swelling belly as its current occupant shifted to a more comfortable position.

"A wish come true for both of us," I said, smiling. "Bill still swears he never went near the wishing well, but I'm not sure I believe him."

You and Bill don't need a wishing well to make your dreams come true, Lori.

"No, we don't," I said, and my smile grew as the baby moved again. "All we needed was a magnificent stroke of good luck."

Sally Pyne's Summer Pudding

Serves 6

Ingredients

7 slices white bread
Soft butter (do not substitute margarine!)
3 cups berries (raspberries or blueberries or blackberries
    work well)
½–⅔ cup sugar (adjust according to the sweetness of the
    berries)
⅓ cup water
heavy cream (optional)

Directions

Butter each slice of bread lightly on one side. Set one buttered slice aside. Line a 3- to 4-cup bowl with the remaining slices, butter side out. Fill the gaps with buttered bread trimmed to fit so the bowl is completely lined.

In a medium saucepan, cook the berries with the sugar and ⅓ cup water for 10 minutes. Pour cooked berries into the bread-lined bowl.

Place the reserved slice of bread on top and fold the edges of the outer slices over to meet. Place a saucer on top and press down, to infuse the bread with the berry juice. Pour off excess juice to serve with the pudding.

Chill at least 6 hours before serving.

Serve in a bowl with heavy cream and a drizzle of the excess juice. (The heavy cream isn't required, but it's highly recommended!)

If you love Nancy Atherton's
novels featuring

Aunt Dimity

go to
www.headline.co.uk
to discover more in the series